FOREWORD

CROSSING LOVE LINES

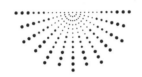

NELLIE KRAUSS

CHAPTER ONE

TEXAS SMALL TOWN murder trials were hell on juries. Alena pushed her mirrored dark glasses up securely on her nose. Thank God it was over. Her blue eyes would probably take weeks to lose their red rims from all the crying she'd done. Deciding innocence or guilt was a heavier than heavy burden, especially when the facts were skimpy and the truth elusive. Listening to a horrific and heartbreaking week of lies and deceit had been unbearable and nobody was satisfied with the outcome, including her. *Remind me never to do this again!*

She scurried past the newspaper photographers on the courthouse steps while reporters fired off questions at both families without waiting for answers. To top it off, the rival gang members standing on the walkways shouted threats at everyone. It was a circus without a ringmaster.

This was not the time for some story-hungry reporter to recognize her. For the last few years she'd lived quietly, keeping to herself when she wasn't at work. Nowadays she wore her hair long and dark, no need for highlights. Head down, not glancing to the right or left, she hurried toward the courthouse parking lot across the street. She wasn't ready to step back out into public view. That day would come, but not today.

Four nights in a row, the Fort Bend County sheriff deputies had escorted the jurors to their cars. This afternoon, no such luck. She was on her own. As long as she kept moving, she'd be fine. A few more steps and she would be able to put it all behind her and never look back. She'd add that to all the other lies she'd been telling herself.

She could see the Mustang. *Don't run, keep it together. You're almost there.* That's when she heard a deep male voice coming from behind her.

"Excuse me, ma'am. I need to talk to you. Please. I just want to ask a couple questions."

Alena didn't answer. *Oh, hell no!* She bolted for her car and prayed she'd get there before some gangbanger grabbed her. When the door slammed shut, she thanked God and Ford for power locks and Mustang GT's. She shoved the key in the ignition. The 5.0-liter V-8 roared to life and she was out of there.

She flew past the rugged looking guy in military style camo pants and t-shirt damn near running him over. Years spent behind the wheel allowed her to maneuver accurately enough to miss him while maintaining control in the narrow aisle.

~

Gabriel stumbled back a step and yelled, "Hey, watch it." Adjusting his cap, he shook his head and walked toward his car parked in the back of the lot. He couldn't blame juror number six for being scared; he recognized the signs, but she was the one he needed to talk to. Everyone else was hanging together like a heard of sheep in front of the courthouse. She wasn't answering any questions or smiling for the cameras. Whatever was going on, she didn't want any part of it.

This was not the homecoming he'd envisioned flying back from his last tour of duty in the Middle East. He'd arrived in time to hear the closing arguments and sentencing portions of the trial. It had damn near killed him to see his younger brother dragged away in handcuffs. Twenty-five years in prison was a lifetime, especially if Carlos wasn't guilty.

He looked down the four-lane road that was the main street through the middle of town. Her flashy red Mustang wouldn't be hard to find.

2

The Medical Center parking sticker on the rear window was a dead giveaway that she worked in Houston. There were only two roads that would get her there. He'd wait. Marines were good at waiting for the opportune moment to achieve their objective.

He'd see her again. Until then he'd have to make sure nothing happened to her. He needed to keep her safe from the fools posturing on the courthouse steps. It didn't add up. Carlos wasn't tough enough to run with a gang.

Without the ugly sunglasses, juror number six was actually kind of pretty. She'd caught his eye sitting in the jury box. If the circumstances had been different... Well, there was no point in going there. He shrugged and rolled his shoulders. Thinking about things like that would only distract him from his mission.

Once the stress of the trial had a chance to wear off, he'd find a neutral place to approach her again. He only wanted to talk, to ask about all the evidence and testimony that had been presented in the courtroom before he'd gotten there. What he'd heard didn't make sense. How had his brother gotten mixed up in a murder?

She was the key to finding the truth and getting justice for Carlos.

CHAPTER TWO

HER SHIFT in the Southwest Houston Hospital emergency room ended at eleven-thirty, same as always. That hadn't changed in the last two weeks. Traffic was still abundant in town as she took the freeway South. Houston didn't sleep, but she lived out in the quietest part of Fort Bend County near the state park so she could.

Out there she had comforting solitude. She kept to herself and let the world roll on by.

She crossed the Brazos River and the next exit put her onto the familiar farm to market road leading home. She reached over and changed the radio station looking for some oldies rock and roll with pounding drums and screaming guitars to keep her awake. It took the place of roaring engines and cheering crowds. There was zero grease under her carefully manicured and scrubbed fingernails. She hadn't been that girl for several years but lately she'd begun to miss it.

A regular job and a quiet ride home at midnight was her routine commute. Thirty-six miles of dark and lonesome blacktop was her time to unwind and cruise. She needed to forget the man from the parking lot. The sound of his voice shouting at her reminded her of a day she desperately wanted to forget—the panicked warning, the gunshots that followed and terrified screams that haunted her.

She shuddered, shook it off and checked her rearview mirror.

Headlights blinked on behind her and she pressed down on the accelerator. This was the third time these clowns had pulled this stunt. It didn't matter which gang was after her, she wasn't playing their intimidation game and she wasn't going to make it easy for them to catch her alone in the middle of nowhere at midnight.

She'd called the county sheriff and they'd wanted the license plate and description of the car and driver before they could to do anything about it. If she knew all that, she should be on their payroll. They were not coming to help. And she was tired of being the mouse in a cat and mouse game. It was time to be the cat.

The pursuing car kept up. Damn. She'd outrun them twice before and changed routes every other night but they hadn't taken the hint. Time to change tactics.

The GT's brakes grabbed and she spun the steering wheel sending the Mustang GT into a pretty one-hundred-eighty-degree spin. The tires smoked burning rubber and Alena came to a stop facing the oncoming car. She winced. That was gonna cost her. GT tires were expensive and she'd just left lots of good rubber on the road. Now she really was pissed.

"Okay. Let's see who's chicken." She grimaced, and snarled, "Meow." Pulling the gear shift into second, she stomped down on the accelerator, slowly let off of the clutch, the back tires spun, smoked, and grabbed sending her flying forward.

The oncoming car changed into the left lane and shot past her. She caught a glimpse of the driver, for her money he was one of the gang members from the courthouse. Not a split second behind the first car was another relic. That driver looked like the same man that had followed her in the parking lot. His car was an old gun-metal grey, Monte Carlo. On its best day it would have been almost fast enough to catch her Mustang GT. This was not that day.

She drove back as far as Rosenberg and across town to Highway 36. No way was she letting any of those second-rate hoodlums follow her home. Nobody needed to know where she lived, especially not the goons from a small-town gang.

She took the long way around through Fairchild.

Once inside her house, she double locked the door, put her heavy purse down and turned on the kitchen lights. A tired sigh escaped as she peeled off her scrubs and dropped them in the hamper by the washing machine.

She could change her clothes, change her profession, change her name and still she couldn't find peace. Nobody ever said life was fair. It was about time she fixed that. She had the weekend off to think about it. First thing in the morning she'd work on a plan to reclaim her life. The one she had lived and almost died for.

CHAPTER THREE

ALENA KEPT her eyes open and checked her rearview mirror often. It would take longer than a couple of weeks for the dust to really settle and people's lives to move on to more pressing matters. She did her shopping in Sugarland and avoided downtown Richmond staying out of local sight.

On Saturday evening, she went to a movie and stopped for dinner at the Steakhouse on Highway 6 in Sugarland. Coming out of the restaurant she smelled a change of season in the air, subtle but it was there. Cool air blowing in from the North caressed her skin.

A gentle breeze blew her hair off her shoulders and lifted the ruffles on her baby blue sleeveless blouse as she moved across the parking lot. She tilted her head up, inhaled a deep breath, and enjoyed the moment. When she refocused on walking to her car, it took a fraction of a second for Alena to process a tall, very muscular man leaning against her Mustang GT's custom paint job. It was him, the man from the parking lot, wearing camo pants and a matching t-shirt. Must be his wardrobe of choice.

She raised her voice just below a shout. "Hey, get off my car. You're scratching the paint."

He looked straight at her. "Sorry, but I didn't have any other way to find you. I only need a few minutes." His head dipped and he sighed heavily. "Please, I need your help. That's all I want."

Oh, hell. Alena slowed but kept walking being careful not to trip on any loose debris littering the parking lot. This was not the time to fall off her strappy wedge sandals. Her jeans could handle a fall but not her ankles. She fished the pepper spray out of her purse and snarled, "I said, get away from my car."

He pushed off from her Mustang and straightened to his full height. "Okay. I'm off." He shifted his weight adjusting his stance. "I'm sorry if I scared you but we need to talk."

"You've got the worst manners of any person I know." Alena stopped just out of arms reach and glared at him.

He turned to the side and brushed his hand over the fender he'd been leaning against. "It looks okay." He refocused on her. "You gonna spray me with that stuff or just point it at me?"

"Depends."

"On what?" He turned back and crossed his arms over his chest.

"If you can act like a civilized human being."

He chuckled. "I can be civilized if I have to."

"Good. So, for the sake of this conversation, you're going to pretend to be civilized and I'm not going to pepper spray you." Her eyes narrowed and her lips thinned. "Yet." If he irritated her, all bets were off.

One side of his mouth hitched up in an almost smile and he grunted, "Deal." He held out his hand. "I'm Gabriel."

Alena lowered the pepper spray while keeping her eyes trained on him. "What do you want?" He was not getting his hands on her. She wasn't falling for that old trick.

He shoved his hands in his pockets. "I need to know what happened."

"What are you talking about?" Her forehead crinkled and she exhaled heavily.

"What do you think?"

She shrugged one shoulder. "With you, it could be any number of things. First, you chased me through the courthouse parking lot. Second, you followed me down a long, dark, deserted road in the middle of nowhere at midnight, twice. And you lost a chicken match to a girl."

"My little brother, Carlos. I need to know what happened."

Alena's eyes got big and her lips parted, allowing her to inhaled sharply. "Carlos DeLeon is your brother?"

"Yeah." Gabriel stared and angled his head slightly to one side.

"I'm so sorry. I did the best I could but nobody wanted to listen."

Gabriel's forehead wrinkled and his eyes turned to slits. "Nobody wanted to listen to what?"

Alena didn't back up. She stood rooted to the asphalt. *Never show weakness, no retreat, no surrender, don't back down, hold your ground.* She looked up into Gabriel's dark and now dangerously glittering eyes. Of course, he would have questions.

She said, "I tried to make them see reason but they wouldn't. They just wanted to get it over with and go home. There were eleven of them and one of me. I was outnumbered."

Gabriel glanced past her toward the restaurant entrance. "People are starting to look at us. We can't talk here." He took Alena by the arm.

She rolled her shoulder and pulled away. "No." She did her best to wrench her arm free. "Let go of me."

Gabriel released her instantly.

Alena checked to see if anyone had noticed. Yep, curious heads were turned in their direction. Not good. She refocused on Gabriel. "We can't stay here."

He pleaded, "I need to know what happened. Please."

"I understand that. Give me a minute. I'll meet you someplace quiet where we can talk without the audience over there."

"Where?"

It was more of a demand than a question. She needed to sit down and she didn't want to be alone with him. "You're not dressed. How about City Club? It's a dive. We can get a table in the back."

Gabriel rolled his eyes. "No, too many rednecks. We can go to Cazadores."

Alena's brows crinkled and she squeaked, "No. I can't go in there." Was he crazy? Somebody'd be bound to recognize her and she

9

couldn't tell him that. Damn, damn, damn. "Think of someplace else."

Gabriel rubbed the back of his neck. "McDonald's."

Alena muttered, "Too bright. How about the Malibu Café?"

"Too white." Gabriel glared at her.

"Ninfa's." Alena looked up and smiled.

"Okay. Meet you there. And don't try to out run me. You won't make it."

"I'll be there." Alena huffed, "You are so suspicious."

"Damn straight on that."

She got in the Mustang and pulled the door shut, temporarily locking out the world. She melted into her seat letting it cradle her tense back, leaned her head against the headrest and stared up at the black head-liner. At long last, the chickens had come home to roost. Gabriel was Carlos DeLeon's brother. Her heart slammed against the inside of her chest, bounced off and landed in the pit of her stomach. What the hell was she going to do now?

Minutes later, she parked at Ninfa's and got out. Under the lights her custom, high-gloss, metallic red Mustang GT sparkled like rubies in a jeweler's case. No wonder he had been able to find her. The beautiful silly thing stuck out like a sore thumb and she loved it. In a world gone to hell, it could still pull her out of darkness and make her smile. She was caught off guard by Gabriel's voice coming up behind her.

"What are you thinking about so hard? You could get mugged not paying attention to what's going on around you."

She flinched and spun around. "How did you find me earlier?" Alena turned her most intimidating evil eye on him.

"I've been following you for days. At first, Michael's crew was on your tail and I followed them to see what they were up to. I couldn't find you in town and you have to take Highway 59 to get back and forth to Houston. So, I watched and waited."

Alena took in his solemn expression. "It's not nice following people. You could scare someone doing that."

"Right, and I wouldn't have had to do this if you'd have talked to me at the courthouse."

She shook her head. "You followed me on my way home. That's called stalking, you know."

"I had to make sure they didn't hurt you. I need to ask you some questions. It's important."

"Okay, so ask." She flipped her hair over her shoulder and adjusted her purse strap.

He put his hands on his hips. "What's your name? Or do I call you *Chica*?"

"Alena. You can call me Al. Everyone else does." He didn't need her last name. That was none of his business.

He dropped his hands back to his sides. "Come on. Let's go inside."

They walked into the cantina & grill like any other couple out for the evening and were shown to a table along the wall by the front window. The waitress took their drink order and left a basket of chips and a bowl of salsa.

Alena looked around the dining room and then at the basket of chips. "Well, here we are." Looking over at Gabriel she did her best not to cringe. Big, rough, shaved head with ink. He had "gang" written all over him. "What do you want to know? And why are you asking me? You're in the gang, ask them."

Gabriel folded his hands, rested them on top of the table where she could see them and leaned slightly forward. In the low light, he was even more dangerous-looking, if that was possible. And handsome. Good god in heaven, why did he have to be so handsome? His eyes were dark brown, gentle and soulful. They did not match the rest of the man. He was a walking contradiction.

His voice was low when he finally started talking. "I've never been in a gang. I'm a Marine. When I left town, Carlos wasn't in any trouble. He was supposed to finish high school and go to college. I sent him the money to buy that Camaro so he could use his paycheck for the tuition."

She studied Gabriel. The tense set of his jaw, the downturned corners of his mouth, the flex and extending of his fingers were all signs indicating his concern for his brother, but she didn't know what she could do to help him.

11

She leaned forward and lowered her voice. "The way they talked during the trial it sounded like the Camaro was paid off. I guess his folks could keep it for him if he changes his mind about letting Sonja have it." That was something even if it wasn't particularly encouraging.

His body went rigid. "What do you mean, let Sonja have it?"

"That's what the defense attorney said. Sonja was going to keep it until he could get out and marry her." Alena sat up straight, putting some breathing room between them. "His old boss agreed to hire him back if he got probation."

"You need to start at the beginning cuz this doesn't make any sense. Do you have any idea what it felt like to get home in time to watch him being taken away to prison? I need to understand what happened."

Alena quietly asked, "Didn't somebody tell you what was going on?"

Gabriel shook his head. "No. Our grandmother only said Carlos was in trouble with the law."

"Well, I guess they had their reasons." She pressed back against her chair, wrapped her forearms across her chest and tucked her hands in tight, holding herself together. She did not want to do this. She did not want to be the bearer of bad news and this was definitely in that category.

"What reasons?" His tone left no room for anything less than a full accounting.

She wasn't going to get out of this without telling him the horrible details she'd had the misery of listening to. She swallowed hard and glanced around the room.

"It's not going to be an easy story to tell." She stared at the table top buying time and gathering her thoughts.

She searched to find the right way, the right words to tell Gabriel his brother had killed a young man from their neighborhood. Only the circumstances were in doubt.

Her voice tended to carry. This conversation needed to stay between her and Gabriel. She cleared her throat and softened her tone.

"There were things that came out at the trial. I think lots of people got called out. You should ask your mom."

"That's a little hard to do." He flattened his hands on the table top while his eyes held hers. "When I got into town, I went home. Mom answered the door and told me Carlos was in jail because of me. None of this would have happened if I'd stayed home and taken care of my little brother like I was supposed to. Then she slammed the door in my face and left me standing on the porch. My grandmother is letting me stay with her."

"Oh. Wow. I don't know what to say. But I don't see how any of it was your fault."

"My dad's not answering his phone. I don't know where he's staying these days."

He clearly expected answers from her. The military training was rolling off of him in waves. It might be the only thing keeping him in his chair before the night was over.

The waitress returned and put their drinks on the table and disappeared.

Gabriel leaned forward. "Please. I need to know. Did I do something to cause what happened?"

Alena untucked her hands, took a sip of her drink, and cleared her throat. "No. It wasn't you." She glanced around the room. There was no escape. "We need nachos. This is going to take a while." She reached for a chip. "These chips are fine but I need something more to chew on."

When the waitress walked by, Gabriel waved her over and ordered fajita nachos with everything on them. He turned back to Alena and grumbled, "Okay, tell me what happened to my brother."

She swallowed the chip she currently had in her mouth and took a gulp of her Margarita. She needed tequila and lots of it. Gabriel looked worried and desperate. He needed answers from somebody but why her? This was gonna hurt him.

She let out a sigh. "Your brother was sitting there at the defense table looking so defeated. He fell asleep a couple times during the trial. I don't know if he was that tired and worn out, but his life was hanging in the balance and it seemed like he didn't care anymore."

"Go on. We haven't got all night."

Alena's head popped up, she spoke slowly with exaggerated calm, "Actually, we have as long as it takes me. If that doesn't suit you, I'm outta here."

He blew out a breath and pressed his lips together. "Fine. Keep talking. Let's try to get at least half way through this story of yours before closing time."

Leaning forward, she grumbled, "It's not my story. It's your brother's. And it's the most twisted story I've ever heard. Do you want the details or not?" He'd already worn her patience thin. She hated trials and testimony. She wanted to be left alone. And he had no way of knowing that.

Settling back, he gripped the edge of the table and shifted in his seat. "Okay. Tell it your way. What happened to my brother?"

Out of the corner of her eye, Alena caught the waitress approaching with their food and waited until she'd put the platter on the table and walked away.

He watched her intently like she might disappear in a puff of smoke. If only she could. She watched the considerable muscles in his arms flex and momentarily relax. She was afraid he was going to choke the story out of her if she didn't say something soon. The problem was she didn't know where to begin.

"You've got food. Now, talk." His eyes narrowed on her with laser intensity.

She muttered, "I can tell you were in the service. You have absolutely no patience at all." Reaching for the pile of fajitas, beans, cheese and jalapeño slices, she pulled a loaded chip loose from the rest and bit into it. "Umm. These are good. Have some." Anything to lessen the tension. Maybe if he bit something besides her, he'd feel better.

Gabriel pulled a loaded chip out of the pile, shoved it in his mouth and chewed.

While she watched, he devoured his half of the plate and started working on hers. The man was starving and didn't even know it. That was a sure sign of him being too worried to take care of himself. A body like his needed fuel. She needed to stop gawking. His body wasn't hers to worry about.

After taking a calming swallow of her drink, she jumped in as close to the beginning as she could remember. "Carlos and Michael were both interested in Sonja. Your parents and Michael's parents encouraged all this macho fighting for the girl stuff through the years. Carlos got beat up a lot."

Alena pulled another chip from the pile. If she did all the talking, he'd do all the eating and she'd get zip. She was still full from her dinner but she needed something to pick at and chew on when she was nervous.

More than anything else, she wanted to go home, lock the door and forget all of it, everything, including the last six years of her life would be good.

Gabriel muttered, "I'm listening." Without looking up, he reached for another chip.

"They all made it to their senior year in high school." She licked the salt on the rim of her mug and took a sip of her margarita. It was cold and she turned a puckered face to Gabriel. "This place has the best margaritas. The sangria swirl is my favorite."

"Keep going," he grumbled.

"Carlos made the grades, Michael made it onto the wrestling team, and Sonja played both ends against the middle."

"What?" He straightened up and shifted closer.

She picked up her mug and wrapped her lips around the rim and sucked up some of the frozen slush so she wouldn't have to look at him.

His hand wrapped around hers and tightened over her fingers as he lowered the mug slowly down onto the table. "Please, put that down and answer me."

She stared at their hands. His were a lot darker than hers and a whole lot larger. He'd been out in the sun and it showed. He had big powerful warm hands, rough skin, straight, strong fingers, and a firm grip. She was in damn big trouble.

In different circumstances, she might have even put her free hand over his offering support. He was going to need it. But she wasn't ready for letting those kinds of feelings back into her life. She scowled and pushed an old memory down. It all started with one touch. She nodded toward their hands. "Let go of me, now."

Looking up, she caught the stunned look on his face. He was lost somewhere in his own world for two seconds. Then he focused and gruffly said, "Sorry," and let go of her.

"Okay. That's better. You stay on your side of the table." She put her hands in her lap. "I don't know how to tell you this part so it won't hurt so bad."

"Tell me the truth. How hard can that be?"

From the exasperated sound of his voice, she could tell he was losing patience. Well, tough. This was no picnic for her either.

She sat up straight, shortening the distance between them, and employed her most soothing tone in the hope it would lessen the pain she was about to inflict.

"Real hard when I know it's going to break your heart. He's your brother and what happened to him was wrong. His life didn't have to get screwed up like that. For years, people pushed him toward the tipping point. When he shot Michael, they all deserted him. He took the fall for all their mistakes. He went to prison and they're still walking free."

"Who are you talking about?" He quirked an eyebrow.

She drew in a deep breath and let it out slowly. "All of them, your parents, Michael's parents, Sonja and her mother. His friends added their share of rumors and stories to ratchet things up a couple notches. They were happy to talk about Michael's gun and how he said he was going to shoot Carlos. But under oath they admitted they'd never actually seen the gun, only some bullets. Lots of drama to go around." She inhaled and exhaled slowly before continuing. "They all helped Carlos box himself into a corner. When he used a gun to level the playing field, none of them would own up to what they'd done."

"He's in prison." Gabriel rubbed a hand over his mouth. "Do you have any idea what they'll do to him in there? He was never a tough kid. How's he supposed to survive that? And you helped put him there."

She stared defiantly across the table at him and switched into defense mode. She kept the volume down but any gentleness was gone.

"You aren't going to pin that on me. I did the best I could to keep things fair. But I wasn't the only juror and the others wanted him to go away for life."

Dropping her gaze, Alena picked up her mug, took a long drink. She needed to calm down, get a grip. "I started with probation, then maybe five or six years but they wouldn't go for it. He killed Michael. There was no way around it. You don't get to walk away from something like that. It was all I could do to get them down to twenty-five years."

"I saw you at the courthouse walking past us like we weren't there, weren't good enough to be acknowledged. You hid behind your sunglasses and never looked at us."

"I couldn't talk to anybody outside the jury room. Those were the rules. I didn't want to give anyone any excuse to disqualify me. Carlos was in a bad place and those people didn't care. They wanted to go home and get on with their lives."

"Don't lie to me. You didn't want anyone to see your face in the news connected to my brother's trial."

Thankfully, Alena's hands were still wrapped around the cold mug so she couldn't slap him. Instead, she gave her drink a shove into the middle of the table and snarled, "I'm done here!" She launched out of her chair, grabbed her purse and slung it over her shoulder. With her head up and her back ramrod straight she grumbled, "When you can speak to me respectfully, try again." She marched out without looking back, leaving him to pay the check.

She was out the door, in her Mustang, and down the highway. To hell with him. She'd be happy to call the devil and let him know Gabriel was on the way. He didn't know a damn thing about her. He didn't have to say it. She could read between the lines. His insinuation that she was more concerned with her reputation than his brother's life opened a Pandora's box of old hurts.

She did not need him resurrecting the past.

Maybe someday he'd figure it out, or not. It didn't matter.

Papi and Romero had taught her to be strong but that girl had been lying low the last few years. The trial had rubbed her the wrong way but she'd held it together until Gabriel stomped on the wrong frayed nerve. He was lucky she hadn't dumped her drink over his head.

The only thing saving him had been the crowded restaurant. She did not want to be recognized when the whole world had cell phones with cameras. She liked her privacy, her anonymity. He was a disturbance she didn't need or want. He was also a Marine. He would be loyal and determined. She could hope, but the truth was, she likely hadn't heard the last of Gabriel DeLeon.

CHAPTER FOUR

GABRIEL DISCREETLY CHECKED on Alena for a week waiting for her to cool off and making sure she was safe. He'd handled her and the situation all wrong. He'd have to do better. He was getting nowhere on his own. As much as he didn't want to admit it, he needed her.

His mother still wasn't speaking to him.

His dad was missing altogether. Word on the street had him staying at his girlfriend's house and she wasn't answering her door.

His grandmother had done her best to tell him what she could remember but it didn't fill in the blanks that still bothered him. Carlos had pleaded self-defense. That was a long way from murder. There had to be more to the story. How had Carlos gone from an enamored boyfriend to a murderer?

Gabriel's old friends were his age, married, working, and struggling to survive. They hadn't kept track of Carlos. Carlos's so-called friends didn't want to answer any questions and were making themselves scarce. He hated to admit it, but he was at a dead-end. As a last resort, he was on his way to her house on a sultry Saturday afternoon. *Into the valley of death rode the six-hundred...or whatever. He wouldn't underestimate Al again.*

Alena was a soft pretty name for a pretty girl. Al was the tough little *chica* who had handed him his ass, twice. Once in the steakhouse parking lot and again in the restaurant.

In his younger days, he wouldn't have approached her at the courthouse or anyplace else. She was off-limits. Becoming a Marine had changed him and taught him a whole lot about life outside of his neighborhood. Nowadays, he didn't back down, didn't quit, and he didn't run from a fight. It was time to suck it up and give Alena his best effort. He would be taking a chance and stepping way outside of his comfort zone.

He pulled up in her driveway and eyed the house. She was in there. The Mustang sat partially shaded in the carport next to a pretty cream with tan trim triple-wide. Nothing fancy from the looks of it. Pretty much standard for Texas country living.

All he had to do was park his Harley, walk up on the porch, and knock on her door. Then she'd take out a shotgun, blow him off the porch, and no one would think anything of it. He could imagine the headline: *Female Juror Shoots Brother of Convicted Gang Member on Her Front Porch in Self-Defense.*

Heaven help him. He stopped close behind the Mustang and shut off the bike. She might think twice about putting shotgun pellets in her fancy little Mustang GT.

Gabriel grinned. The girl liked to drive fast and had the perfect car for doing it. He looked it over carefully. The custom modifications were there for a trained eye to see. Her Mustang wasn't stock. It was refitted to race. The rear stabilizers were barely visible under the custom ground treatment. Since they were there, he'd bet so were the shocks and struts necessary to hold the track at high speeds. The expensive paint job distracted people from looking too closely at the air intake system masquerading under the hood scoop. Damn. His hands itched to touch it, to look under the hood, to drive it.

Down boy. That's never gonna happen.

He got off the bike, walked up her front steps, and pushed the doorbell.

Amazingly enough, the door opened and Alena eyed him through the screen. "How did you find me?"

"I followed you home." He didn't take his eyes off her. She was so pretty and so fearless. Some Marine that outweighed her and could rip her screen door off its hinges didn't faze her. *Beautiful.*

"Why?"

He kept his eyes fixed on her. "I need you to tell me the rest of what happened. Nobody's talking. It's like they've got something to hide." Her curly chestnut-brown hair was tied back in a ponytail. Her oversized t-shirt hid her shape. He grinned to himself. He'd interrupted her house cleaning day. That ought to irritate her. Interrogation tactics: Make the person uncomfortable. He was on it.

She glanced past him to the driveway. "What happened to your car?"

"It's messed up. It's gonna take me some time to fix it."

Gang style vengeance had busted out the headlights, taillights, windshield, and sliced the tires. She didn't need to know that.

"Oh. So, that's your ride now." She nodded toward the black Harley parked in her driveway. "It's a relic."

"Yeah, but it still runs." He grinned as he watched her blue-grey eyes dart back and forth from him to his Harley. In the daylight, the blue came out. At Ninfa's they'd looked grey.

"If you walk around to the back, we can sit in the shade and I'll do my best to finish telling you what I know."

Gabriel jerked to attention and speared her with a stare he reserved for people who were treading on his last lick of patience. What? He wasn't good enough to come inside her house. "Around back like some low-life biker trash?"

Al glared back.

"No, more like an uninvited guest I barely know." She stood up straighter. "Considering the circumstances of our last meeting, I'll be damned if I'll invite you into my home." Gripping the edge of the door she raised her eyebrows and glared. "So, haul yourself around to the back porch where we can sit in the shade or sit out here on the front steps in the sun and roast. Better yet, get on down the road. It's a no-never-mind to me."

Before she could slam the door in his face, Gabriel gave a curt nod. "Fine, back porch." He turned, stomped back down the steps and around to the back of the house. In order to get his answers, he'd play nice. Well, he'd try to play nice.

He took a seat at the patio table. The colorful tropical printed seat cushions provided a cheerful ambiance but he wasn't in the mood to be cheerful. The Marines had drilled manners, discipline, and self-control into him, but around her it all went out the window. She pushed his buttons like a pro. He couldn't, wouldn't hurt her, but he had to get a grip and fast before he did something stupid like strangle her. She was no ordinary girl, no way, no how.

The back door opened and Alena stuck her head out. "Would you like some iced tea?"

"Sure. That's fine." He glanced her way then back out over the yard. He'd made it this far but it hadn't been easy. He needed to hold it together a little longer. Talk about a mean girl. Al was tougher than old boot leather. He grinned. He could deal with it. He got the plain ugly truth from her. There was no guessing, no reading between the lines where she was concerned.

But he'd like to get to know Alena better. He only had to get past Al to do it. The left side of his upper lip twitched. Getting past Al wasn't going to be easy.

He loved a good challenge.

～

Alena poured two large, insulated tumblers of iced tea, and picked up some packets of sweetener on her way to the back door. Once outside she put the tumblers on the table and dropped the sweeteners in the middle. "I don't know if you like your tea sweet or not so I brought those."

Gabriel glanced down and then looked up at her. "Thanks. It was a long ride and it's hotter than hell today."

"I don't like being followed." She stared at him. He was even more handsome in the bright light of day. Damn the bad luck.

"I didn't have any other way to get in touch with you." He tore a strip off the sweetener packet, dumped it into the tea, and sat back against the thickly padded cushion. "Are you gonna sit down?"

"If you hadn't been so awful the other night you might have been able to get the rest of the story, or maybe ask nicely for my phone number. You were supposed to be acting civilized. Remember?" She sank slowly on to the edge of a chair while keeping the table evenly between them. She clearly recalled the warm firm grip of his fingers, and she didn't want to think about it.

"I'm a Marine Corps Sergeant. I expect answers to my questions. You weren't being very cooperative, and you weren't making it easy to talk to you."

"Sorry to hear it, but it's not news." She slid back in her seat, raised one foot, hooked her toes under the edge of the nearest foot stool and moved it around to where she could rest her bare feet on it. "Being nice got me a lot of grief. This is me now, take it or leave it."

Gabriel's eyes directly focused on her. "All right. I get that, I guess." He drank half his tea in a few swallows. Still holding the tumbler, he asked, "Can we try again? I'd appreciate any help you can give me."

Alena nodded once. "Okay, I will if you will." She didn't want to but she would. She had to give him credit for trying. He'd gotten into town too late to help Carlos before the trial. Judging by the look on his face, he was discouraged and losing hope. That bothered her conscience. She lowered her eyes and sipped her tea.

"Deal." He rearranged his fingers on the tumbler. "Where did my brother get a gun?"

"After graduation from high school, he moved in with some guy he knew. I don't remember his name but the gun belonged to him. He wasn't home the evening of the shooting, so he didn't testify. The pistol was kept in a kitchen drawer making it easy to get to."

"But why did Carlos have it?"

Alena scrunched down in her chair. "Sonja. It was all about Sonja." She peered over at Gabriel. "Do you know her?"

"Yeah, I saw her around the house a few times when we were kids. She was always coming around looking for Carlos."

"Neither attorney asked Sonja why she kept going over to your house when it always ended up in a fight with Michael beating up Carlos. At first, I got the impression Carlos and Sonja were an item."

She sighed and shook her head. "Anyway, she would get Carlos to drive her around in the Camaro running errands. But in between times she was seeing Michael, the wrestling star, and going for rides in his Wrangler. She was using both of them, pitting them against each other."

Alena stopped to catch her breath and gauge how Gabriel was doing. His head was turned away from her, facing toward the back fence and the open field beyond. When the world got to closing in, it had a calming effect. She'd spent plenty of evenings gazing at the tall grasses swaying on the breeze. It was a good place to escape reality for a few minutes. She could give that to Gabriel.

The sun rested low in the western sky and her afternoon had slipped away. It would be dark soon. She studied the melting ice in her tumbler, gave it a swirl, and took a few sips of tea while resting her voice a minute. His silence prompted her to go on.

"One evening, Sonja got Carlos to drive her to the laundromat. While they were there, she saw Michael pull up at the Exxon station across the street. She went over to talk to him and he drove her back to the Laundromat. When they got there, Carlos walked up to the Wrangler and told her to get out but she didn't. She kept visiting with Michael."

Gabriel's attention snapped back to her. He looked like a man about to commit a murder of his own and she was the only other person around. Not good.

She put her tumbler on the table. "Look, I'm only telling you what was testified to in court. Don't get mad at me."

"I'm not mad at you. I'm just angry, period. It's that same old trick girls pull to get boys all worked up and make them jealous." Gabriel's fingers dug into his thighs right before he rubbed his hands down toward his knees. "Don't stop now. I need to hear the rest of this."

"Maybe we should take a break." Alena studied the tense set of his jaw, the strain around his mouth, the flexing of his biceps. She was staring at a human stick of dynamite. If she struck a match, he'd explode and take out half the county. Couple that with the tired sad eyes and she had a man at the end of his rope. "It's going to get worse.

And it's getting late. I haven't eaten anything since breakfast. I'm going to fix dinner. There's enough for two, if you want some?"

He glanced at her out of the corner of his eye. "What? Are you gonna put it out here on the porch in a dog bowl for me?"

"You know something, you can be absolutely hateful. I don't have a dog, or a bowl for one, but right now, you'd be lucky if I threw it on the deck and let you fight over it with the ants." She glared at him.

He faced her, squared his shoulders, and glared back. Then he cracked a smile followed by a snort, then a short laugh. "You're crazy, *chica*."

"Yeah, well that's not news either. Since you haven't tried to kill me yet, I figure it's probably safe enough to let you come on inside while I fix dinner. Nothing fancy, just food." Alena put her feet down, stood, and plucked her tumbler off the table.

He launched out of his chair so fast she was instantly reminded of his military training. The only thing missing was the salute. Manners, not many men were trained to stand when a lady leaves the table. *Guess the Marines taught him something.*

She was acutely aware she wasn't dressed for company as she padded ahead of him on her bare feet. Saturday was cleaning, reading, listening to music, and resting day. That was until he'd come stomping up her steps. She glanced behind her. Nope, he wasn't wearing combat boots. Looked like he'd traded them in for biker boots.

Earlier, she'd been comfortable in her oversized t-shirt and leggings. Now, she resisted the urge to pull her t-shirt down around her knees. Not that it would stretch that far. She wasn't dressed for company, no matter how uninvited he was. Her work uniform and her jeans were her outer armor. They put a safety barrier of confidence and distance between her and the world. Without them she was vulnerable. If she went to change, dinner would be delayed, but if she hurried up, finished the story, and fed him, he should go away. That was a better strategy.

He followed her through the dining room and on toward the kitchen. The soft thick pile light tan carpet muffled his footsteps, but she could still hear him just fine. T-Rex was right behind her all the way.

She walked around the raised counter and into the Tuscany styled cooking area. She'd spent a fortune upgrading and customizing that room. Imported Italian tile had been added to the walls behind the cooktop and counters. Arches framed all the alcoves with smoky glass-front cabinets and recessed lights were the finishing touches. Racks hung from the ceiling for the gourmet endorsed pans. Yeah, she liked to cook when she had the time. This was not one of those times.

It was also a spacious room that allowed her to turn and see everything in the living room, including Gabriel. Him, she watched like a mongoose watches a cobra. She wasn't sure she trusted him all that much, but they couldn't sit outside forever. The blood-sucking insect population came out to party at sundown and feast on any naked skin they could land on. Maybe she'd screen in the back porch, someday.

"If you want to wash up, the guest bath is that way, first door on your left." She pointed toward the back of the house behind the kitchen area.

"Thanks." He walked in the direction she'd pointed, went into the bathroom, and closed the door.

She let out the breath she'd been holding. There was a man in her house. A tall, dark, and handsome man. He needed to go away. She didn't want to go there again. His voice, his eyes were too perfect, too easy to lose herself to his alpha- maleness. *No, no, and no. Not happening.*

By the time he'd washed up and taken a seat at the counter across from her, she had their dinner ingredients lined up on the butcher-block cutting board.

She didn't look up. "Bacon and spinach stuffed hamburgers are the only thing on the menu tonight with grilled herbed veggies and country fries. Hope that's all right."

"Sure. Sounds good. Lots better than what I've been eating the last few years. Fix it and I'll eat it."

"I can do that." And fast. She could put it together quick, stuff it in him and shove him out the door.

She glimpsed in his direction. He seemed okay. Not as uptight as he had been earlier. That was good. She eyed the counter that curved out into the living room giving her a safe zone. Either it had shrunk, or

26

his broad shoulders were taking up a lot of room. She moved her placemat a little farther away from his. It was a good thing he wasn't going to be around after tonight or she'd need a bigger house. His ink and rugged good looks were playing havoc with her visual senses and he smelled good too, all warm leather and woodsy aftershave. He made her heart beat a little faster. Something it hadn't done in years. This was not a good time for that nonsense to start.

She had already arranged the items in the order she'd fix them. Staring at them wouldn't get them on the grill. Damn. She spread her fingers out on the countertop next to the cutting board and exhaled. "Okay, where was I? Oh, yeah. Carlos was upset when Sonja wouldn't go with him. So, he got in the Camaro, drove to the apartment, got the gun, and went back to the laundromat."

She picked up the razor-sharp, porcelain paring knife. "See, that's where things went really bad. Carlos had been hearing from guys in the neighborhood that Michael had a gun and was going to shoot him the next time they fought. So, Carlos's lawyer told us that this was all self-defense. But the catch is that when Carlos left, he wasn't in any danger. He was fine. He could have simply stayed away and let Michael take Sonja home. Or let Sonja find her own way home, but he went back."

She stopped slicing and watched him sitting stone-cold still on his bar stool. His forearms rested on her granite counter with his one hand crossed over the other where she could see them. The top hand gripped the bottom one with a strangle hold. If that was any indication of what was going on inside of Gabriel, she hoped it never got out.

She asked, "Are you okay?"

"No, but keep going. Let's get this done."

"If you're sure?" She didn't like the worrisome signals his body was sending out. The muscles along his jaw bulged, his neck veins visibly pulsed, his breathing had grown heavy and irregular and he wasn't meeting her eyes when she spoke. These were not good signs. She waited a few seconds, giving him a chance to call it off. If she took his blood pressure, she was sure it would be in the high-risk for stroke category.

"Yeah, I'm sure."

She needed to stall. She did not want him passed out on her floor.

She walked over to the pantry and rummaged around in her spices. There had to be something she could pull out that she could use. Ah, yes, dried parsley. Good for the digestion. Perfect. She walked slowly back to her work area.

"When Carlos drove back to the laundromat, Michael and Sonja were still sitting in the Wrangler. Carlos testified that when he walked up to Michael's side of the car, it looked like Michael was reaching for a gun under the seat. He got scared and the gun went off." Alena stopped to collect her thoughts and breathe. "Carlos told Sonja to get out of the Wrangler and get in the Camaro."

She studied Gabriel carefully. If he was going to detonate, this would be the time.

"I'm sorry, but Carlos did shoot Michael." She kept quiet, letting it sink in.

"Yeah." He stared down, maybe at his hand or the top of the bar. She couldn't tell. But he wasn't looking at her. "At least that much is true."

"Sonja said they went to the Brazos River and Carlos threw the gun off the bridge. The deputies found it on the riverbank and sent it to the lab in Austin." She chopped two slices of crisp bacon into tiny bits.

"Then what?" He interlaced his fingers and tapped the edges of his hands against the counter top. "Let's get this over with."

"Well, they went to the apartment where Sonja lived with her mom. Carlos and Sonja sat on the couch. They could hear the police sirens out in the street. Then Sonja's mom came out of the bedroom with Michael's father, Mister Juarez." Alena ducked her head. "He left without knowing his son was dead."

Alena looked up and caught the incredulous expression Gabriel shot her way. If looks could kill, she'd be so dead and bleeding-out on her pretty cream and mocha-swirl tile floor.

He grumbled, "Go on, finish it. What happened?"

Gabriel wasn't smiling, but he wasn't foaming at the mouth. His jaw relaxed and he unclasped his hands. This might be one of those times where looks could be deceiving and he was really one breath away from putting his fist through her granite counter top.

"I'm so sorry. This has to be hard to hear."

"So, rip the bandage off and get it over with."

Alena's fingers worked to pinch the hamburger pockets stuffed with chopped spinach and bacon closed. "Um, the police found Carlos at the apartment and took him in for questioning and he confessed to shooting Michael but he kept saying he thought Michael had a gun."

"Did he?"

"Nobody would admit to anything. Being summer, the Wrangler had the rag top but there were no doors on it. Nobody at the Laundromat would admit to seeing anything at all. If there was a gun in there, somebody could have taken it before the cops got there. Nobody knows. Or if they do, they're not telling."

"Are you done?" He stared at her with narrowed eyes.

"Almost. Are you sure you want me to go on? This gets worse."

"Stop stalling and spit it out." His stare turned into a frustrated, intense glare.

She faintly bobbed her head acknowledging she'd heard him. "Carlos swore that he loved Sonja and they were going to get married. He was going to let her keep the Camaro for him if he went to prison and they'd get married when he got out. His attorney tried to convince us to give him probation or at least a short sentence. He reminded us that Carlos had a boss who would employ him and a girlfriend who would help him live a respectable life."

Alena stopped to catch her breath again. She really hated this next part. She looked around the room. There was no escaping what came next and nothing was going to change it. This was where she was going to gut punch Gabriel.

He glanced up at her but didn't say anything.

She dropped the sliced vegetables in a bowl with herbed olive oil. Since he didn't look like he was going to cut her up and stick her in the bowl with the green beans, onions and squash, she ran out of time and verbally trudged onward.

"When they put Sonja on the stand, she told us how she loved Carlos and was going to wait for him. But then the prosecutor brought out some fancy greeting cards she'd sent to Michael. She'd written on them how much she loved him and that he was everything she wanted. Carlos looked like he was going to die right there in front of us. He never knew, or if he did, he'd ignored it. She really put it over on him." Alena turned away, walked over to the stove, took a cast-iron grilling pan down from the overhead hook. She casually tested the weight, just in case she needed to swing it in self-defense.

"And?"

She inhaled deeply. "I reminded the other jurors that Carlos had lots of help getting to where he was that night. The parents on both sides who kept pushing him to be a man and fight for Sonja weren't innocent. Sonja used Carlos for all she could get while she went after Michael. Their so-called friends spreading rumors that Michael had a gun and was going to shoot Carlos." The only sound in the house was the turquoise, enamel coated, pan hitting the gas burner grate.

"So, what happened?"

"When Carlos drove away, he should have stayed away. He made the choice to go back. I voted for probation so I'd have room to negotiate. When they wouldn't go for probation, I said ten years, the same amount of time as all this squabbling had been going on. He'd be out in four since he'd already spent one year in jail. But the others wanted life or fifty years. We argued back and forth. Things got so loud that the bailiff came in to check on us. To avoid a hung jury, I was forced to agree to the twenty-five so he could get out in twelve."

"You sent my brother to prison for twenty-five years." Gabriel stared at her while his fisted hands rested, white-knuckled, on her counter.

She stared back. "Look, those people weren't interested in the mitigating circumstances. They had businesses and jobs to get back to. One woman had retired and was packing to move to Tennessee. They just wanted to get it over with."

Alena stopped, took a deep breath and focused. She slid the hamburgers onto the grill and reached for the vegetables.

"It wasn't supposed to be a murder trial. We were picked for a drunk-driving case, but that got settled out in the hall. Since they had a jury selected, they used us for Carlos's case. They love having nurses on juries. We understand the science behind the evidence. We get the psychological issues. I did the best I could. I tried to make them see how important it was to consider everything leading up to that night."

She used her cooking tongs to grab the marinated vegetables and drop them on the grill. The sound and aroma of sizzling meat and vegetables filled the kitchen.

His eyes focused on her as he grumbled, "Is that supposed to keep my brother from being raped in prison?"

"What was I supposed to do? He walked up and shot Michael in the back of the head. I saw the pictures. Nobody knows if Michael even saw him coming. Carlos had parked on the far side of the parking lot. Sonja swore she didn't see him until after he shot Michael."

Gabriel wasn't moving. It had to be awful to hear what his brother had done from a stranger, but he needed to hear the specifics that he wasn't getting from his family. They'd had their part in the circumstances that had pushed Carlos to do what they expected of him. Now, they wanted to say what a good boy he was and how it was all Michael's fault. Michael's family was telling the same story with Michael as the innocent party. Alena didn't even want to start on what she thought of Sonja. It wouldn't change anything.

Alena lowered her voice and gently said, "There's a difference between the law and justice. I tried to get justice for Carlos but the law wasn't on my side."

She watched out of the corner of her eye as Gabriel put his elbows on the bar and held his head between his hands. She had unintentionally stunned a Marine into dead silence. She murmured, "I'm so sorry."

He said, "I need to go."

Panic shot through her. She scrambled out from behind the counter saying, "Oh, no. Not right now. You've just been hit with this disaster and you're in no condition to ride that motorcycle. I understand if you're not hungry but you're not leaving till you've had time to let this sink in and settle."

She stopped beside him so close she could feel the heat coming off his body. Too close. She took a small step back.

Gabriel looked straight at her, then all the way down and back up slowly. "And you think you can stop me?"

A cold shiver ran down her spine but she stuck her chin in the air, screwed up her courage, and mustered up her firmest tone. "Maybe not, but I can try. I'll be damned if I'm going to let you ride out of here and get yourself killed. Motorcycles have no protection. If you're not a hundred percent focused, you can be dead in a second." She snapped her fingers in his face. "And right now, your mind isn't on the road."

She pointed toward the front door. "Over by the power plant, the gators like to crawl up on the road at night because it's warm. Hit one of those and you're dead." She gently put her hand on his chest. "If hitting the asphalt doesn't kill you the pissed-off gator will take chunks out of you. So, no, you just stay put a little while. You haven't got any place you need to be that's worth dying over tonight."

He grumbled, "You're kinda bossy," as a slow grin creeped across his lips.

She dropped her hand from his chest, nodded and smiled. "That's one way of putting it. Come on. What've you got to lose? Hang out a little while. Don't make me ruin dinner because I'm following you home to make sure you get there in one piece."

"Sure. Wouldn't want you getting lost in the low rent part of town."

"Low rent doesn't scare me." *But you do.* She walked to the kitchen side of the counter. "This is almost ready. I'm going to make you a plate. You should try to eat at least a little of it."

Gabriel hitched his hip onto the barstool and grunted. "Why not? Gotta be polite."

Her grip on his plate tightened. She would be totally justified in hitting him over the head with his plate for being such a snot. She glanced over at him. No, it wouldn't phase him but it would break one of her good stoneware plates. She put their food on the counter and retrieved two forks from the top drawer next to the sink. Looking up at Gabriel she asked, "What would you like to drink with your dinner? I've got more iced tea or bottled water."

"Don't suppose you've got any beer?" He cocked an eyebrow.

"Yeah, I do, but then you aren't going anywhere tonight. Nobody drinks at my house and rides all the way to town on a motorcycle in the dark." Alena eyed Gabriel. "You'd have to stay over in the guest room."

"Fine, so give me a beer. I could really use one." Gabriel shifted on the bar stool, settling in. "Unless you don't want some inked biker guy sleeping in your pretty little house, messing things up."

32

Alena inhaled noisily and exhaled slowly. "There you go being hateful, again. You know, I could put you out on the porch and let the mosquitos carry you off." She walked to the refrigerator, opened the door, and plucked a beer off the shelf. She set the can down directly in front of Gabriel. "There you go, sport."

He popped the top and took several swallows. Putting it down, he looked at Alena. "Thanks, that helps."

Gauntlet thrown down, picked up, and thrown back. She nodded in his direction and gave him her *don't-jack-with-me-buster* look.

They ate in silence. Alena didn't want to fight with him. But a nagging thought kept rolling around in her mind. He was a pit bull with a bone to chew on. This wasn't over. She glanced over at his plate. It was empty. The man had been hungry. And he'd been hungry the night they'd gone to Ninfa's. He wasn't eating or at least not eating right.

She slipped off her bar stool and carried their plates to the sink. "Can I get you anything else? I've got some apples if you want one."

"No, but I'll take another beer." Gabriel picked up the empty can and held it out to her.

She rinsed it out and dropped it in the recycle bin. "You can go turn on the TV if you want and I'll bring it to you."

Just like old times, an instant replay. Only it had been a different dark and handsome man in another lifetime. She so did not want to go there again. Not another crushed and broken-beyond-repair heart. Never again. She inhaled a deep breath and let it out slowly. She could do this.

Just this once.

He'd go away in the morning.

Gabriel got up, walked to the living room, eyed the camel colored, micro-fiber couch and finally sat down at the far end. He sank like a stone into the cushions. Soft. Perfect for making out with a nice little *chica* like Alena. Wrong, he rubbed the back of his neck and cleared that thought. Al was not a nice little *chica*. She was in his face and mouthy. But she had soft, gentle hands and smelled like warm summer afternoons. What the hell was wrong with him? He had zero business going there.

The TV remote was on the large square ottoman that doubled for a coffee table. All very stylish and from the looks of things, fairly new. There was a rock fireplace in the corner with a star of Texas carved in the stone. She liked nice things. She'd have no use for him, ever.

"How long you been living here?" he called over his shoulder.

Before he had time to turn his head, Alena walked up alongside of him and handed him a cold beer. "It's been about four years now. Why?"

Gabriel shrugged and took the can from her. "Everything looks new."

"How long were you in the Marines?"

He watched her walk a few steps to the rocker-recliner and sit. She scooted back, pulled her feet up, and settled in cross-legged.

He took a quick swallow and lowered the can to rest on his thigh. "Eight years." He didn't blink, didn't smile. He looked over at her. "Eight years and a lot of miles."

"Did you get to go to Germany? Most of the nurses I work with, their husbands are in Germany."

She rocked gently in the recliner.

Gabriel kept watching her. He was making her nervous. At last, he was getting something from her besides dodge and weave defense. Good, it served her right. She'd sent his brother to prison. "No. I got sent to Afghanistan by way of Iraq."

"Oh. That's rough." She looked around the room. "Things have changed in town a lot over the last few years but you'll get used to it. Lots of new stores."

"Yeah." He watched her rocking back and forth, picking up speed with each pass. "You nervous about something?"

"What?"

"You're power-rocking." He gave a nod in her direction.

"Oh. Sorry, I didn't mean to do that. Rocking usually helps me relax." She leaned forward and stopped moving. "I can't help it. I have a lot on my mind these days."

"Anything to do with my brother?" He raised an eyebrow. There

34

was peaceful rocking and then there was her trying to rock that recliner out the door and down the road. He knew the difference.

She sat back and looked steadily at him. "I think about Carlos. I can't forget the way he looked sitting there at the defense table when the prosecutor read those greeting cards. His heart was breaking. I could see it happening right in front of me. It was terrible and Sonja did that to him."

"Yeah, and seeing my little brother dragged away in chains was no picnic either." Gabriel raised his beer and took another swallow.

She nodded. "I don't remember seeing you in the courtroom."

"I got into town Wednesday. I only got to hear the closing arguments that afternoon. I went to the jail to see Carlos that evening, but he refused to see me. Thursday and Friday, I sat in the back row with our grandmother. I didn't want to make Michael's family any madder than they already were. It wasn't easy listening to the verdict on Thursday but the sentencing on Friday was the worst."

In a nanosecond, Alena disappeared and Al scrunched down tighter if that was possible before she snarled, "I'm sorry for you and your grandmother but I don't really give a rat's ass if Michael's parents were angry. They kept urging Michael to beat up Carlos. They didn't have to do that. They raised him to be aggressive." She sat up and leaned back. "And no, he shouldn't have died over it, but his parents aren't blameless. They need to own their part in his death." Her mouth turned into a seriously disgusted frown. "And that Sonja, she's a piece of work. That girl is seriously evil."

Gabriel sat still and watched her go back to rocking. The pinched-up look slowly relaxed and the softer side of her came back out. She cared. The tears he'd seen leaking out of her eyes when the verdict was read were real.

He exhaled a resigned sigh. "I never thought you gave a damn what happened." He rubbed the bottom of his beer can on his thigh a couple times leaving a damp trail on his jeans. "I watched you walk in and out of the courthouse with the deputies. You always looked like you were trying to avoid us. It seemed to me like something was wrong since you were afraid to face us."

She glared at him and huffed out an exasperated breath. "Did you happen to notice the two rival gangs standing on either side of the sidewalk shouting at us? They didn't need to get a good look at me. I was scared but I still wanted to do the best I could for Carlos and Michael. There were two lives lost when that gun went off. The only difference is Carlos is still breathing."

Gabriel watched her and muttered, "At least for now."

"That's not on me." She shifted around in the chair rearranging her legs to one side.

"Those guys have quit following you. They aren't going to hurt you. They've moved on." He'd made sure of it, Marine style. But he couldn't tell her that.

"What are you, some kind of fortune teller? You don't have any idea what they'll do. Those hoodlums are no joke. They might be just small-town wannabe gangsters but they want to make it to the big time of gang-world."

"I hear things. They tried intimidating some of the other jurors in town. Complaints were called in to the police. Carlos and Michael aren't worth the trouble."

"Good to know." She white-knuckle gripped the arm rests. "Why didn't you act like a decent person and come up and ask me straight out what was going on? Some guy running at me in the parking lot is scary." Alena dropped her feet over the edge of her seat and planted them on the floor.

Gabriel smiled sheepishly. "Yeah, well, you weren't easy to catch." He looked down. His smile disappeared. "I couldn't believe what I heard when the judge read the sentence. It took me a minute to get up and take our grandmother to my car. All the other jurors were surrounded by the reporters. You were the only one I had a chance of talking to and you were already on the other side of the parking lot. I had to hurry to catch up to you."

She continued to stare directly at him. "I figured you were one of the gang members. I didn't have anything with me to protect myself. They wouldn't let me have my pepper spray or Taser in the court house. All I could do was run for my life."

He exhaled slowly. "I'm sorry I frightened you." Would wonders never cease where she was concerned? He wasn't one to apologize but judging by the seriousness of her tone, he owed her that.

She leaned back wiggling herself deep into her chair. "I'm sorry I was rude to you."

Gabriel grinned. "I think I might have deserved it." He turned the can in a lazy circle. "You really scared the crap out of me when you did that one-eighty out there on the road. Where'd you learn to drive like that?"

She hesitated to answer him. For a few seconds, he was afraid she wasn't going to.

She inhaled in a slow deep breath, pulled her feet up onto the seat, and wrapped her arms around her legs. "Back in college I used to race an old Chevy Nova mostly on amateur nights, just for fun."

He swallowed and lowered the can. "Not too many girls into racing."

"No, not too many. It's a tough sport. All grease, gasoline, burning rubber, and sweaty men." Her lips turned down at the corners. "God, how I miss it. It was a long time ago."

"Not exactly the kind of thing I'd picture a girl doing." Gabriel tipped his head to one side, letting her last admission sink in. Okay, this was something new. She missed the race track?

"I dropped out of college to race but it didn't work out. I went back to school and learned to do something useful."

He watched her attempted small smile fail to reach her eyes. What was up with this girl?

She murmured, "I'm tired. I'm going to bed." She stood and stretched. "You saw the guest room there across from the bathroom. Make yourself comfortable. Take a shower if you want. There's plenty of beer in the fridge and if you get hungry, help yourself."

She turned an uncompromising eye on him. "You have to promise me you won't ride that motorcycle tonight."

Gabriel did his best not to laugh. *Chica* was trying to intimidate him. He raised his beer can in a salute. "I promise not to ride the bike tonight." It wouldn't hurt to humor her.

"See you in the morning," she said softly while walking toward her bedroom. "I'll make breakfast, if you want."

The door closed and he heard the lock click. If he had to bet, she was probably pushing her dresser over in front of the door just in case he decided to attack her in the middle of the night. He definitely wasn't that man. He grinned and let out a soft snort. He'd made it past her first line of defense. *Game on, chica.*

For now, he had the living room to himself. He sat on the couch and finished his beer. It was quiet. Peaceful. No noise from the neighbors, no stereos blaring, no car doors slamming, no engines revving. He liked it. He went to the kitchen, dropped the empty can in the recycle bin, and grabbed another one.

He sauntered through the small office area off to the side behind the kitchen checking out the framed photos on the walls. He popped the top on the fresh can. There were several eight by tens with a very young Alena standing between two men. They all wore matching coveralls. The race cars they were standing in front of were classics. There hadn't been anything like that on the tracks in twenty years. Then there were a few of her during what looked like teenage years. There weren't any of her at college age. What was up with that?

Both men were tall but the Latino man was huge. He had long, coal-black hair tied back. Gabriel looked closer. He was handsome if you liked a long moustache. But it was the eyes that really got his attention. Gabriel recognized the war zone stare. Wounds that would never heal. That man had seen the worst and it haunted him. A very young Alena was holding his hand in every shot. The Caucasian man was slender with tousled grey hair. Definitely a man in his sixties. His hand either rested on her shoulder or was hidden from view behind her back. They were all smiling proudly.

On his way back to the living room, Gabriel glanced at the mail at the far end of the counter to get her full name.

He sank back down on the couch and turned on the TV. He put the volume down low. Alena Cordova had to be crazy letting him stay in her house overnight. What was she thinking? Guess she wasn't that scared of him after all. And he'd be finding out where she got the name Cordova. She sure hadn't been born with it.

The elderly man was likely too old to be her father and the Latino man was out of the question. There were some missing pieces to the

38

puzzle that was Alena. And Al was a whole other story. A woman didn't get that strong by accident. She'd learned it somewhere along the way. She was a mystery and he didn't like mysteries. He liked facts. He pulled out his phone and started looking up anything related to racing and Cordova.

CHAPTER FIVE

THE NEXT MORNING, Gabriel watched her shuffle across the living room. He smiled at her from where he sat at the bar. "Coffee's ready."

"Thanks, I think." Alena kept moving toward the kitchen.

His smile turned to a grin. *Chica* was a mess in the morning. Her unruly mop of curly brown hair was everywhere and the awful zebra-striped, fuzzy slippers were enough to give any man nightmares. But the rest of her was pretty fine. The hot pink tank top and black short-shorts she wore had his attention. Hello, she had a pair of inviting tits, legs to die for and that ass was pretty sweet, too. Maybe he needed to rethink things.

She poured a cup of coffee, made an awful face and glared in his direction.

"This could take the enamel off a person's teeth," she grumbled. She added water and shoved it in the microwave. When it dinged, she snatched the cup out and sniffed. "Better. It's a miracle you have a stomach left after drinking this stuff."

He grinned. "It's the Marine way. Lots of caffeine and little volume. Can't be stopping to piss every half hour."

She rolled her eyes. "Oh, yummy breakfast conversation, male pissing habits." She put the cup down and stepped over to the refrigerator. "You okay with bacon and eggs for breakfast?"

"Yeah." Gabriel watched her open the door and bend over to retrieve the egg carton and bacon. His heart slapped the side of his chest and he swallowed hard. It was all he could do to stay in his chair. He wasn't about to get up and have his knees buckle under him, but damn, mama, those shorts didn't leave much to the imagination. He forced his eyes to look at his hands. He tightened his grip on the coffee mug and sucked in a breath. Yeah, he was definitely going to rethink everything.

Alena took a step back, and carried the bacon keeper and egg carton over to the counter. She looked at Gabriel and asked, "Are you okay?"

"Huh?"

"You look weird. Are you okay?"

He shifted in the chair and adjusted his jeans. "Yeah, I'm fine." *Don't even think about it. She isn't gonna let you near that. Well, not today.*

No woman could possibly be that clueless. He watched her move around the kitchen. Her long hair swayed and he caught sight of the scars the straps of her tank top didn't begin to cover.

He'd seen plenty of gunshot wounds and she had one big as Dallas on her left shoulder under her collarbone. She'd been shot. From the looks of it, it had hit her from the front. The edges were too clean to be an exit wound. She really was Al Cordova, the stock car driver and El Diablo's fiancée. He sipped his coffee. That explained a lot. It sure killed his hot mama vibe. He'd gone to bed thinking her name had to be a coincidence but apparently it wasn't. And it explained her carrying pepper spray and a Taser. Thinking back, it was a miracle she hadn't shot him dead in the courthouse parking lot.

"Scrambled eggs okay?" Alena asked as she looked up and met Gabriel's stare. She followed his eyes. "I see you've discovered my souvenirs."

"Sorry." He held her gaze. "Do you mind me asking what happened?"

"You could call it a very bad romance." She opened the egg carton. "How many eggs do you want?"

"Three." He kept watching every move she made. It didn't seem to

41

interfere with anything he'd seen so far. "Um, people don't pull out guns and start shooting for no reason."

She cracked an egg on the side of the bowl. "Another driver wanted to get together. I didn't. I had someone important in my life and we were engaged. It was after a race. Snuffy was losing and we were winning. He got mad and I got shot."

"I'm sorry." Gabriel couldn't take his eyes off her. She just kept cracking eggs like they were talking about a scratch. "Are you okay?"

She threw the last shell in the trash, put both hands on the counter, and looked him straight in the eyes. "I'm as good as I'm going to be. It doesn't let me dance like I used to. No fancy twirling under my partner's arm." She inhaled deeply. "So, moving on. How many slices of bacon would you like?"

"Four?"

She smiled and said, "You got it."

She fixed breakfast and he watched her, carefully.

He wanted to say something to break the silence but nothing came to mind. He settled for what he wanted to know. "Do you have more than one wound?" He looked over at her. The woman in the video had been shot several times.

"Yes. They're not pretty either." She met his gaze.

"I don't get it. You don't shoot someone because they don't want to go out with you."

"It wasn't only that I wouldn't go out with him. I was on the winning team, driving the winning car. We were on our way to the top. Snuffy went after my team and I got in the way."

What was he supposed to say to that? After all the gunfire he'd been party to it didn't seem like there was anything he could add. It was time to spit it out. "Are you talking about El Diablo's team?"

"Yes." She scowled. "It was a long time ago."

"I was shipping out on my second tour and didn't catch the particulars. Only that El Diablo was dead."

"He died at the track." She turned her attention back to the plates.

"Did they convict the guy?"

"Yes. Snuffy's serving a life sentence. I watched the deputies drive him away from the Harris County Courthouse headed back to jail." Her

42

eyes met his and held. "That's what happens when you kill innocent people." She slipped his breakfast onto the counter.

That hit close to home. He hoped he could make it through breakfast without sticking his foot in his mouth, again.

When they finished eating, he looked around the open living space. He wasn't ready to leave but he was out of reasons to stay. He shifted his weight from one foot to the other and asked, "Can I get your phone number? I can give you mine. In case you think of something."

"Sure. I'll get my phone. You can let me know how things are going. If you want to."

After exchanging information, they walked out to the driveway together. He settled in and started up his Harley. "Thanks for everything, dinner, breakfast. It was good."

"Sure. No problem."

He rolled out of her driveway and glanced in the rear-view mirror. She was still standing there in the bright Sunday morning sunshine, shrinking in the distance. For a hot second, he thought about turning around. There was something about Alena that worked for him. He couldn't put a name to it yet, but he'd figure it out by the time he saw her again. And he would be seeing her again, soon.

Some opportunities only came around once in a lifetime. This was one of those and he wasn't about to miss it worrying about the blow back. He'd deal with it when it happened.

CHAPTER SIX

FRIDAY AFTERNOON, Gabriel stopped at the mini-mart for a twelve-pack of beer and put it in his saddlebags. He hadn't found a job yet, but it had only been a couple weeks. He was living with his grandmother, making his savings last and helping her make ends meet. She was always there for him no matter how bad things got.

Fortunately, Houston continued to grow and build. He had experience with heavy equipment. He could fix it and operate it all day and all night long. In the dark, pouring rain, howling wind, blowing sand, he had it covered. He wasn't too worried. Sooner or later he'd find something. That was the way life worked.

What did worry him was his brother. Carlos had been moved from one prison unit to another. No explanation just moved. He'd written and tried calling but Carlos had refused the call. Their mother still wasn't speaking to him. No change there. His father's girlfriend would only say he wasn't there when Gabriel could get her to open the door. It felt more and more like they were hiding something, and he was getting nowhere.

They were all getting on with their lives. Carlos was history in their eyes. Gabriel could fight this battle alone or he could enlist Alena's help.

She was the only one who had told him anything but she only knew what had been testified to in court. People never told the whole story under oath. They answered the questions the attorneys engineered to get the appropriate answers. If it didn't benefit their side of the case, it went unsaid.

He reached out to her first. Two weeks of texting her every other day and calling her every evening to be sure she was okay was his story and he was sticking to it. He liked talking to her late at night when the world around him was quiet. His mind frequently wandered to thoughts of her, especially after the information he'd found on line. Currently there was zip, but the past, now that was something else.

Alena Cordova was Romero's driver and fiancée. He was a devil-mechanic with a wrench. She'd come out of nowhere and he'd snatched her up before anyone else got their hands on her. In person, Gabriel hadn't recognized her from her younger days on the stock car circuit. During the races she wore a flame-retardant suit and helmet. After the race, the helmet came off leaving her with sweat soaked short hair and a flushed face with zero makeup.

His Alena was all fluffy curls, pink lips, and stormy blue-grey eyes that reached inside him and awakened a need that he'd been ignoring for too long.

He grinned passing the power plant. He was in a mood fit to wrestle alligators if one wanted to crawl out on the road and give him a go. It would be a good warm up for his date with Al.

Two nights ago, she'd agreed to feed him if he brought the beer. She'd offered and he'd accepted without thinking twice. He should have kept his distance, but he didn't want to. What he wanted and what he should want were two different things. He'd spent a lot of hours thinking about it since then and he'd made up his mind. He didn't care what people in his old neighborhood would say. He'd changed and she was the one he wanted.

The Mustang wasn't in the driveway when he rolled up to her house in the late afternoon. He pulled the twelve-pack out of the saddlebags and walked around to the back porch. He set it on the patio table and popped one open. She'd be along soon. Settling into a soft padded seat, he put his feet up and got comfortable. He really liked it out there in the country. A peaceful breeze drifted over him. No worries for the time being. He was in a good place. After several swallows of beer, his eyes drifted shut. He could do this. He could take a chance.

The traditional growl of the Mustang's V-8 brought him out of his resting, half-napping haze as the tires crunched to a stop and the engine shut off. Nap time was over.

When he rounded the corner of the house, he saw the trunk open. As he got closer, she stepped out from behind the car.

She called out, "Hey, I saw the Harley when I pulled up. Can you help me with the groceries?"

Damn, she was pretty in that moment. Standing in the bright sunlight wearing Texas tight-fitting, dark-blue jeans and a Galveston souvenir t-shirt, all sea shells and glitter, she sparkled. And somehow it suited her. He really had it bad for Alena, or maybe he liked courting trouble. Trouble was what he was used to.

"Sure. No problem." He walked over and reached for the bags. "You stocking up or what?" He looked at the multitude of shopping bags and grinned.

"There's a pot-luck at work Monday. I'm going to make some simple stuff. It looks worse than it is." She stepped back. "So, what brings you out this way? It can't be my cooking."

"I don't know. I've been wanting to go for a ride and it's been a couple weeks since you cooked for me." He jiggled the bags getting a better grip on the handles and reaching for one more. "You wanna get the door?"

"Yeah." Alena shut the trunk and hurried ahead, digging in her purse for the house key. "I have some pork chops for dinner. We could grill 'em if you'd like."

"Sounds good."

"We could watch a movie later, if you can stay." She glanced over her shoulder at him.

"Great."

Hell yeah, he was staying. She didn't know it, but he had plans for the evening. Hotter than hot plans. He'd been feeling edgy the last couple weeks. No, she wasn't exactly what he'd had in mind when he imagined getting home, finding a girlfriend, and getting on with his life. He'd pictured a sweet, black-haired beauty with dark brown eyes, not some smart mouthed, blue-eyed mystery on hot wheels. But very little had turned out the way he'd pictured it.

The things he'd seen and done gave him nightmares. He'd shut down his emotions in order to carry out his missions and survive. Al challenged him, pushed him out of his comfort zone, and made him feel alive again. She wasn't afraid of him. She didn't back down. He didn't have to handle her with kid gloves. She told it like it was and he could deal with that. And considering where she'd been, he was definitely a step up from El Diablo, Romero Vasquez.

There were plenty of pictures and sports articles about Romero's racing team and their female driver. When Romero put a ring on her finger, speculation had gone into overdrive. He hadn't been the marrying kind and his engagement made tabloid headlines. The day he was killed by a losing driver gone berserk at the race track sent the sports world into turmoil.

Gabriel would employ tried-and-true Marine tactics and wait for the opportune moment to have a talk about what he'd seen in that video. He'd have to take it easy, not push too hard, too fast, and not push her away. If he screwed up, Alena would disappear and Al would come out swinging with both fists and hand him his ass in a sling.

Alena interrupted his thoughts. "I've got stuff for salad to go with the chops. You good with that?"

"Whatever you've got is fine."

He needed to adjust his jeans. He put the bags down on the counter and headed for the back porch. A quick rearrangement of the semi-erection behind his zipper relieved the pressure and let him breathe better. He grabbed the remaining beer and brought it inside.

"Is it okay to put these in the refrigerator to get cold?"

Alena glanced at the cans. "Sure." She kept emptying the grocery bags. "What have you been doing?"

Gabriel put the beer away and stepped out of the kitchen. He perched one hip on the bar stool nearest the walkthrough. "Same old thing. Looking for work and helping my grandma clean up her yard and doing some minor repairs around the house. You know, trying to make the place look a little better. I figure it's the least I can do since she's letting me stay with her."

"I'm sure she appreciates the help." She kept talking as she carried a few things to the pantry. "I saw her in court. She's too small to wrestle with heavy yard work."

He watched her move around the kitchen on auto-pilot. They were talking like they were old friends. Boy, was she in for a surprise. He'd been envisioning all the things they could do later. It had been a long time since he'd actually been with a woman and the throbbing bulge in his jeans was definitely onboard with the plan.

"Yeah, I'm giving her some money for the room and groceries. She's on social security and doesn't have much. When I get working, I'll do some fixing on the house for her." He shifted his weight.

"Every little bit helps. What kind of work are you looking for?" She carried an armful of cans to the pantry.

"Construction, heavy equipment." His heavy equipment was getting heavier by the second. What was it about this girl?

She glanced over her shoulder at him. "Houston is probably your best bet. The companies building out here are pretty much based there."

"Yeah, lots of roads are being built out this way." His eyes followed her movements. She moved easily. The old wounds didn't seem to slow her down any. His fingers itched to peel her clothes off and see them for himself. He wanted to know everything there was to know about Al.

She moved back to the sink, peeled open the pork chops, rinsed them off, and dropped them on a plate. "Do you like spiced or plain?"

He shrugged. "However you like them is fine with me. I could get into spicy." Where the hell had that come from? The last thing he needed was her any spicier than she already was.

She sprinkled mesquite spice over the chops, put the bottle up and said, "There, let those sit while the fire gets hot and we're good to go."

Gabriel grinned. "Where's the grill?"

"Follow me, I'll show you." She was already moving toward the back door.

Once outside she walked down the steps and over to a small manufactured shed and opened the door. "Here we go." She tugged on the grill to get it rolling.

Gabriel reached past her and took ahold of the handle. "I've got it from here. You go work on the rest of dinner."

"Sure. I'll just leave the grilling to the man. Works for me." She grinned and winked at him.

He wasn't sure how to take that wink, so he grinned back and let it go. Had she seen his semi-hard on? He'd damn near lost it when she'd leaned over to drag the grill out of the shed.

He found a bag of charcoal, built a nice layer in the old-fashioned grill and got things going. He went inside and found her standing next to the sink putting the salad together. "I'm letting the charcoal burn down a little."

"Okay." She kept slicing the cucumber.

He opened the refrigerator and grabbed one of her cold beers, the light version of his brand. If he pressed it against his dick, it might go down temporarily. He grinned and popped the top. He glanced her way to see if she noticed or if she'd say anything but *nada*, nothing.

He asked, "Doesn't driving all the way to Houston for work get old?"

"It doesn't bother me. It gives me time to think." She quartered the cucumber slices and scooped them into the salad bowl.

He ran his hand over the granite counter top. "When did they start putting tile floors and granite counter tops in trailers?"

"I wouldn't know. This is a modular home built to HUD standards."

He caught a hint of irritation in her voice, like maybe he'd insulted her house. Nobody was going to call her trailer-trash. *Recalculating.*

Gabriel grinned. "So, how'd you find this place? You got some family around here?" Before Romero, there was nothing on her. She was still a mystery except for the photos in her office. Where had she come from? Who was she really?

"No, no family around here." She kept slicing.

"You don't like to talk about yourself much, do you?"

Alena shrugged and reached for the avocado. "There's not much to talk about. I'm pretty dull. It would be a very boring conversation."

49

He blinked. "How do you know I'd be bored? Try me."

She peeled the avocado. "I grew up in San Francisco, went to college, quit my junior year. I met a boy, fell in love, we had big plans, but it didn't work out. I went back to college, got my nursing degree and here I am. Nothing the least bit exciting. That's me in a nut shell."

He leaned back against the counter next to Alena. "Uh-huh. And what have you left out?"

"Nothing you'd care to hear." She glanced his way.

He frowned and grumbled, "How do you know?"

She softly said, "Really, it's all the average girl stuff. Bad prom dates and a miserable senior trip."

Gabriel shrugged. "Okay. The charcoal should be ready. I'll put the meat on." He picked up the plate and walked out the back door. The girl was stonewalling him but that was okay. He'd get her in the next round. He wasn't finished.

The chops hissed and sizzled when they hit the grill. He took the plate back inside and got a clean one.

What kind of girl could deflect his questions, cut green beans and smile like nothing was out of the ordinary? He made a mental note to never play poker with her. She could guard information like nobody he'd ever met. But the internet did not keep secrets. That boy she'd hooked up with was a full-grown man. Romero was a hot-tempered, mean bastard by all accounts and eight years older than her. Alena being hooked up with that guy did not add up.

The evening was just beginning and so was he. The Marine Corps had taught him patience. Wait for the right moment to attack.

The chops were done and the salad was ready. Their dinner plates landed on the counter top and nobody was talking. Dead silence was about as boring as it could get.

Gabriel stabbed a piece of meat onto his fork. "You know you'll have to tell me about those big plans of yours sooner or later."

Alena swallowed the salad she'd been chewing, washed it down with a sip of chardonnay and said, "No, I don't." She stabbed another forkful of salad.

Gabriel watched all this with an amused smile plastered on his face. "Wanna bet?" He loved a challenge.

She grinned back at him. "I don't need to bet. I haven't asked you about your life before you barged into mine."

"No, but if you did, I'd tell you. Friends don't hide their pasts." Gabriel glanced her way and took another bite of his supper.

"So, now you're a friend of mine?"

"Absolutely." He smirked.

"Why?"

"That's easy. We've been getting to know each other for a couple of weeks." He smiled. "I like you and I want to get you into bed." There, he'd said it out loud. He could be blunt when he had to. Score one for stepping way outside of his boundaries.

Alena stopped chewing, turned and stared at him. She shook her fork in his direction, went back to chewing long enough to swallow and not spit her food half-way across the kitchen. She gulped down her wine and carefully returned the glass to the counter top. "What the hell? Have you lost your mind?"

"I'd like to know who I'm getting in bed with."

"Whoa there, fella. Is this some kind of Marine thing? Announce your plan of attack and expect to win?" She inhaled and stared at him. Then she started to laugh. "Oh, hell." She put one hand on her chest, "This is your version of shock and awe. Well, you got me. I'll give you that one."

Gabriel reached over and gently touched her arm. "I'm not joking."

Alena looked directly at him, still chuckling. "Sure you are."

"No. I'm not." He shook his head once.

"Okay. Slow down and think a minute. This isn't a good idea." She lost the smile.

"I like it."

"I'm good with being your friend." She still had her serious face on. "Come on, quit kidding around and eat your dinner before it gets cold. We can watch a movie when we're done if you want."

She turned away from him, refilled her wine glass and went back to her food.

"You got *Zorro* in your collection?" He wasn't getting sucked into an argument with her. She was pretty, strong and honest, and plenty good at making him hungry for more than his dinner. And they hadn't even gotten to the best part yet. Dessert.

"Yes, and I've got the Expendables with Banderas. He's so hot." Alena snickered softly and took a long sip from her glass.

Gabriel sat still and just stared at her for several long seconds. *Banderas? Really?* He gave up, temporarily, and ate his dinner without saying another word. *Recalculating, again.*

After they cleared their plates, Alena got him a fresh beer. When she closed the refrigerator and turned around, he had planted himself firmly in her personal space.

She held the beer can between her chest and his with very little room to spare. "Here, I got you a cold one."

Gabriel took the can, placed it on the counter, and put both hands on her shoulders. "I'm not kidding."

"Well, you have to be." She met his gaze.

"Why?" That was the burning question. Wasn't he good enough?

"Look, I get that you're angry at the people on the jury. And I get that you've got questions you can't put into words yet. I've told you everything I know." She glanced away. "So, romancing me won't help. Is this some twisted revenge or some kind of macho thing?"

Gabriel gently squeezed her shoulders. "Hey, look at me. Don't try that stereotyping crap on me. That scar of yours caught me by surprise, but considering my scars, it's not a big deal. Battle scars are just a part of a warrior's life. This is me wanting to get closer to you."

"Yeah, no, it's not." She shook her head.

"Well, then what is it?" He released her and put one hand the counter and the other on the refrigerator. She wasn't getting past him. He wanted to hear her say it. Tell him flat out what was wrong with him.

"You tell me." She fixed him with her sternest stare. "Maybe you need to get laid. You know, back from war, haven't had any in a while, and tired of jacking off. I'm better than nothing." She crossed her arms over her chest and glowered at him.

Gabriel dropped his arms, stepped back and chuckled. "You're the only girl I know that says what she thinks. I get the truth from you."

"It's still not a good reason to hook up. I don't know. Maybe you're trying to make a point or something. Whatever it is, it's not working on me." She slid past him into the living room.

He followed her. "Okay, so we'll slow it down a little but I'm not giving up. We could ride over to Galveston tomorrow? Play in the water?"

War had taught him how fast life could end. Moving slowly was not his way of doing things, not anymore. He'd found her through some twist of fate and he only had to ask himself one question. Did he want her, yes or no? That was easy. Hell yeah. A woman with the courage to speak up and say what's on her mind didn't come along every day in his world.

Alena pursed her lips, then cocked her head. "Are you kidding? Is this some kind of diversionary tactic?" She drew in a breath and shrugged. "I don't have a helmet. We'd have to take the Mustang."

Genuine happiness spread warmly through Gabriel followed by a satisfied smile. He'd take the victory and try not to gloat. He pushed for one more. "You gonna let me drive?"

Her lips pinched tightly as she squinted at him. "Really? Let you drive my car?"

"Yeah. The man always drives." He kept grinning like a cat about to eat a canary.

She angled her head to one side. "Okay. As long as you're careful and don't wreck it."

"Hot damn, I get to drive that fine red racing machine." He started to reach for her.

She stepped back. "If you stay over, we can leave early."

Gabriel wasn't sure if she meant stay over in the guest room or really stay over. He was in the mood to be all over her and he was through waiting. He moved fast putting one arm behind her back, and the other under her knees. He scooped her up, turned and headed for the master bedroom.

Alena squeaked, "Hey, chico, what do you think you are doing?"

"Screw Banderas. This is where I get the girl."

"You're loco." She giggled.

He lowered her into the middle of the champagne-pink and pale-gray satin comforter, and followed her down.

Alena put her arms around Gabriel's neck. She caught and held his gaze. "Are you sure about this?"

Gabriel pulled back, breaking her hold. "I'm sure. We're here and we've got a chance at something real. I can sleep in the guest room if you don't want me tonight." Gabriel watched and waited. "Well?"

"Honestly, I've thought about you and me but I didn't think you'd be interested. I can't imagine why you'd want to get involved with me. I didn't get any condoms when I was at the store."

"We're good. I've got it covered and I wouldn't be here if I wasn't ready to give us a chance." What was there to explain? It was what he wanted.

"Okay, but you've been warned it's not pretty."

"And I told you, I've got scars of my own and lots of ink. Some girls don't like it." Gabriel cocked an eyebrow. "Well?"

"I like ink. I like it a lot." She squeezed his shoulders and pulled him down.

Gabriel let a slow grin spread across his lips. "Good."

At two o'clock in the morning, he was awake and she was sound asleep next to him. He lay on his back with one hand tucked under his head and stared at the ceiling. He was right where he hoped he'd be. He'd been expecting a certain amount of heated passion. She wasn't shy. But when the lights went out, Alena disappeared and Al turned into one wild chica.

Worn out after the most challenging and hottest sex in his life, he'd tried to get her to talk about her past but no go. She'd given him a lazy satisfied smile, slid off of him, rolled over and gone to sleep, thank you very much. The quiet, post-sex pillow talk thing wasn't her style.

He had more questions now than when he'd arrived in her driveway. All he had was what he'd found online. The girl who could hold Romero Vasquez had to be *una chica loca,* a crazy girl, for sure. The tabloids had that part right. And he'd experienced it for himself. He wouldn't be forgetting this night ever.

She was hell-on-wheels and Romero had put her in the fastest cars on the race tracks. She'd disappeared after the shooting at the Valley Raceway. Gabriel considered himself the luckiest man in Texas to have found her, even if it was under the worst of circumstances.

The drab brown ceiling fan blades whirled slowly and silently overhead.

Romero was a mixed blood, the son of a crack whore and a drug dealer. He had a notoriously dangerous reputation and nothing an uptown girl would touch with a very long stick. Al's temper colliding with Romero's would have been like fire and gasoline. There was more to the story.

They were the mismatch of the century. The night she beat Romero's driver, he'd gone nuts. His man had come in second to a girl in a crap car and Romero wasn't having it. The sports reporters were in gossip heaven. Romero marched over to her pit. Nobody knew what he said but he was next to her every race after that. Not in front, not behind, but next to her. Often times with his arm around her shoulders. Protecting what was his?

The unsolved mystery that nobody could figure out was why he'd asked her to marry him. She was definitely not one of the glitzy, long-legged hotties he usually had hanging on his arms. And she was a different culture altogether. Even calling herself "Cordova" didn't cut it. Looking at her snow white next to his dark, dark brown in their pictures was like looking at day and night.

Plenty of guys would have stepped up to be her man back then, but she was spoken for and nobody was insane enough to challenge Romero.

Gabriel exhaled, stretched his leg muscles and uncurled his toes. She'd taken everything he had and worn him out. Usually he'd get dressed and leave after sex but not this time. He was staying. He was home from war and he was stepping up. Thinking about her made him ache in all the right places. He should have brought more condoms. He'd do better next time.

Only the strong survived. He made a habit out of being tough. It was a Marine thing. Al met him head on and Alena held him with a reassuring firmness he hadn't expected. She wasn't intimidated by him. He wasn't sure what to make of that but he liked it.

He glanced over at her sleeping form curled up under the comforter. Thank god, she was blissfully unaware of his thoughts. She didn't need to know all the things he wanted to do with her: the ways he wanted to touch her, taste her, get her hot, and take her.

His hand brushed over the smooth sheet. Finally, he was right where he belonged. He didn't know how it happened, only that the relentless longing to find what was missing in his life was gone. This was not a one-night-stand.

She had no obvious reason to be in Needville. She'd dropped out of racing, dropped out of sight, and disappeared from public life. From a distance and away from the track she wouldn't be easily recognizable. No one looking at the local newspaper would connect her to Romero but if the story had been picked up in Houston, some sports reporter could have made the connection. The high ceiling and dark wood paneling shadowed the courtroom but outside in the bright light of day the cameras would capture a clear shot. Her sunglasses, walking with her head down, and avoiding the reporters made more sense now.

If she decided to run and hide again, he might not be able to go with her. Gabriel wasn't kidding himself and he wasn't going anywhere until he had done everything possible to get Carlos a fair trial. Keeping her close while he sorted out his family problems was definitely his next biggest challenge.

He'd get the real story of her relationship with Romero out of her one sentence at a time if he had to. He wasn't going to quit. He'd been taken down, sucked, fucked and put up wet. Damn, she'd sure lit him up. He rolled to his side, his body spent and satisfied. He draped his arm over Alena, pulled her skin-to-skin close and drifted off to sleep. *Mi chica, my girl.*

CHAPTER SEVEN

THE GALVESTON FALL season was easy going without all the hustle and bustle of the summer crowds. They had plenty of open beach to enjoy. The sun's lazy afternoon heat tempered by a soft breeze fanning over the sand hinted at quiet days to come. An idyllic day, the sort that people hoped for when walking along the tideline or strolling along the seawall.

Alena watched Gabriel inhale the sea air, relax, and laugh at the seagull's antics. The ever-present loneliness that had been her constant companion for the past four years was temporarily forgotten. They were in no hurry to get anywhere or do anything. Time slipped away with the sun sinking slowly on the western horizon casting shadows along the sidewalks.

That evening, they sat at a secluded table upstairs on the outside deck at the pier restaurant. Gabriel looked happy for the second time since she'd met him. The first time had been that morning. A blush creeped over her cheeks and the ocean breeze blew her hair around her face, hopefully in time to hide it from his eyes. Ever vigilant, he didn't miss anything. She giggled as her hair tickled her face, then swiped at the flyaway strands and looked right at him.

The dishes had been cleared and they were enjoying their drinks, sitting high over the water in the fading light. She loved Galveston. It was perfect.

He asked, "What's so funny?"

"You are. We drive all the way to Galveston and you won't stick your feet in the water."

"I don't want to get sand in the car." He leaned back in his chair.

"Sand is not a problem. It'll vacuum out." She smiled. "Who drives fifty miles to look at sand? You gotta stick your feet in it to really appreciate it. This is the day you have. Enjoy it."

"Is that what you do?" He shifted slightly forward.

"It's what I try to do." Her smile held on. "Some days I'm more successful than others."

His voice took on a somber tone. "How am I supposed to make that work? My brother's in prison and I'm supposed to be happy because I've got sand between my toes." He leaned toward her, folded his hands on the table top and pinned her with a cold stare.

Her eyes shifted from his to their almost-empty drink glasses sitting on the table in the fading light. "Are you mad at me?"

"Don't do that."

"What?" Her eyes flicked to his.

"Stereotype me. You're thinking I've got some hard liquor in me and I'm turning into an angry drunk."

"Some people don't handle alcohol very well. One minute, they're fine and the next, they're pissed at the world. So, it's either the booze or maybe you're bipolar. Which is it?" She stared at him waiting for an answer.

"Neither." Gabriel's face fell as he looked out at the waves. "It's my brother being locked up while I'm here eating and laughing at the beach. It doesn't seem right somehow."

"You didn't cause his problems and they can't be fixed tonight. You need a reason for a new trial. Keep looking. Maybe with time something will shake loose." Alena picked up her drink and took a slow sip. "I know you're hurting and I'm sorry for that but it's not my fault."

Gabriel's eyelids drew down as he inhaled deeply. "And Romero?

What about him? That wasn't your fault either. Who were you before Romero? What is it you're afraid of telling me?"

Alena straightened, shifted in her chair and frowned. He'd just hit her below the belt. She'd let her guard down, let this guy get close to her with his hard body, soft voice, familiar accent, and now she was screwed in more ways than one.

She muttered, "Oh, hell, that was a low blow. I take it you've been online snooping. Well, aren't you clever?" She finished her margarita. She reached out and flipped over the stop sign for the waitress.

"I need another drink, this one is gone."

Gabriel stared at her. "Fine, I'm driving. You can drink, loosen up and tell me the truth. Who are you?"

"You can really be a jackass." She cocked her head and nodded slowly. "I should have known better."

"Yeah, well, you aren't the first person to call me that.

I'm waiting, so how about you start talking?"

"What are you gonna do?" She lifted her glass, wiggled it and put it down. "You gonna fill me full of truth serum and choke it out of me? What do you want to know?"

"Alena, I'm not kidding here. Start at the beginning. I want to know how you met him."

He'd called her out. No more friendly, good-time, easy-going short version. Damn. Fine. *You want it? Okay, you got it.*

"That's easy. Back in college, I was trying to prove I could make it on my own. My old Nova was falling apart. I took it to a small garage to see if the guys could keep it running. We started talking and next thing you know they'd fixed it up good enough to race. We took it out to the track on amateur night. If we wrecked, it wouldn't be a big loss. Romero came over to take a look. Curiosity must have got the best of him."

Alena glanced up at the evening sky and then back at Gabriel. "He just laughed. He laughed at the car, he laughed at my mechanics, and then he laughed at me. That was a mistake."

She twirled the empty, ocean-blue, thick swirled glass by the stem, and snorted softly. "Hmm, he wasn't laughing when I passed his car like it was standing still and won."

Gabriel unfolded his hands and rubbed circles on the wooden table top with his index finger.

She watched the corners of his mouth soften. Not quite a grin but better than his poker face.

He asked, "Yeah, and then what?"

"I'd all but wrecked the Nova to get to the finish line. We pushed it up to the trailer and were trying to figure out how to load it when he walked over. He handed us a couple of come-a-longs and said if I'd give him my number, he'd come over and help us work on it for the next race." She inhaled slowly, bit her upper lip and exhaled. "One thing led to another. I quit school to race full-time. We won a lot of races with that old car, scored a lot of points, and started moving up in the ratings."

Gabriel looked up from the wet spot on the table. "Go on. Then what happened?"

The waitress put a fresh drink on the table in front of Alena and left.

She took several sips before saying, "We won a national qualifier. Romero pulled me out of the car at the end of the race like always, but that time he kissed me." She looked at Gabriel. "First on my cheek but then on the lips. It started out casual, but it changed into something more. He was different that night. He dropped his guard and let me get close to him."

"Uh-huh."

"Look, what's the big deal? Boy kisses girl. We had stars in our eyes. It happens. We were an item. But Snuffy, he was always crazy, thought he was God's gift to women. I wasn't interested in leaving Romero for him, not ever. Even *Papi* said Romero was good for me."

She stopped talking, took a long sip from her fresh, melting margarita and looked out at the water. She hadn't meant to bring up *Papi*. He was hers and hers alone. She didn't share him with the outside world.

Gabriel growled, "I'm waiting."

"When Snuffy was high on his drug of choice, he was a maniac on the track. But he was getting sloppy. The drugs were taking a toll on him. Paranoia was setting in. I beat him that day and he lost it. He

60

climbed out of his car and started walking toward us. I saw the gun. Snuffy shot me first and then Romero." She turned cold eyes on Gabriel. "I tried to get to him, to protect him but I wasn't fast enough. I held his hand and watched the life fade from his eyes until he was gone."

"Yeah, the videos are pretty clear on that. But I don't understand what you were doing with a man like him."

Alena's glass landed on the table with a *clunk*. Her eyes narrowed and she frowned at Gabriel. "What are you talking about? A man like what?"

"A guy with a bad temper, drinking, fighting, partying, and lots of different women all the time."

Her mouth morphed into an ugly scowl, the muscles in her jaw tightened. She forced her mouth to move. "Yeah, no. I'm leaving now." She flipped the stop sign again and pulled five twenties from her wallet. "That should cover the check."

She slapped the money on the table, glared daggers at Gabriel, and marched toward the stairs.

Gabriel jumped to his feet. "Hey, wait a minute. Come back here."

No, not happening. Her feet kept right on walking.

He was a resourceful Marine. He'd get home just fine without her. Alena cruised slowly along the Seawall headed toward her favorite hotel. Smart girls always carry a spare car key in their purse just in case they lock themselves out by accident or are stupid enough to give them to a man. *Ugh! Why had she been so stupid?*

She pulled in at one of Galveston's finest. They weren't booked up and she got a nice room with an ocean view of the gulf. But a nice view wasn't good enough, not when the sky was so clear. It was a good night for star gazing. She'd spent so many wonderful island nights there. She wanted them back.

She caught the elevator to the ground floor, got a drink from the bar, and found a cushioned seat out on the patio. It had a much better view of the night sky and she could hear the waves washing ashore.

There was reassurance in the sound and the reminder of the endless cycle. All was not lost. Good would come around for her again, someday.

Leaning back in her chair, she put her feet up on a stool and sipped her peach margarita. There were a few wisps of clouds but not enough to count. The stars twinkled, giving off a soft golden glow. *Beautiful.* The lights from the rides on the pleasure pier were perfect in their rainbow of colors and brilliance. The distant sound of the waves rolling in helped her slip far away to a happier time.

She was shipwrecked, sitting on the sand safe and warm in Romero's arms.

CHAPTER EIGHT

GABRIEL WALKED along the seawall trying to come up with a way to get back to Rosenberg. He looked across the street at the hotels, contemplating if he could afford a room for the night and spotted the Mustang.

And there was Alena sitting casually on the tropical patio with her feet up relaxing. The tiki torches were a romantic touch complementing the fading glow of the setting sun. *Well, why not?* Most women would have stayed in their chair, maybe sniffled and cried before giving in and answering his questions. Some might have even accused him of being mean. Then he'd have driven them home while they pouted. But not Al. No. She'd left him alone and stuck on a pier fifty miles from home. There was a reason that girl was still single. No ordinary man would be able to handle her.

He crossed the street, walked through the bar and out to the patio. She had that gone-to-another-planet look on her face. He pulled out a chair at her table and sat down.

He said, "It figures I'd find you here. This hotel is about as nice as it gets. Did you get a room for the night?"

"Yes."

"You wanna share?" He hoped she'd take pity on him.

"No."

He watched her closely. She didn't blink, didn't frown, and didn't look in his direction. He was falling off her radar. He needed to change that. This was not the time to lose what he'd barely found.

"I need a ride home, you know."

"In the morning."

The weariness in her voice, the tiredness in her eyes told him more than her words.

He'd pushed too hard. He had to fix this and fast. "I'm sorry if I said things wrong, but I'm trying to talk to you."

She blinked but did not turn her head in his direction. "It doesn't sound like talking to me. It sounds like you've judged me and Romero, and we don't measure up to your standards."

He sighed and grumbled, "That's not what I meant."

"I don't get it. First you want to have sex with me and then you drag my past out like I should be ashamed of it." Al was back and she glared flaming daggers at him before she went back to staring out at the Gulf of Mexico. "I'm not sorry I loved him. Now, go away."

Ouch. If looks could kill, he'd be dead and buried.

He exhaled. "I'm not going anywhere. We're going to talk about this."

"Never bad mouth him again. Do you understand me?" She picked up her drink and brought it to her lips.

Gabriel stared at her and leaned forward taking in the stranglehold she had on her frozen mug. Condensation dripped into her lap and she didn't even blink.

She'd slapped him down hard; the girl was tough. She should be in hysterics or ripping him to shreds, not calmly drinking a girly drink on the patio.

He squared his shoulders. "What made you put yourself between him and a man with a gun? Was he worth it?"

"Yes, absolutely. I'd do it all again."

"You loved him that much?"

"Yes." She finished her drink and stared into the empty mug.

He hoped he didn't look confused. His poker face had deserted him.

She put her feet on the floor. "I need another drink." Standing up, she looked down at him and asked, "Do you want something?"

"Sure. Tequila, straight shot." He kept his eyes on her.

"Good choice," she muttered as she got up. "I'll be back." As she walked away, she muttered, "Eventually."

Gabriel watched her until she disappeared into the dim shadows inside the bar. He closed his eyes and reran the film in his head. By the time she'd crawled to Romero, he was already as good as gone with only seconds remaining and Snuffy was shooting at the pit crews. The EMTs had to peel her off of her man's lifeless body.

Gabriel opened his eyes and gave the patio a quick glance. Everything was good. There was only one couple in the far corner lost in their own romantic-rendezvous world from the looks of it. He could still pull this out of the crapper if he was careful.

He looked toward the inside door for Al. She'd stared death in the face and chose to hold on to her man even when he couldn't hold her anymore. Gabriel wasn't sure he deserved it but he wanted a woman like that. One that would stay with him and not run away when things got rough. He was an ex-Marine with no college degree. The next few years were going to be tough till he got himself established. And even then, he wasn't going to be in the big money. He needed Al to keep him on track. And he needed Alena to help heal his battered heart and soul. He didn't want to be alone anymore.

He breathed a sigh of relief when he saw her carrying two very large frozen mugs of margaritas, one peach for her and one golden for him. She put his down in front of him, and hers on the table by her chair before she sat down.

Thank his lucky stars she hadn't deserted him.

Once she settled in, she picked hers up and held it toward him. "Here's to starry, starry nights. I had them put an extra shot of Patrón on the top of yours."

Gabriel clicked his mug against hers, lowered it and took a bold drink. "Good thing I'm not driving tonight."

"Right. This should make me comfortably numb. And you still have my keys." Alena extended her hand palm up. "Give 'em over."

"Why won't you tell me what happened with you and Romero?"

65

"Because it's none of your business. What part of that don't you understand?"

"Okay, we've got a communication issue here." He cleared his throat. "I joined the Marines to get a better life. After three tours overseas, I'd seen enough death to last a life time. I wanted to come home and settle down. When I get here, my brother's headed for prison and our mother is blaming me."

Gabriel took a long swallow of his drink. Bless the extra shot of Patrón floating on the top. It really hit the spot. He needed courage to go on.

He looked directly at Alena. "You practically ran me over in that parking lot. What kind of girl does that? Talk about a pain in the ass. Like it or not, I needed facts, information, something to go on. You gave me that."

He stopped talking. Her eyes were glued to the horizon. He lifted his mug to his lips and swallowed more cold tequila.

"I'm not the same guy who left town on a bus wanting to become a Marine and make something of himself. They made a different kind of man out of me. I never counted on that. Being around you feels good. But I need to know what I'm getting into."

Alena sat silent as the Sphinx, staring toward the ocean and not even blinking. Gabriel took another big gulp of liquid courage and put his mug down. "I clicked through hundreds of pictures online and then I hit on the videos. I've seen a lot of shit but I've never seen anyone even try to do what you did. In a war zone, we get our guys to lay down some cover fire when we go in to rescue."

He watched her finally take a slow sip of her drink while still looking over the salted rim at the ocean. The silence was killing him.

He'd been honest. There was nothing for him to do now but wait for her response.

Her voice drifted to him, a soft lilting sound that he had to lean in to hear.

"Romero took a silly, stubborn girl with a broken-down Nova and a dream, and he made it happen. He believed in me. He wanted me." She stared at Gabriel. "He went against everything he'd learned growing up. Girls don't race. Uptown girls don't go with tattooed, back alley

66

boys. We didn't fit in most places, so we lived in a world of our own, the racing world. In that world, nobody cared what we did off the track as long as we won."

"But what were you thinking? Pushing him out of the way like that and getting yourself shot."

She exhaled and sucked in a deep breath. "He had terrible wounds from a childhood we can't begin to understand. But I'd seen that kind of hurt before and I understood him. I loved him and he loved me." She took a couple swallows from her drink. "He was a hard man and real rough around the edges like my *Papi*. He had a big heart that he kept hidden. He liked to laugh." She let out a little giggle. "He was a terrible tease when no one was listening."

She sipped her drink and looked dead on at Gabriel. "I did what I had to. What would you do to save the one you love?"

"Kill, if I had to." He focused on her face illuminated by the tiny lights strung around the edge of the patio. "You could have kept racing. You were a great driver and you still had the rest of the crew."

Al turned back toward the ocean. "We used to come here and stay on the beach and pretend we were shipwrecked together on a deserted island."

She smiled an easy smile that let him relax a little. With patience, he might be able to get them back on track. He was not ready to give up, not yet. Only now, he had a new mystery: who the hell was her *Papi*? She'd mentioned him a couple times. He put that on his list of things to do in the future.

He had to stick to the current subject. "Why did you quit racing?"

Al licked some salt off the rim of her mug and took a long swallow. She put her mug down and took a deep breath. "He wasn't there to catch me at the finish line."

Gabriel's brow wrinkled. "What? I don't understand."

"Some people race to get away from their demons. Back then I was pedal-to-the-metal with no brakes. I didn't know when to stop. After I met Romero, I raced to get to him. He was always at the finish line to catch me. He kept me from crashing."

Gabriel shrugged. "I never thought of him that way. He was always

67

fighting his way into the winner's circle. If he could do it, so could we."

"Well, now you're back home and you can tell the boys you've slept with Romero's old lady. You'll be a hero. You win!" She held up her drink in a salute.

His jaw clamped down tight and an angry red heat crawled up his neck. Any second it would be staining his cheeks. That was not a good look on him. She had a way of pushing him to his limit.

Taking a white girl to bed was a totally new experience for him. It was scary as hell and he wasn't sorry he'd done it. But every passing second served to drive home the message that he would have to live with the consequences.

Alena was strong in so many ways. Romero had respected her enough to ask her to marry him. Gabriel had underestimated her. He wouldn't make that mistake ever again.

It took him a minute to unlock his jaw and snarl so low only she would hear, "Don't you ever say anything like that to me again. Not ever. Do you hear me?"

When she didn't say anything he insisted, "Answer me."

"Yes, I hear you but I wish you'd shut up. I'm trying to listen to the surf."

Gabriel jerked back. "What the hell? Did you tell me to shut up?" He ran his hand over the top of his head and down the back of his neck. "Romero would have slapped you for talking to him like that."

Alena grinned around the edge of her mug and glanced his way. "No, he wouldn't. And that only goes to show you really don't know much about him at all."

She nodded toward the ocean. "We were sitting out there at sunset. The sand was still warm and I wanted to listen to the waves make that hissing sound coming ashore. There's something reassuring about it. He was trying to talk me into changing cars for the next season. I told him the same thing I told you."

Gabriel shook his head and grumbled, "And you're still alive. That has to be some kind of miracle."

"He wrapped his arms around my shoulders and whispered in my ear with that soft accent of his." She looked at Gabriel and grinned.

"He said he had something that would keep me warm all night long." A tear rolled down one cheek while she swiped at the other side with her free hand. "Well, that was a long time ago. It doesn't matter now."

Gabriel moved his chair closer to hers and laced his fingers through hers. It wasn't exactly a plan for keeping her warm all night, but it was a start. He asked, "So, did you let him change cars?"

"Of course I did. Anything he wanted was all right with me. He fixed the cars. I only drove them." She tilted her head back and looked at the heavens. She took a deep breath and let it out slowly.

Gabriel dropped his gaze to their joined hands. Well, he'd asked and she'd told him. He'd gotten his answers, some of them at least. It was enough for now.

Alena was still stargazing when she said, "You still haven't told me why any of this is important to you. It's not the kind of thing a man asks."

"I want to know what I'm getting myself into. War taught me things about people I wouldn't have believed until I saw it."

"Do you have nightmares?" She glanced his way.

"Sometimes. Not often, but when I do, they're bad."

"Can you tell me about it?"

"It would take too long tonight. Years of killing and death can't be explained in a few hours. The things we did and the things we saw, there's no way to explain them to someone that wasn't there."

"I understand. But why so interested in me and Romero?"

He should have seen this coming.

"There was this kid in my squad who had it bad for a local girl. We were working every angle to get her out of there and back to the states so he could marry her. Her family found out and killed her. They made sure she suffered before she died and left her body where we would find it."

He heard Alena murmur, "Oh, lord no."

Gabriel took two big gulps from his drink sorry it wasn't a double shot of straight tequila that would dull the memory.

He cleared his throat. "He went freaking nuts. One night, he snuck off base and killed the whole family. Not just her brothers and father but everyone. He took his time and did to them what they'd done to her." Gabriel looked at Alena. "I don't get what makes a person do something like that. I've seen both sides and I'm still trying to understand."

Alena stared at her glass and whispered, "I hope you never find out the hard way what it feels like to have your heart ripped out while you're still breathing."

"You lost me." He stared hard at her.

"It's a pain so bad you can't think straight. You can barely breathe and you'll do anything to make it stop." She looked out to sea. "You're dead inside when the pain finally does stop. It takes a long time to fight your way back to the land of the living."

Gabriel sat there in silence and heard her words echo in his mind. He finally said, "I've never felt anything like that."

She turned her head and looked him in the eyes. "When you find someone to love with all your heart, you'll understand."

Gabriel squeezed her hand gently and kept quiet. She'd walked away from her safe middle-class life for a very low-life man. She'd been willing to die for him. If Al was his, he'd fight his way through every kind of hell to keep her.

"It's late and I'm worn out." Alena stood up. "Come on, I'll get you a room."

"I'd rather sleep with you." He held on to her hand and hoped she'd hear the wanting, the hope in his voice. There were things he couldn't say, not yet. That didn't mean he wasn't thinking and feeling them.

"I have to warn you, I've been drinking, so I'll probably snore all night." She gave him a crooked grin.

"Doesn't matter." He wanted to be close to her. He needed to feel her next to him and pretend she was his, really his, long-term kind of his. Yeah, crazy thoughts were creeping in and teasing him with ideas that he'd never imagined could happen.

"I don't get you. You're a complicated man." She shook her head slowly and stared at him.

"I can't help it. It's the way I feel, all right?" He stopped just short of grumbling, *you're mine*. But that would set off a shit storm he wasn't prepared to deal with.

She huffed, "Fine. I'll tell the desk clerk so they don't get upset about the additional guest."

They caught the elevator to the third floor. Alena opened the door and led Gabriel in to a luxury room.

He let out a low whistle, "Yeah, this is nice."

Picture perfect, warm, and inviting with high-end everything to pamper the guests.

Alena looked at him with a cheeky smile. "It's the Galvez, of course it's nice. What did you expect?"

"I don't know. Never been in a place like this." He hung the "Do Not Disturb" sign on the outside handle, closed the door, and secured the locks. If things went his way, they were going to need their privacy till check-out time tomorrow.

"When I'm in Galveston, this is where I stay. If you want to sleep with me, you'd better get used to it." She let out a sigh. "I'm tired. I've had plenty of tequila, so I'm taking off my clothes and going to bed. That's it. You can have that side of the bed." She pointed at the side away from the window.

"Okay by me. Do you mind if I take a shower?"

"Don't mind at all. Be my guest. Just don't disturb me when you come to bed." She was already peeling off her jeans.

"Yes, ma'am. Got it." He gave her a half-assed salute.

CHAPTER NINE

GABRIEL TOOK a shower and toweled off. He felt better, but his lazy day at the beach had turned into a near-disaster. Only by the grace of God was he not walking back to her house. He turned off the bathroom light and opened the door.

Moonlight filtered through the window casting shadows around the edges of their room. He silently padded over to the window and looked out at the Gulf of Mexico. Alena sighed and rolled over in bed but didn't wake up. He glanced her way and then at the moonbeams playing on the dark glistening waves. This was perfect. A night a man like him could only dream about.

Funny how his words were coming back to haunt him. What kind of man was he? And look what had happened to him. If his mother was right, he didn't deserve this. Not as long as Carlos was in prison. He had abandoned his brother and he needed to fix it.

In Gabriel's real life, he could camp on the beach or stay at a motel several blocks away from the beach. Maybe he could eat at the restaurant on the pier for a special occasion. The Galvez would have been a honeymoon destination. And Alena, well, being with her was one of those things that would have never happened.

But things were different now. And she was right about one thing. Being with her was going to come with a lot of issues he'd have to deal with eventually. As long as he was dreaming, he might as well go all the way.

She was going to be cross with him but she'd get over it. At least he hoped she would. The temptation was too great to resist and he had to try. The tequila made him do it. One side of lips turned up in a mischievous grin.

He didn't turn around, he was afraid of the look he'd get. He said loud enough to be heard, "Alena, wake up. I want to go walking in the surf."

Behind him, she grumbled, "Uh, now? What's gotten in to you? Are you drunk?"

He picked up his jeans and pulled them on.

He smiled. "I'm not drunk. Come on. You're the one telling me to live life and I'm taking your advice. It's beautiful out there. Look." He tipped his head toward the window.

She threw back the covers, stuck her legs over the edge of the bed and muttered, "I'm in bed with a crazy man."

Gabriel grinned, and said, "No, you're not. I'm not in bed at the moment."

"Whatever!" She got to her feet. "This better be good."

Gabriel handed her the jeans first then held up her t-shirt. "Come on. You don't need your shoes. Roll up your pant legs."

He tugged her out the door and down the hall. While he pushed the button for the elevator, he chuckled. "You're running barefoot in the hotel with your jeans rolled up to your knees. There's something to tell your friends."

"Really? You don't know me very well. This isn't even a blip on the radar."

The elevator pinged and the door opened. Gabriel pulled her in and wrapped his arms around her. "We're on camera."

"Great. We'll be online by morning." She laughed softly, "You really are easy. Your reputation will be totally ruined. I've turned you into a hotel call-boy." She pressed her head against his chest and sighed.

Gabriel chuckled. "Fine, you've ruined my reputation. I can live with that, as long as you're the one calling me." He hugged her close and whispered, "Call me real often, lady. I live to please."

She pinched his sides and mumbled into his shoulder. "I'll put you on speed dial."

When the elevator door opened, Gabriel dragged her across the lobby so fast she could barely keep up. His long legs ate up the distance to the beach.

"Slow down."

He slowed temporarily when they got to the steps so she wouldn't trip, but they didn't stop till they stood knee-deep in the surf.

He still had her by the hand. "Look, the moonlight on the waves makes them shine like silver."

"Yeah, okay." She looked up at him. "And?"

Gabriel let go of her hand and wrapped his arms around her. He leaned down slowly, and when she didn't pull away, he pressed his lips to hers. He started with a slow kiss that flared into a full blooming passion in seconds. The slow burn deep in his belly turned into a fire that the cool water swirling around his feet couldn't remedy. This was his version of heating things up and keeping her warm all night long.

He pulled back to catch his breath. "I wanted to kiss you out here under the stars. It looked so perfect, something to remember when we're hit with those freezing-cold winter days."

She tilted her head back and gazed at the heavens overhead. "Sometimes fate is written in the stars." An incoming wave hit them and Alena gasped when the brisk spray hit her face. "Okay, now I'm going to need a shower before getting back in bed. This is all your fault." She broke out laughing. "But it's good."

"Yeah?" He didn't want to stop looking into her eyes or holding her and feeling her body plastered to his.

She nodded. "Yeah."

He still had one arm around her waist as they made their way out of the surf and back up on to the sand beyond the tide line. He imagined crawling up out of the water and pulling her with him. They had just survived being attacked by pirates and had made it to shore. He'd have to work on the rest of the story. He muttered, "This is gonna be a mess."

Alena giggled, "It'll wash off. It's only sand."

"Yeah." Only he wasn't talking about the sand.

They walked back to the hotel and rode the elevator up to their floor. Gabriel pushed her up against the elevator wall, pressed his body to hers and kissed her until the doors opened.

Alena fished the room key card out of her pocket and got the door open with him running his hands over her butt and hips.

She hissed, "Stop it. There are cameras in the halls for security."

"Then get the damn door open before it gets X-rated."

"The only thing X-rated around here is your mind." She laughed and pushed the door open. "There, saved by our right to privacy. I get the shower first."

"Sure, and what am I supposed to do? These wet jeans are cold." He frowned and sent his most pitiful look her way.

She looked over her shoulder and leered at him. "Take them off. Let's see what you've got."

"Throw me a towel, will ya?" Al wasn't falling for his tricks. No sympathy from her. *Recalculating.* It was going to take more than his shriveled balls to get her to feel sorry for him.

"Spoil sport. Here." She winked, tossed him a hand towel and disappeared back into the bathroom.

She finished her nice warm shower, wrapped her bath towel around herself, and walked out into the bedroom. Gabriel sat looking out the window.

"All yours." She ran her hands down his arms. "You're cold. The shower will help warm you up."

Gabriel put his hands over hers. "And what are you gonna do to warm me up?"

Alena whispered in his ear, "I'm going to start a fire you can't put out."

Gabriel stood and faced her. "You promise?"

She reached around and lightly squeezed his butt. "Count on it."

"Keep doing that and I'll skip the shower."

"You need to get warm. Get a move on." She gave him a quick kiss.

"Just give me five minutes."

She swatted his taut butt cheek when he walked past her. "I'll be waiting for you."

He threw his head back and laughed, "You're gonna get it now."

"I certainly hope so." She watched him disappear around the corner.

Another hard man with rough edges and a few soft spots. She could so easily fall for him. Hell, she was already on the roller coaster. Who was she kidding?

Romero had been gone over four years. When was she going to move on? It hadn't been an issue before because no man had caught her eye until now.

Gabriel was a man worth having but it was going to cost her. Facing the past, conquering her fears, putting her barely healed heart on the line came at a price. She'd never been any good at gambling. Give her a fast car and she'd give you a run for the money. Was Gabriel her fast car or a deck of dark, tarot cards? Did they have a future together? The harsh voice of experience crept in around the soft edges of an old-fashioned love song. Tonight, love was only a heart-beat away.

Tomorrow she'd get her forever friend Banji to read the cards. Maybe there was a clue in there somewhere.

CHAPTER TEN

ALENA OPENED the variety pack of condoms they'd picked up on the way to Galveston, put them on the nightstand, and slid into bed. She flipped through the TV channels. When she heard the bathroom door open, she hit the power button.

She asked, "You feeling better?"

Gabriel walked out of the bathroom with a towel wrapped around his waist. He sat down on his designated side of the bed. "Yeah, I'm good."

When he didn't get in and roll her way, she crawled over and put her hands on his shoulders. "What's the matter?"

She felt him tense. Her hands caressed the soft skin and the hard muscle underneath. The heat that was the man radiated from him and lured her closer. She pressed her front against his back. Gabriel was a good man. She wanted to wrap herself around him and protect him from all the hurt coming his way.

"Nothing's the matter. I just can't believe I'm here with you. I've looked at this place from the road a dozen times but never dreamed I'd ever get my foot through the door."

She twisted around to his side so she could see his face a little better. "This is where we are and this is the night we have." She caressed his cheek. "We can rev on the red line or shut it down. It's up to you. You tell me."

His head turned and their eyes met. She searched his face looking for a clue. She wanted him. His strength, his heat, and the touch of his hands spoke to her. She asked, "What do you want?" He had to make that decision for himself and they'd both have to live with the answer.

"It's too late to shut it down," he said softly.

Alena leaned back, gently running her hands over his shoulders and down his sides. He had some small scars scattered across his ribs and back.

He muttered, "Shrapnel. Hit us from behind. I was lucky."

There was lots of ink. But no wings. He was a fallen angel. She could fix that. Get him his wings back. It would take work, but she could do it. She skimmed her hand over his shoulder blade where the missing wing should be.

She whispered, "Gabriel the archangel." She wrapped her arms around his shoulders and kissed the back of his neck. He smelled warm and male, clean and tempting all at the same time. "A good name. It suits you. You are magnificent." She dropped one hand down lower and loosened the towel from his waist.

He asked, "You sure you're okay with this?"

Alena drew her hands down and back over his hips. "Perfectly fine."

She let go of him and scooted back to the middle of the king size bed. "Come closer, we've got all night and plenty of moonlight."

He put one knee up on the mattress and crawled toward her, saying, "This only ends one way with you and me."

"It's you, me, and the night." She crooked her index finger. "I'm waiting for you."

Gabriel pulled her in close.

She watched as his eyes took in everything about her. It had been a long time since a man had looked at her with hungry eyes. When he was done looking, he snuggled her tight to his body and kissed her. Gentle, hot, and working up to an inferno that wasn't going to be put out anytime soon.

His skin was hot to the touch; the muscles moving underneath were relentless in their efforts to get closer to her. She pushed back, pulled her lips free for a hot second, and softly said, "You're going down."

"What are you going to do to me?"

"Everything," she softly purred. "Absolutely everything." She reached over and grabbed the first square packet her hand landed on and tucked it close to his hip.

Gabriel grumbled, "I don't know how to take that."

For a second, he was motionless until she pushed him over on his side and rolled him onto his back.

She straddled his thighs, looked him over from head to groin and whispered, "You'll take it like a man. I'm going to start slow. We have all night. Stay very, very quiet and remember to breathe." She smirked. "No screaming in the hotel."

He watched her without making a sound.

She wasn't kidding. She smiled slowly as she leaned forward and kissed the pulse point pounding in his neck, moved lower, licked one nipple and then the other. "You taste so good. I'm going to kiss you and lick you and suck you till you beg me to stop."

She watched his pupils dilate, turning his eyes black. No sound escaped his lips.

She moved up his body and nibbled his ear lobe, then ran her tongue along the pulsing vein in his neck. She was back to his chest. Lick, nibble, suck one nipple while caressing the other. She felt his pulse kick up a notch. She moved lower, trailing her way to his navel. Her tongue invaded the hollow then moved midline to his groin. She raised her knee, rubbed it across his thigh and shoved it slowly between his legs and whispered, "Open your legs for me, Gabriel."

His hands fisted as he grabbed the sheet and sucked in a breath.

She crouched between his thighs and ran her tongue around the tip of his cock. He sucked in another breath. Her tongue licked a trail to his balls.

His head came up as he clenched his teeth and groaned, "God almighty, what are you doing to me?"

He was smart. He'd figure it out. Her mouth was occupied with something more important at that moment. She sucked one ball into her mouth and rolled her tongue around it and hummed gently, very gently.

Gabriel's hips jolted off the bed. "Stop. Stop or I'm gonna come."

She turned him loose and asked, "Would that be so bad?"

"I want to be inside you."

Alena crawled up his body, straddled his hips, and tucked her toes under the edge of his thighs. She could feel the hard length of him between her folds and the tip of his cock nudging her clit. "I'm going to make you come hard, real hard. You understand me?" She peeled open the wrapper and rolled the condom down his length.

He nodded and choked out, "Yeah."

His hands grabbed her thighs and held on.

Alena slipped forward until his cock rubbed her opening, then she reached between her legs, tipped him up just enough to catch her edge and pushed herself onto his shaft as deep as he'd go.

Gabriel's back arched off the mattress; he sat up, wrapped his arms around her and groaned. "You're killing me. I can't take this anymore."

He'd done enough sit-ups to have the six-pack to show for it and right then it was Alena's undoing. She caressed his cheek, looked him in the eyes, and murmured, "You'll take a lot more than this before I'm through with you."

Gabriel grunted, "You started this, but I'm going to finish it." Then he rolled her onto her back.

Alena smiled up at him. "So show me what you've got."

Gabriel loomed over her with his forearms on the mattress.

She whispered, "Come on. Do it."

He buried his cock inside her till she was stretched tight. She could barely breathe, it was so good. She grabbed his sides with her hands and wrapped her legs around his thighs. "Don't stop now." She tipped her pelvis. "Oh, yeah, that's got it."

Gabriel slowly drew back with a grin and began a slow slide back and forth till Alena was making little whimpering sounds. His thrusts were long, deep and steady.

Alena was quickly reaching her point of no return. She pushed against him, meeting him mid-thrust. She pushed with every muscle she had against the hard body that was Gabriel. Her head tilted back, his lips brushed her neck and her legs trembled as he slammed into her hard and fast. The quivering began between her legs and then traveled outward to all parts of her body. She clamped tight around his cock and he groaned. His muscles contracted and his body progressed to completion. Hot and pulsing, hot semen gushed from deep inside his body. She was barely aware of her hands pulling at his shoulders. He collapsed partially off to her side with his cock still buried deeply inside her sheath. Her legs tangled with his while her inner walls tingled with tiny ripples of pleasure.

They were hot, sweaty, and exhausted. Their bodies entwined, their heavy breathing the only sound in the room while their wildly beating hearts returned to something near a normal rate.

Gabriel was done fighting his feelings for her. It was time to roll with it, but there were things he needed to know before he fell in any deeper. He started to pull out, anchored the condom to the base of his shaft while the warm sticky fluid clinging to his cock cooled. "You made me come hard, just like you said."

"Yeah, it was so good. Um, I might have to do it again." She brushed her hand down his arm.

He sat up on his side of the bed and removed the spent rubber. He walked to the bathroom, disposed of it and cleaned up.

He called out, "I'm getting Carlos a new attorney. Are you gonna be okay with it if he gets a new trial?"

She flung her arm over her eyes. "I knew it, I knew it. There was more to your temper tantrum at dinner. Why didn't you man-up and say what was on your mind?"

"I know you went through a lot with the first trial and this might be hard for you. I was trying to figure out where to start." He climbed back into bed and faced Alena.

"I won't be on the jury. It's not going to have anything to do with me. You, your family, the witnesses, that's a different story. They haven't changed. You said it yourself. You think they're hiding something."

"Sonja is the only person who would know if Michael had a gun with him that night."

"She won't tell you. And if she did tell you something, you couldn't count on it to be the truth. She'll say whatever it takes to get what she wants. You can't trust her. Why don't you go see Carlos? Find out what he wants."

Gabriel winced. "I tried but he refused my visit. I can't stand by doing nothing."

"Okay, so do what you have to and find out as much of the truth as possible. Once you have that, you'll be able to make a decision you can live with. Go see him in a couple months. Maybe after he's had time to think about things, he'll be ready for a visit. It had to be awful for him at first. He probably didn't want anyone to see him in there."

"It's a long ride to Palestine. Would you go with me?"

"I can do that. Find out when visiting days are and I'll request some time off. We can ride up there together but you'll have to go in by yourself."

"Yeah, that's fine."

Gabriel wrapped his arm around her and anchored her to his side. Her breathing turned soft and slow as she drifted into peaceful sleep.

He watched the shadows drifting across the window and welcomed the gentle sounds of their seaside hideaway. For a few hours he could take comfort in the prospect of loving Alena.

He still wasn't to the bottom of the mystery surrounding her. He didn't like that her *Papi* had been a man like Romero. That meant she would have grown up rough and that wasn't right either. She was too soft, too well spoken, too educated. No way in hell was her father a man like Romero. He'd have to keep digging for answers.

A few hours later, the sun peeked over the ocean on the horizon and Gabriel was awake with a hard-on that wasn't going away anytime soon. She was still curled up asleep next to him. He sheathed himself with a warming sensation condom, nudged her onto her stomach, moved her legs aside and sank himself deep inside of her welcoming passage with not so much as a good morning kiss.

Alena hissed, "Oh, yes. Yes. That's good."

Her hands slid out from under her pillow brushing over the cool sheets. Gabriel's hands covered hers and his fingers curled around hers. His mouth was by her ear. He whispered in between thrusts and grunts, "I've got you now, *chica*."

"Yes, yes, do it." She groaned softly. "Harder, make me come."

Gabriel let go of her hands to caress her warm, damp center. Her clit was plump and easy to find. It didn't take but a few strokes to have her screaming into her pillow. She was smoldering hot and wet when she came, squeezing his cock so tight he thought he'd rupture. In response, he slammed into her harder and deeper with each stroke until he found release.

He flopped to one side, heart pounding and breathing heavy. "You're killing me. It's never been like this. It's like I can't fuck you hard enough or something. I just want more."

She squeezed his arm. "I promise you, there is more. This is a work in progress."

"I can't move." He aimed a lopsided grin at her.

"It's okay. We've got plenty of time before check out." Alena snuggled closer to his side.

"And we need to shower." He kissed the top of her head.

"Not right now. Later. I'm not through with you." She tweaked his side.

Thank goodness cuz he wasn't done with her either.

When they pulled into her driveway late that afternoon, she squeezed his hand. "It was good to see Galveston again, but we stayed longer than planned. I'm sure you need to get back and check on your grandma. She's probably starting to worry about you."

"She's used to me." Gabriel tilted his head and shrugged one shoulder.

Alena kept her happy-poker-face firmly in place. "Well, I'm sure she'll be glad to see you."

"I'll see ya soon." He leaned over and gave her a quick kiss.

"Sure, sounds good." She let go of him and got out. Her legs were a little stiff from sitting so long on the ride home or maybe it was all the rolling in the sheets. It had been a long time since she'd done that. She needed to exercise more so she could keep enjoying Gabriel.

He straddled his Harley and let the engine warm up while he zipped his jacket and pulled on his gloves. Watching him could easily become an addiction. He was so damn handsome. This was the second time she'd stood in the driveway watching him ride away. She looked up at the clouds drifting overhead. "I'm going to need some help with this."

When he was out of sight, she went inside and called *Papi*.

CHAPTER ELEVEN

THE NEXT MORNING, Gabriel sat across the worn kitchen table from his grandmother sipping the fresh hot coffee she'd made him. The dark circles under her tired eyes told him that the trial had taken a toll on her. He hoped that what he was about to tell her wouldn't make it worse.

He said, "I'm sorry."

"Sorry or not, that Sonja is no good. You stay away from her."

"She's the only one who might actually know if Michael had a gun in the car that night. If he did, maybe Carlos could get a new trial."

"If Michael had a gun, she would have said so at the trial they already had. There was no gun. That lawyer made it up."

Gabriel swallowed hard. "Maybe somebody took it before the cops got there. It's the only chance Carlos has."

"You listen to me. Your father and mother pushed Carlos to stand up to Michael. It was stupid. Carlos wasn't a fighter. Not like you. He should have gone to college. But Sonja, she didn't want him to go. She's selfish, wanting him to stay here and take care of her while she chased after Michael. Now, you forget about her."

Gabriel put his cup down on the table and leaned back in his chair. "It's not about me. I need to help Carlos and she was there."

"Time will help Carlos." She sighed. "You are home and should get on with your life, find a good woman and settle down."

He leaned back in the aluminum framed chair and stretched his legs out in front of him. "What if I told you I have someone?"

"Oh, *Mijo*. Who is she?" She stepped away from the sink and slid onto the chair across from him.

"That's just it; she's not from around here."

Gabriel watched his grandmother's eyes narrow and get that suspicious look.

"Where's she from?"

"California." That was the truth.

"Oh." She smiled. "There's lots of Spanish blood out there."

"And lots of others." He rested one hand palm down on the table.

"*Madre de Dios*, you've taken up with a white girl!"

"Yeah. I'm afraid so."

"And you're sure she's the one for you?"

"Yes, I'm sure." Gabriel nodded.

"How do you know?"

"Alena sticks up for what she believes in. She stays with her man, no matter how bad it gets. I have peace in here…" he put his hand over his heart, "…when I'm with her." Gabriel lowered his hand and wrapped it around his coffee cup. "She was on the jury. She told me what happened."

"How did you make her do that?"

"I followed her home after the trial was over."

She shook her head. "Maybe you frightened her and she said things you'd want to hear so you'd go away."

"Not this girl. She's got no problem getting in my face. She tells me straight out how it is."

"Just because she told you what people said doesn't make her anything but honest and maybe kind."

"I know, but there's more to it than that. I'm comfortable around her. She doesn't run away crying when I get edgy. There's no guessing where I stand. I want to make it work."

"A new trial won't help that."

"I know. If we say the jury did something wrong, she could get in trouble. She won't want anything to do with me after that."

She leaned back in her chair and stared at him. "These days, men go from girl to girl for fun. It's not right to start something if you aren't serious."

Gabriel took in the somber look on his grandmother's face and said, "That's not me. You raised me better than that." He'd stayed out overnight with Alena and this was his grandmother's way of calling him out.

"She won't fit in with most of your friends here. And your children will be stuck in the middle of two worlds. That will make things hard for them."

"I know. I didn't go looking for this, but it found me. I've been places and seen things that changed me. I don't want the same things that I used to. Being a Marine has shown me I can have more."

She nodded and sighed quietly. "Is she the one with the big ugly sunglasses?"

"Yeah. She was Romero Vasquez's *novia*. After he was killed, she moved out to the country to get some peace and quiet. She didn't want the reporters to catch on."

"She's a brave girl. She could have told the judge she didn't want to be on the jury."

"She was trying to do the right thing for Carlos."

"If you decide to marry her, don't tell anyone till it's done."

"What? I don't believe my ears. What are you saying?" Gabriel leaned forward in his chair closing the distance between himself and his grandmother. "Why?"

"Because if you tell people, they will try to stop you. They'll tell you it's a mistake." She reached out and put her hand on his wrist. "When I was a young girl, I fell in love. We wanted to get married, but my parents objected and made us promise to wait until he came back from Korea." She shook her head. "He was a Marine, like you, and he was going to South Korea for a year." Her eyes were glassy when she looked away. "He got killed over there. I never loved anybody the way I loved him. If you have to blame someone for this, you blame me.

There'll be problems, but you make her a promise to be faithful and marry her quick before anyone figures out what you're doing."

Gabriel sat back and let his grandmother's words sink in. Marines were faithful, no problem there. Marry her quick? The picture of the big man standing next to Alena in the old photo crossed his mind. Really big problem there, especially if he was her *Papi*.

CHAPTER TWELVE

SHOPPING MIDWEEK MEANT the stores were less crowded. Alena placed the books she'd selected on the worn counter at the secondhand bookstore. Kat and Ann Marie owned the place and they knew everything that went on in town. They had comics and collectables, as well as books. Sooner or later all the local news filtered through their door.

Ann Marie checked the books and rang them up. "The word around town is that Gabriel has taken up with Sonja, his brother's girlfriend. Everybody's seen her riding with him on his Harley. I just can't imagine what those boys see in her. She's nothing but trouble if you ask me."

Alena grimaced. "Yeah, you don't know the half of it, but I'm sure he has his reasons. He's not stupid. Sonja was the only person in the car with Michael when he was killed."

Kat leaned on the counter. "So, what's up with you these days? You haven't been around much."

"I'm trying to keep a low profile. I don't want any trouble from Michael's people or the gangs. I'm thinking maybe I'll have to move. Being on that jury has really messed things up for me. I see why people avoid it like the plague."

The bell over the door jingled and Kat sucked in a breath and whispered, "Well, look what the cat dragged in. He's even better up close."

Alena looked toward the door. Yep, Gabriel was fine in anybody's book.

"I saw the Mustang out front. Thought I'd catch you and see what's going on."

"I'm getting something to read for those nights when I need to wind down and have trouble falling asleep."

"Yeah." Gabriel winked at her. "I could help you with that."

"I'll keep that in mind." She picked up the books she'd paid for.

Gabriel chuckled and asked, "You doing okay?"

"Sure, always." Alena kept a grip on her books. "How about you?"

"I'm okay. I went up to Houston. Stopped at The Finish Line tavern and had a nice visit with Emilio."

Her heart skipped a beat and she gripped her books tighter. "Oh. Um, how is he?" She hoped she hadn't turned a ghastly shade of pale.

"He's good, has his own crew now. I saw your pictures on the wall."

Alena looked at the front door. "He'll be a good pit boss. He's a good mechanic." She wanted to run. "Those pictures are from a lifetime ago."

Good hell, what else had they talked about? She and Romero owned the Finish Line and, when he died, she got his half. Emilio got a ten percent cut of the profits on top of his salary to manage the place and keep her name out of things. It was way past time she sold the tavern but that didn't mean she could actually do it. Romero had been so proud of it. No, it stayed put for now. She'd suck it up and deal with it. Whatever *it* was.

Gabriel asked, "Are you off today?"

"Yeah, I'm working the weekend."

"How about I come by later?" He leaned against the counter and glanced at the books in her arms.

"Sure. I'll be home."

"Great." He gifted her with a one-sided cheeky smile and walked out.

Kat sighed. "Wow, how hot is that man?"

Alena's cheeks flushed rosy. "He's very hot."

"Um, is he dating you or Sonja?"

"I'm not dating anybody." It wasn't exactly a lie. Sleeping with the man was not dating.

Alena waited a few minutes to give him time to leave before she went out to the Mustang. He undoubtedly had his reasons for spending time with Sonja, and whatever was going on, she didn't want any part of it.

She dropped into the driver's seat, threw her books over onto the passenger side and headed home. The miles gave her time to pull herself together. She was half way in love with the man and he was complicated. No, this wasn't a good idea. Racing wasn't a good idea. Owning a tavern wasn't a good idea. Hell, nothing she liked was a good idea.

She parked in the driveway next to the Harley. Gabriel had gotten home first. No surprise there. The man rode like the devil was chasing him.

She walked to the back porch and found him stretched out on the lounge chair. His eyes popped open when her foot hit the bottom step.

He smiled. "Hey, you got home fast. I thought you might stop for groceries while you were in town."

"No. I'm good." She sat in a chair facing Gabriel. "Are you really doing okay?"

"Yeah. Talked to my grandma. She thinks the same as you that there was no gun. The defense attorney made it sound possible since nobody could say for sure."

"It was her job. She needed something to make a case for self-defense."

"All Sonja would tell me was she didn't know for sure. I could tell she was lying."

"That's the same thing she said at the trial."

"I wish I'd been there for that part." Gabriel looked toward the far end of the field behind Alena's house. "Sonja rode to Houston with me when I went to The Finish Line to talk to your old crew."

He let that revelation hang in the air between them.

"Why would you want to talk to my crew?" She watched him intently.

"Wondered what happened to them after the shooting at the track and felt like taking the bike for a ride."

"You could have asked me."

"I get the feeling you don't like talking about those days."

"You're right, I don't." She didn't look away. "If you have questions about me, you can ask. I'll tell you the truth so be careful. Be sure you want the answers."

"Deal." He leaned forward. "I didn't tell anyone we were seeing each other. I only said I'd been a big fan and wondered what had happened to everyone after the shooting."

"We lost some good people that day. Things weren't the same after that and I couldn't bring myself to go back to the track. I wasn't ready and didn't have any idea when I would be." She leaned back in her chair.

Gabriel winced and nodded slowly. "Seems like everyone was hurting pretty bad. But being able to go in there has given them a place to meet up and talk about the good times they had."

"We did have some good days." She chortled. "Some really good days. Those are the memories we all need to hang on to."

"Sonja's not a kid anymore. She's over twenty-one and playing with the big boys." Gabriel lost his grin. "She's old enough to know better but she did me like she did Carlos. She went to flirting with the guys and then she left with one of them."

Alena nodded. "Age hasn't changed her. She'll be back, and when she gets home, you can be sure she'll be blaming whatever happened on you."

"Naw, she'll be blaming it on Julio."

Alena's eyes opened wide and she went on full alert. "Julio is a player. I don't think he even stops long enough to sleep eight hours."

"Seems like a match made in heaven, if you ask me. She needed two men here to keep her satisfied. Maybe one Julio will be enough."

Alena inhaled deeply and stared at the roof overhead. She needed to put lights on the rafters. It would make things more cheerful. "Michael and Carlos were really still small-town young men. Julio is seriously all alpha-male in overdrive. He doesn't play games and he has no limits."

"If you're trying to make me feel sorry for her, it's not working. All she had to do was stay with the guy she came with, but we know that's not her style." Gabriel sat in silence for a couple seconds then added, "I got the visiting days and hours for the Coffield Unit."

"Good. I'll put in for some days off on the next schedule."

"Are you sure you feel like doing this?"

"You shouldn't go alone. I thought we were sort of together now, since we're friends and all." Alena focused her full attention on Gabriel.

"Thought we were more than friends." He shot her a questioning look. "A lot more than friends. Unless taking me to the fucking limits with a mind-blowing finish in Galveston wasn't a big deal to you."

"All right then, more than friends and we help each other through the rough spots." She stood. "It's getting late. I need to fix myself some dinner and get ready for work tomorrow. You want something to eat?"

"Sure, sounds good."

"Come on. Let's get this show on the road." She rummaged in her purse, pulled out the house keys. "I think I've got some chicken I can throw in the oven."

"Great." He got up and followed her inside.

He planted himself on his barstool, the one he'd appropriated on his first visit, while she fixed the chicken and put the pan in the oven to bake.

When she turned away from the stove, he said, "You haven't kissed me yet."

Looking in to that man's eyes turned her to mush. How did he do that? She was so screwed. She softly said, "I wasn't sure you wanted me to. Rosenberg is a small town, and you know I was bound to hear you were keeping company with Sonja." Alena walked to him and pursed her lips to one side. "Maybe you're tired of me and moved on."

Gabriel put his hands on her shoulders and pulled her between his legs. "Not in this lifetime. You want to go in the bedroom or do it here? It's been a while and I'm gonna make real sure you sleep extra good tonight. You're my girl and I gotta take real good care of you."

She brushed her hands over his shoulders and down his arms. "You seem a little tense. I could help you with that. We could take our time after dinner." She whispered in his ear, "You like it when I take care of you real slow."

His hips shifted and he pulled her tight into the center of the V between his legs. "I've changed my mind. You're not going to get much sleep tonight."

CHAPTER THIRTEEN

ROLLING southbound on Interstate 45 toward Houston in stony silence signaled Alena that Gabriel's meeting hadn't gone well. It had been a long day and a very quiet ride with her driving the speed limit set on cruise control. Brilliant Red Mustangs tended to attract cops and they didn't need any complications.

She glanced at Gabriel and then back at the road ahead. "If you're hungry we can stop for dinner in the Woodlands."

Gabriel grumbled, "I'm not hungry."

"Okay." She kept her eyes on the traffic.

"Thanks for driving." He looked out the side window.

"No problem. You've got a lot on your mind."

"Al?"

"Yeah?" She rearranged her fingers on the steering wheel.

"It was Sonja."

"Okay. We already knew she was involved."

"She wouldn't get out of Michael's car. She said she needed a real man." He looked over at her.

With a quick glance she caught his look and turned back to the road, "Well, damn. She never testified to that and Carlos didn't either. It's not a game changer but you can see where it could have pushed him over the edge. Something like that could set a man off. Never mind a young man in his prime with parents and peer pressure pushing him to prove his virility."

Alena's stomach growled and she changed lanes moving over to the right. She'd been hungry for a while and Gabriel looked like he could stand a break.

"Al?"

"Yeah?"

"I'm gonna be sick."

"Okay. Barf bag's in the console. I'm taking the next exit." She flipped on her blinker.

Alena looked right and changed lanes again. "Hang on a little longer. Take some deep breaths."

Gabriel opened the center console, grabbed the plastic bag, and leaned forward.

Alena took the first exit she found, rolled across the access road lanes, and pulled to a stop in the first strip mall she came to. She put the Mustang in neutral and pulled the parking brake.

He hadn't hurled yet. She waited. He was taking deep breaths and looking at the floor.

"I'm so sorry. What happened in there?"

"They've got him on his knees. I gotta get him out of that hell hole."

"What did he tell you?"

"She wouldn't get out of the damn car. He went and got the gun to prove he was just as much a man as Michael. He thought if he pointed the gun at them and told her to get her ass back in the Camaro that would take care of it. When he walked up to the Wrangler, he saw Michael lean over. He thought Michael was reaching for a gun and his just went off. He doesn't remember pulling the trigger."

"Okay, so for right now, keep breathing slow and steady. You haven't eaten all day. You're partly car sick and you can't think straight like this. There's a drive-thru over there. I'll go get you something to eat. It'll help settle your stomach."

Gabriel raised his voice, "I'm not hungry. How many times do I have to tell you?"

Alena sat back in her seat and gave him as much space as the Mustang would allow.

"All right. It's all right," she said softly in a tone she would use if she was talking to a snarling grizzly bear.

She turned up the air conditioning, released the park brake, put the Mustang in gear. "I need something or I'm going to throw up."

"Fine, get whatever you want." He hung his head over the bag.

She got an order of French fries and pulled back out onto the access road. She took the first entrance ramp she came to with no plans to slow down again till she got him home. She obeyed the traffic signals and speed limits all the way to Gabriel's grandmother's house.

She nibbled on the fries hoping he'd at least steal a few but no luck. He spent the rest of the trip staring out the passenger window not saying a word.

She breathed a sigh of relief when she stopped in front of his grandmother's walkway. "Here you go. Delivered home in one piece. Get some rest. Nothing looks good when you're tired."

"Right. Thanks for the ride."

He got out and walked away with his shoulders stooped and his head bowed. Defeat weighed heavily on him and there was nothing she could do about it. She'd been afraid this would happen. Seeing it tore at her heart. He didn't deserve this. And she couldn't fix it.

She waited until his feet hit the porch before she pulled away from the curb. She checked her rearview mirror. He'd gone inside. Best place for him at the moment but she knew it wouldn't last. He wasn't going to take this lying down.

She'd known him long enough to know he'd take some time to process what he'd learned, form a battle plan, and come out fighting. Problem was he didn't have much to fight with as far as she could tell but that wouldn't stop the Marine in him.

Sonja's inflammatory statement wasn't hard evidence and it sure wasn't enough for a new trial. He'd have to come up with something else. Maybe he could go with ineffectual counsel. Good luck with that. What lawyer would want to point fingers at one of their own? The interrogation tapes did not show any coercion by law enforcement. Those had been seen during the trial. His best bet was to file an appeal on whatever grounds the new attorney could come up with and pray. Whatever they came up with would stir up trouble. That she knew for sure.

CHAPTER FOURTEEN

THE FOLLOWING EVENING, Alena crawled into bed and settled down for the night. She'd just gotten comfortable when her phone rang. She glanced at the caller ID and answered. "Hey, how are you?"

Gabriel said, "I'm sorry for waiting so long to call and thank you for the ride yesterday."

He sounded so pitiful. If he was there with her, she'd wrap her arms around him and tell him everything was going to be okay. And maybe it would be. But she didn't want to give him false hope.

She said, "No problem. You need time to sort through what you heard."

Remorse interlaced heavily with his words. "That's no excuse for the way I treated you."

"You're forgiven this time but don't do it again." Her best scolding tone lost its impact when she snickered.

"I'll do better."

"I believe you." They talked a little longer until she yawned.

They had long ago established yawning was the warning sign that she was about to fall asleep. In a few more minutes he'd be talking to the night.

He said, "I'm going to take care of this thing with Carlos. I have an idea. Get some sleep and I'll call you tomorrow."

After that he called every night for a quick check to make sure she was okay. She still kept an eye on her rearview mirror in case the gangs got bored and came looking for her. So far, nothing interesting had happened. The flip side of the phone call was him letting her know he was all right. If that's what he needed, she could give it to him.

His somber tone conveyed what he didn't say. He needed breathing room so she wasn't surprised he didn't come to see her, lounge on her couch, and watch sports on the big-screen TV. Pain and anger did funny things to people. He might need help but he wasn't going to outright accept it. At least not from her. He had his pride. She was an expert on that one.

What did surprise her was a call from the district attorney's office two weeks later. She resented being called in without any explanation. Sitting and waiting in his reception area for God-only-knew what disaster to descend on her was straining her disposition to the max. She'd give him five more minutes and then she was walking out. If he wanted to talk to her that bad, he could get a judge to issue a warrant and arrest her. She did not like being pressured.

The secretary looked at her and went back to her typing. Hooray for the perpetual wheels of bureaucracy. Alena looked out the window. She really hated this courthouse. If she ever got out of here, she was moving where they'd never find her.

An inner office door opened and a man that she recognized from the trial said, "Ms. Cordova?"

"Yes."

"I'm D.A. Hardy. Thank you for coming. Would you come in, please?"

She marched into his office, and waited next to the chairs in front of a desk piled high with files and papers.

She asked, "Why am I here?"

He walked around behind the desk, extended his hand in her direction and said, "Have a seat."

Alena perched on the edge of the nearest chair and waited wordlessly while he settled into his executive chair.

He cleared his throat. "An appeal has been filed in the Carlos DeLeon case. There is a possibility of some juror misconduct. Do you know anything about that?"

Her forehead wrinkled and her eyes narrowed. "What? No."

"We have reason to believe some of the jurors might not have been impartial." He leaned forward.

"Impartial? Oh, they were definitely impartial. They didn't care what happened as long as they could move to Tennessee on time and get back to their offices. They had mail to sort and messages to answer, and filing to do. Look, I don't know what you're hunting for, but leave me out of it. I did the best I could to be fair. I had plenty of paid time off and I could stay as long as it took to do it right. That's it. That's all I'm responsible for."

"But you are seeing the brother, Gabriel DeLeon. You may have been prejudiced in the defendant's favor."

"I didn't know Gabriel existed until the trial was over." She glared at the district attorney. "Your timeline is flawed. The trial started before he even got in to town. I was picked for a drunk-driving case that settled at the last minute. Your people moved us to the murder case with no questions asked. Check your records."

He sat back, and appeared to be studying her. Probably contemplating his next move.

Finally, he nodded at her and said, "I see. Well, thank you for coming in. I believe that clears things up."

"Good." Alena stood up and walked out on shaky legs that miraculously held her up all the way to her car.

She'd been accused of juror misconduct. The one thing she'd done her best to make sure didn't happen. This nightmare was never going to end. At least not in a good way. She didn't want anything to do with any of it. Not again. She needed to get away. Far away. Maybe Australia?

She started the Mustang and looked up. Gabriel stood on the sidewalk across the street staring right at her. She inhaled a deep breath and let it out slowly. Her heart beat faster recalling the touch of his hands and the sound of his voice. She shook it off, she wasn't going there. He'd betrayed her trust. She put the Mustang in gear and rolled out of the parking lot, pretending she didn't see him and didn't have a care in the world.

A few blocks later, she pulled over into the grocery store parking lot and called in sick to work. She was in no shape to take care of anybody other than herself and even that was questionable at the moment. She wanted to be left alone. The slow drive home through Fairchild allowed her a change of scenery and gave her time to put things in perspective.

The fields were plowed under and ready for winter. Some winter crops were in the ground, but not many. It had been a dry year. In the spring, new crops would be planted. There was a cycle to things. It was time for a change.

She slammed her front door shut, leaned her back against it, and sank to the floor. Her shouting filled the house. "No, I'm not doing this. Not again. I'm not going to sit here crying over things I can't change. I'm moving on."

She pulled her knees up and cried until she was all cried out. Then, she wandered to the bathroom, pulling off her clothes and dropping them on the floor as she went. Her reflection in the mirror would pass for a ghoulish haunted house poster girl. She could audition for Frankenstein's next bride or Dracula might need a new girlfriend.

The mascara and eyeliner had run rampant on her face and she reminded her of the red-eyed vampire on the cover of one of her books. She muttered, "You look awful, you're a mess girl. Better get a grip. He used you to get what he wanted. Talk about being thrown under the bus and run over. Twice!"

She put her phone on silent, pulled on a soft pair of pajamas, and fixed herself a strong drink. That was putting it mildly. She'd get the numbing effects started and watch old movies until she fell asleep in the rocker-recliner. A couple drinks and several hours later she woke up in time for the credits to roll on the screen. She'd missed the happy ending. Again. Not a big surprise. There was nothing enchanted about her world.

She turned off the TV and the lights. A short walk and long fall into bed was what she needed. It would all look better in the morning after a good night's sleep. Who was she trying to kid? No way was it going to look better.

It was definitely time to go home. She pulled her suitcases down from the closet shelf.

CHAPTER FIFTEEN

COME MORNING, she didn't feel better. She lay in bed and stared at the ceiling. Thank goodness it wasn't a mirrored ceiling. That would be too scary first thing in the morning. Her cell phone vibrated and lit up. She glanced at the screen and blinked back a tear. Gabriel smiling on the beach in Galveston. She hurled it at the wall. It missed, flew into the living room, and landed with a muffled *thunk*. So much for technology wrapped in a shock absorbing case.

She needed *Papi*. He'd know what to do, how to get over this latest and greatest mistake of hers. He didn't like talking on the phone for more than a couple short minutes. She'd have to go see him. She could do that. The more she thought about it, the better she liked the idea. She missed him and his wife, Carmen. They were her family.

She finally sat up and looked out the window. It was all gray sky and leaves being ripped off tree branches by the north wind. A storm was blowing in. Old man Winter was definitely coming soon. She crawled out of bed and made her way to the kitchen. Coffee sounded good. Kahlúa sounded better. Mix them together and she had a morning-after the night-from-hell, good old-fashioned painkiller.

She curled up in her rocker with her favorite coffee mug and a soft blanket. A couple hours later, she recognized the sound of Gabriel's boots stomping across the porch. Then the pounding on her front door started.

She shouted, "Stop, already. I'm coming."

She would get there eventually. She wasn't in any hurry to see him, talk to him, or fight with him. She slid out of the rocker and eyed the distance to the front door. It was a long way to go for an argument she was in no mood to have.

She opened the door and stepped back as he pushed his way past her. She glared at him with one eye. The other one was too numb to care.

He shrugged off his jacket. "Shut the door and just listen to me. Then if you want to throw me out, I'll leave."

He flung his black leather biker jacket at the couch.

Alena closed the front door shutting out the cold, ambled back to her cozy chair and crawled in. "I'm listening."

He sat down on the far end of the couch, the same arrangement as their first evening.

She watched him watching her. It looked more like he was calculating his next move. She wasn't so deep into her pain-killer remedy that she didn't register the conflict behind his stoic, tortured eyes. He'd never admit he was afraid he'd screwed up royally.

He finally asked, "Are you okay? You're not rocking."

She took a sip from her mug. "I'll be fine."

"Coffee?"

"With Kahlúa."

"Isn't it a little early? Don't you have to work today?"

"Define early, and I called in and quit." She tightened her grip on the mug.

"Quit? Why?" He rubbed his hands down his thighs.

"Because I wanted to."

She glared at him with both eyes this time. She wasn't that numb, yet. What right did he have to ask her anything, especially after what he'd done?

He shook his head. "I'm sorry. I didn't know the D.A. was going to question you. I only want Carlos to get a fair trial."

Hot. Her temperature instantly rose and radiated to her cheeks. She'd be flaming red in seconds. Screw it.

She shouted, "Well, you got what you wanted." She looked wildly around the room and inhaled a deep breath. She needed to get control of the anger and disappointment bubbling up inside of her. "And I want my life back." She put a death grip with her free hand on the arm of the rocker-recliner to keep herself from launching out of it. "I want to enjoy living. I want to be shipwrecked with someone that actually gives a damn about me. But we don't always get what we want, do we? No. We get stuck with whatever life dishes out." She wiggled to the edge of her seat.

Gabriel pulled back like he'd been slapped. "It's not about you. I have to do what I can to help my brother."

She tipped her mug up to her mouth and drained it.

He leaned forward and lowered his voice. "He's my brother. I was there when Mom brought him home from the hospital. I was there when Dad walked out and Carlos ran after him crying. I pulled him out of the street so he wouldn't get run over. I gave him the down payment for that Camaro. I can't turn my back on him now."

"Yeah, got it. Go take care of your family. I'm good. No problem. I'm going to go visit mine for a while." She leaned forward and her feet hit the floor.

"What about your job?"

"What about it? It was just a job. I think it's time I did something for me for a change. I have a bad habit of taking care of everyone else, while my life goes to hell in a handcart. Well, I'm done with that." Alena eyed the bottom of her empty mug.

"If it wasn't for you, I wouldn't have anyone to help me. I owe you." Gabriel half-cringed into the cushions. "We have something, you and me. I wasn't looking for this but it happened. It's going to be tough but I don't want to lose what we've got."

Alena stared at the floor in front of her feet and inhaled deeply. Calm resignation took hold. "We had a couple good nights. No big deal. Great island memories. A walk on the wild side for you. It was fun."

"That's it? It was fun?" Gabriel sat back and angled his body

106

toward her. "For a girl who just had so much fun, you sure look rough."

"Yeah, well, it was a rough night."

"Yes, it was." Gabriel took a deep breath, exhaled and asked, "So, is San Francisco still home?"

"No. My mother's house is not a home. Better to live on Alcatraz." Breaking eye contact, she glared at her empty mug. She needed a refill in the worst way.

"What about your dad?" Gabriel watched her closely. "Where does your father live?"

"What about him? He calls and writes when he has time. He lives outside of Carmel. I get the occasional email letting me know how things are going with him."

Alena focused on the kitchen, plotting how she was gonna get to the coffee maker. She'd run out of painkiller and needed more, lots more. Now. Right now.

Gabriel looked away. "How long are you gonna be gone?"

"I haven't even left yet. How should I know when I'll be back?" Why couldn't he leave well enough alone? Carlos was getting a new trial; Gabriel could get a girlfriend and go on with his life. She'd be in sunny and warm California with *Papi* and Carmen. Everybody's problems would be solved.

Carlos's attorney thinks we'll be able to get a new trial before Christmas since the court takes the holidays off."

She nodded and interlaced sympathy with her words. "That'll be good. It would be nice if you both could have Christmas together with your grandmother. She'd like that."

"So when will you be back?"

"I don't know if I even want to come back. I need to talk to *Papi*." She untangled herself from the blanket that was rapidly smothering her and let it fall to the floor. "You can help Carlos and get on with your life."

"Don't do this." He fixed his gaze on her following every move she made.

"Do what?" She grumbled. The bottle of Kahlúa called to her.

"Don't leave. Stay here."

Alena pushed herself out of the chair grumbling, "I need a drink." She kicked free of the blanket threatening to wrap itself around her feet and unceremoniously trip her.

"You need to stay here with me."

"The D.A. won't like that. It could go bad for Carlos."

She stumbled crookedly to the kitchen with Gabriel following close behind. She poured a generous amount of Kahlúa into her mug, and added a splash of coffee for warmth. She held up her mug, "Cheers," and gulped it down.

Gabriel stood next to her blocking the path back to the living room.

"Then stay here at the house. Be here for me."

"That's asking a lot. I don't want to go through all that mess again with the lies and manipulations. All the who's sleeping with who, the gun nobody saw, and the gangster garbage. I've already heard it. I'm up to my eyeballs in small town Texas machismo bullshit. No thanks."

"It's not like you to walk away?"

"No? Well watch this; I'm going to drive off as fast as the Mustang will roll. And that's pretty damn fast. So stand back." She glanced around the room. "As soon as I get this house closed up."

"I'll call you. We can text."

She muttered, "We can't."

"Why not?" He cocked his head to one side, his brow furrowed and his eyes narrowed.

She caught him studying her. If he was waiting for her to fall apart, he'd be waiting a long time. She was already in pieces. He'd missed that part of her melt down.

She said, "I can't find my phone."

"When was the last time you had it?"

"This morning. I chucked it out of bed and now I can't find it."

Gabriel loomed over her. "Okay, that's enough. What's going on, really going on?"

Alena braced her hands on the counter and looked down at the floor. "I can't watch you die. I can't do it. I don't have it in me to go through that again."

Gabriel wrapped her in his arms and drew her back against his chest. "What are you talking about? I'm not going to die anytime soon."

"Michael's family wants revenge not justice. It's either Carlos or you. Somebody is going to pay for what happened."

"You're not making sense." He hugged her a little tighter.

He was so warm, so strong, and alive. It was too awful to think this might be the last time she'd be held in his arms. She swiped at her runny nose. "It's not adding up. Is there some old grudge from way back or something? Michael's dad is sleeping with Sonja's mom, Sonja playing Carlos and Michael against each other. What's that all about?"

"Nothing that I know of, why?"

"Your mom telling you that you should have stayed home and protected Carlos. Didn't you wonder what you were supposed to protect him from?"

"No. She's been telling me I needed to look out for Carlos since we were kids."

"There's more to it. Something worth letting her son go to prison over."

～

Gabriel worked Alena around to face him. He got it. He understood she was hurt and that was his fault. She was handing him his walking papers if he wanted them. Problem was, he didn't want to lose her, not over this. No, he wanted it all. He wanted time with Alena and to help his brother. It was going to be rough, but he was a Marine. He could and would make it happen.

His girl looked like she'd been in the worst bar fight ever. Matted hair, smeared makeup, red rimmed eyes surrounded by black smudges that made her look like she had two black eyes. And it was his fault she looked so awful.

He'd never imagined she'd be hurt enough to cry over him. Mad, yes. But hurt, no. Apparently, she wasn't so tough when it came to him. Who'd have guessed he'd already made it through her outer armor. He'd figured they'd have to go together a long time before she'd let him get close enough to make her cry.

She ran a hand through her hair brushing it out of her eyes. It flopped back, covering half her face.

She blew out a breath, moving the hair away from her mouth. "I give up. I can't do this. You need to go so I can finish drowning my sorrows and pack."

"I'm not leaving yet. We need to get some things straightened out first."

"I don't feel like straightening anything."

"Okay, fine, less crooked."

"You used me. The D.A. came after me." She sucked in a shuddering breath.

"I was out of options. I told him about the other jurors, not you."

"Well, he didn't make it sound that way." She sniffled. "I tried to help you."

"You did help me." Gabriel scooped her up, walked to the couch, and sat with her on his lap.

He brushed her hair out of her face. "I want you to listen to me. Carlos will get an impartial trial this time with better representation. When it's over, we'll have to live with the outcome, same as Michael's family. It doesn't have anything to do with me."

He wrapped both arms around Alena's shoulders, holding her close. Her head rested against his chest giving him a temporary sense of relief. He'd envisioned her clawing her way off the couch, trying to get away from him.

She hiccupped. "There's no guarantee it'll be any better than the first one. There's more to this than simply getting Carlos a new trial. Michael belonged to a gang and so did Carlos. They'll be back."

"Michael and Carlos were barely fringe members on a good day. Their gangs have moved on."

"This is not as simple as it looks."

"You're right and it's not simple. I've got the attorney looking into Sonja. She never gave me any straight answers. She's hiding something. I can feel it. It might not change the outcome but it's worth a shot."

"What if Carlos gets sent back to prison?" She rubbed at her nose.

"I'll have to live with it. Don't give up on us. You're the one woman on this planet brave enough to stand by me. You don't scare easy, and I need that." *I need you.*

"You're so wrong. I'm a terrible coward. You'll hate me someday when you figure that out."

"You damn near ran me off the road, and walked out on me twice in restaurants leaving me looking like a fool. If I was going to hate you, I'd have done it from the start. Instead, I chased you down and carried you off to bed."

"You probably weren't in your right mind. It happens when men don't get laid regularly." Alena sniffed. "I need my coffee."

Gabriel stifled a laugh and hugged her tighter. "You need to remember who you are. You're the brave woman who fought a maniac with a gun trying to save her man."

"Let go of me." Alena struggled in his arms, feebly pushing against his chest. "I'm the reason he's dead. Big difference."

He held on tight until she gave up. He had her right where he wanted her. "Romero was a grown man. He could have walked away from you but he didn't. He knew a good thing when he had it. I'm not walking away either."

"That's a mistake. There's more to this mess and nobody is talking."

"No, they're not, but this time the truth might come out. Or at least something closer to the truth."

"I'm not sure anyone really knows what the truth is."

"Maybe not, but I have to try." He rearranged his arms getting a better grip on her.

Alena yawned and rested her head against his chest. "I'm going home." She mumbled, "I need *Papi*. He'll know what to do." Her eyes drifted shut.

Gabriel looked down at the hot mess in his lap.

"Alena, is *Papi* your father?" She'd mentioned him a couple times but it didn't sound right.

"No, he's my *Papi*. He raised me."

"That doesn't make sense. *Papi* is Spanish for father."

"I don't care. He's mine. I have *Papi* and my dad." She burrowed into the last tiny remaining spaces on his lap.

Gabriel gave up. "God help me, chica. You're killing me."

She mumbled, "Never. I love you too much."

Too stunned to take his next breath for a couple hot seconds, Gabriel's thoughts flew to the first logical explanation. It had to be the Kahlúa talking.

Right about the time he thought he could relax, she hit him hard with a gut punch that would have knocked him to his knees if he'd been standing up. *I love you, too.* He'd keep that to himself for now.

Damn! Women were confusing, especially this one.

He'd ridden to her house thinking they'd be over if she didn't listen to him. He understood that what he'd done looked bad and she wasn't answering her phone in retaliation. If he wanted to talk to her, he'd have to do it in person. Thankfully, she'd heard him out.

He only needed a chance to show her how strong his love could be and how dedicated he was to making their relationship work. And if he was very lucky, she might love him back. He inhaled deeply and closed his eyes. No way he was already there. When had all that happened? How'd he miss it?

He had to know. "Are you gonna come back after you visit your *Papi*?"

"Maybe. Probably."

He suggested quietly, "We'll find your phone so we can talk and text while you're gone."

"Okay." She wrapped her fingers around his shirt bunching it up and wrinkling the hell out of it.

"You want me to watch the place while you're away?" He rubbed a hand up and down her arm gently and slowly, hoping to keep her talking.

"If you want," she mumbled.

"You gonna give me a key?"

"It's in the shed." She settled in for a nap.

"Okay." He brushed the hair away from her face again. "You're my *chica* and I'll keep an eye on things for you."

Translation, I'll be here waiting.

And he had a new mystery to solve. Who was this man who had raised her, if he wasn't her father? The guy had done one hell of a job.

What kind of man raised a little girl to be fearless, determined, and more independent than most of the men Gabriel knew? She'd march into hell and come out the other side holding the devil by the scruff of his neck if she took a notion to.

The insistent urge to rub the back of his neck was overwhelming but he didn't dare let go of Alena. She was harder to hang on to than an angry wet cat. He'd almost lost the battle several times. The only thing going for him had been the calming effects of the Kahlua.

While she slept snuggled up against him, he had time to come up with his next plan for keeping her with him. This girl was too good to let slip away. How the hell far was it to California anyway?

CHAPTER SIXTEEN

SEVERAL DAYS and a lot of miles later, Alena stood on the wide stone porch at the front door of her father's family home. Her home. The Spanish colonial hacienda sprawled on top of the cliffs outside of Carmel and had been in his family since the day it was built. It was the old oceanside house, as opposed to the San Francisco house. Her mother liked to make fun of the hacienda and all its outbuildings. She said it was faded glory and she wouldn't have dreamed of setting foot in it.

Alena loved the old place. It held her most cherished childhood memories and it was where she'd found *Papi* and Carmen.

Alena had called ahead so her dad would know she was coming. She rang the bell and waited. The door was immediately answered by a uniformed housekeeper.

"Yes, may I help you?" She looked expectantly at Alena like she might be making a delivery.

"I'm Alena Betmunn y Cordova. I'm here to see my dad." Alena stood up straighter.

"Come in and I'll let Mr. Betmunn know you've arrived."

Alena stepped into the entry hall and gazed at the blazing crystal chandelier. It must take days to clean that thing.

The housekeeper closed the door. "If you'll wait here, I'll announce you. Mr. Betmunn is expecting you."

"Yes, thanks." She watched the woman disappear down the hall on silent feet.

She glanced around. The large open rooms with huge windows let in the California sunshine. She took in a deep breath and it still smelled good, comforting. Furniture polish and Grandad's pipe smoke. It smelled like home. She hadn't been there in years. Not since she and Romero had visited.

Thank God her mother hadn't gotten a hold of it. It would have been sold off and the money spent on another French château in some quaint little town with a name Alena couldn't pronounce.

The housekeeper was back. "If you would follow me, please?" She turned and glanced over her shoulder smiling as she started walking away. "I'm Bonnie, household manager otherwise known as the house-keeper. Let me know if you need anything."

"Sure." Alena followed Bonnie down the hall to the open door of her father's office. It had been her grandfather's office when she was a child. Times had changed things a little. There was a new executive chair.

She waved her hand once and said, "Hi! Dad."

"Hello, Al, what brings you to the coast?" He watched and waited. She couldn't blame him for being cautious. She'd been distant, emotionally and physically, since Romero's death.

"I wanted to see you. It's been a long time and we're family." She took a few tentative steps farther into the room.

He didn't look like he'd aged a day in five years. Maybe if she really studied him, he was a little greyer at his temples. Still fit and trim, dressed for a casual day in his home office.

Montgomery Betmunn glanced at the family photos and portraits on the wall to his left. "Yes, we are. Have a seat." He gestured toward the chairs across from his desk.

Alena selected a comfortable looking chair next to a round occa-sional table in front of her father's desk and settled in. "Thanks, it was a long drive."

"Are you tired? Do you need to rest? I had the maid prepare your room." He reached for the intercom.

"No, I'm okay." She looked around. "I always loved this library. It was granddad's favorite."

He leaned back in his chair. "It hasn't changed much." He glanced at his desk then back at her. "How do you like living in the country?"

"It's quieter, peaceful. I sleep better out there with the fresh air and all."

"Of course, just like your grandfather. He never cared much for living in town. Too much noise and smog he said."

"Right." She smiled. "He liked the open air. He was always going somewhere with me running along trying to keep up." She softly laughed, "Until he turned me loose on *Papi* Cordova."

Montgomery smiled. "Exactly. Let's have a drink and we'll get caught up." He buzzed the kitchen and asked for iced tea with lemon.

"Great." She had questions that needed answering.

"You were too young to understand back then, but your grandfather was a bit of a scoundrel."

"No?" She quirked an eyebrow.

"Oh, yes. You see he married an actress, my mother. In those days, it was a family scandal. You look a bit like her. When you became fascinated with cars, people talked. Racing and scandal became the family curse."

"I guess I must take after your side of the family." Alena twisted her fingers nervously in her lap, and cleared her throat. "See, that's why I'm here. I'm seeing someone that's all about family. He's trying so hard to help his and it got me to thinking I should try to do better with mine."

"And you've come to see me?"

"It's taken me a while to get strong enough to get back out and go places that might remind me of Romero." Talk about racing and scandal. She had the market cornered on that.

"Well, I'm glad you're here. Last time I made a mess of things. I had no idea your mother had completely misrepresented the situation." He shook his head and frowned. "I was afraid I'd pushed you away. Romero made it very clear he was an honest man who was deeply in love with my daughter. I offered him two-hundred-thousand to walk away and make your mother happy." Her dad snorted. "He told me exactly what I could do with that money. Santiago told me I'd made a terrible mistake. He was right, of course."

Alena grinned. "I know, they told me."

"It was a terrible shock when Santiago charged in here saying you and Romero had been shot. I couldn't believe it."

Montgomery glanced away and took a deep breath. "I was afraid we were going to have to lock him up. I'd never seen him like that, storming through the house yelling. I put him on a chartered flight with Carmen. I didn't dare let him drive, and I sent Hector with them to do the driving when they got to Houston."

"Why didn't you come with them?"

"I didn't know what to do. Santiago and Carmen had seen that kind of thing before they came to America. They'd know how to take care of you. They'd been taking care of you for years teaching you every-thing we couldn't. I thought I'd only be in the way."

"Mom didn't even call." She looked down and then back up at her dad. "I didn't want to see any reporters. I wanted to go home."

"I tried to contact your mother but she was in France and not answering her phone."

"It wouldn't have made any difference. I'm an embarrassment to her. What about you?" Might as well address the elephant in the room. "Are you ashamed of me, too?"

"I could never be ashamed of you. Santiago raised you right. You are strong because of him and spoiled because of me and Granddad. You're the best of the three of us combined. You come on home anytime you feel like it."

"Until Gabriel came along, I didn't really have the strength to look at myself and admit I've been hiding from life."

"I can see we need to clear up a few things so we can move forward. He rested his folded hands on top of his desk. "After Granddad passed, your mother told me you didn't want to spend summers here."

"She told me you were too busy to have me around."

The internal conflict playing-out in his eyes came through in his tentative voice. "I knew you were safe and I was afraid she'd take you to France permanently. I was never too busy for you, only terrified I'd lose you forever. I thought you might go and never come back."

"She did take me to France, but I didn't like it much. I missed *Papi* and Carmen. I missed the beach and Granddad. I made her life miserable so she'd send me home. I didn't understand why you didn't want me anymore."

"It's not that I didn't want you, but your mother can be very difficult when she wants to be. Fighting with her didn't seem like a good idea at the time."

"Difficult is her standard of living." Alena quirked her mouth to one side. "Everything has to make her look good or it's out."

Montgomery nodded once and grimaced. Taking a deep breath and putting a cheerful smile on his face he said, "I'm hoping you can stay a while this time. This is your home. Remember, Grandad left it to you with a life-estate for me."

She sighed heavily and with a certain amount of resignation admitted, "I'm going to have to move back here eventually so I can take care of *Papi* and Carmen. There's plenty of room in this house for all of us."

"I like the sound of that." Montgomery pulled his hands back and rested them on the arms of his chair. "While you're here, I'd like you to meet the neighbors next door, Esmiralda Kington and her family. That place has been in their family longer than we've been here."

"This is as good a time as any. It's good to know the neighbors." Alena had only seen Kington House from a distance. Two stories of palatial grandeur. White stucco and black wrought iron balconies overlooking the Pacific Ocean. Their front gate was nothing to be sneezed at. They had better security than Fort Knox. They also had the reputation to go with it. Challenge a Kington at your own risk.

Her dad clicked the intercom to his assistant. "Laurie, call Ms. Kington and invite her to dinner later this week. Tell her I'd like to introduce her to my daughter." He released the intercom and turned his attention back to Alena. "Now, that's all set." He settled against the back of his chair. "Have you talked to Cami lately? You two were inseparable when you stayed here."

"I called her when I got to San Francisco. She's living in Texas now. Her little boy is fine and she sounds happy."

Montgomery nodded. "Are you working? Are you getting the money I send to your account every month?"

"I quit my job. It wasn't a good fit. She shrugged. "I get my allowance. I'm saving it for a rainy day, you know, just in case."

Montgomery tapped his fingers on the arm of his chair. "You sound like a broken record of your grandfather. He always had a little extra stashed away in case of disaster."

"Oh, well, I guess. Anything's possible." She lost her smile. "So, Dad I was thinking I'd like to go back to school."

That was the thing. She'd changed her mind so many times already when it came to settling on a career. She wasn't sure he'd be willing to hear that she was making another move.

There was a soft knock on the library door before a casually dressed maid entered with iced tea. She served it with all the usual pleasantries and then left as quietly as she came.

Montgomery took a sip from his glass and asked, "And do what this time?"

His expression didn't change. Alena tried not to wince. "If I finish my Business degree, I can do something that will make a real difference."

"All right." He tipped his head slightly, presumably studying a spot on his desk. "Don't you like nursing?"

He wasn't fooling her. She could almost see the wheels turning inside his head.

"It's good knowledge to have, and I'll be able to take care of *Papi* in his old age. I'll never put any of my family in a nursing home." She kept her eyes trained on her father. When he didn't flinch, she continued, "I want to do something that will reach more people before they get hurt so bad they end up too traumatized to fully recover. Kids like Romero who need a safe place to live. His life could have been so different. If I go back to racing, I can donate a portion of the winnings and build a shelter."

Montgomery's face lit up with a huge smile she hadn't seen in years.

"That's my girl. Any chance you'll come to Betmunn Racing? It was your grandfather's dream. He and Santiago were sure you'd be a winner. He said you were a chip off the old engine block." He leaned forward resting his arms on the desk. "We have strict orders to provide you with any racing equipment you need. And your car is sitting in the garage right where you and Santiago left it. It's been waiting for you to come back. We could establish a division for supporting your shelter."

Alena sat up straighter. "Are you kidding?"

Her father's smile became a gentle laugh. "I'm afraid not. Granddad made it very clear we were not to touch your car until you came home. Once you roll it out on the track, it becomes our new company logo. We can back your shelter. Other companies are doing things like that, but we haven't found one we like. Yours would be perfect."

"I miss working with *Papi*. He'd have to be part of the team."

Montgomery nodded. "You were either with Santiago or Granddad. Back then, Santiago was our top mechanic." He gazed out the window. "I remember when he came to us all branded and tattooed. A monster. The first day Granddad took you down to the garage, you walked right up to him and it was over. You had him from the start. Our little beauty and her big beast. I'd never seen him smile until the day you took his name. He's so proud of you."

"I'd like my family…" She looked her dad straight in the eyes, "… you, *Papi* and Carmen, to meet Gabriel. He got out of the Marine Corps a few months ago. He's getting back into civilian life. He doesn't give up when things get tough. That's important. I'm not easy to live with."

He laughed and lightly slapped the armrest. "Happy to meet anyone you want me to and of course Santiago and Carmen are family. Have been since you latched on to them. I'll never forget him swearing and walking away with you jabbering and running along behind him. I was going to say something to him about his language, but Granddad told me to leave it be. You would hear worse before it was over and as long as you were with Santiago no one would dare lay a hand on you."

Alena grinned at her father. "I'm pretty sure I've heard it all some-where along the way." She took a couple swallows of tea.

"Yes, well, when Granddad would work the pedals and you'd steer, we'd hear you squealing and shouting for him to go faster. When the two of you would finally get out of the car, he'd spin you in circles just to make you laugh some more. Granddad loved that about you. You were fearless."

"That explains the way I am at the end of the race."

"Santiago would shake his head and mutter that it was impossible to keep the two of you speed-demons from wrecking his beautiful engines."

"Is *Papi* here today?" She'd walk over to his house if he wasn't. She had things she needed to talk to him about. Like how to start over. And how to let Gabriel into her life without feeling like she was abandoning Romero.

"I'll call down and find out. He's semi-retired, but he lives in the same house. If we couldn't find you in the garage, we'd send a car over to his place to bring you home. You were very fond of his wife's cooking and you were always hungry. That French nanny your mother sent was afraid you'd get fat. She was always fussing about not over-feeding you here at the house. You spent more time with them than you did with us."

"Carmen taught me how to cook and understand people. She taught me to use my intuition to keep myself safe." Alena glanced out the window. "They needed me."

"I know. You were a blessing to them. He won't tell you, but he almost lost his mind when you got hurt. I think it would kill him if he lost you."

"*Papi* will know how to help me get back on the track. I feel like it's time for me to stop hiding and go back to doing what I love. I have a good mechanic in mind but he's not Romero or *Papi*."

"I'll call the garage and let Nate know you're coming. He's the best we've got. You can have all the parts you need. Esmiralda's niece has a trucking company. We've used them for parts delivery. They're very reliable and the price is reasonable." He looked extremely satisfied with himself. "We can talk to them about transportation."

Alena inwardly breathed a sigh of relief. Everything was falling into place. She finished her tea. It was going to be okay.

Her dad lost his happy face. "Just do one thing for me, please."

Alena nodded. "Okay, what?"

"Take your grandfather's seat on the Board of Directors. I'd like to retire."

Later that afternoon, Alena walked to *Papi's* house. She could find her way in the dark. And she had many, many times. In the really old days it had been part of the estate. Granddad had left it to Santiago. Carmen was the best cook in the world and *Papi* was special. He was hers and she was his *pequeño tigre*, little tiger.

She walked past the old house to his garage and found him bent over the engine compartment of a classic race car. He enjoyed restoring antique cars and his skills were always in demand.

He still wore the white t-shirt and dark blue work pants he'd always worn. Betmunn provided dark blue work shirts for the mechanics and somewhere around noon, *Papi* took his off and spent the rest of the day in his signature white t-shirt. How Carmen got them clean was a mystery.

She called out, "Hi! *Papi*. I'm home."

His head popped up like he'd been stuck in the butt with a hat pin. "*Tigre*! Where did you come from?"

"I just got here."

He stood up straight; well over six feet tall and built like a locomotive, broad shouldered and powerful, even though he was coming up on his fortieth birthday. He was a Christmas Eve baby. This year she'd be there to celebrate with him. He'd help her find the strength she needed to keep going.

Tears ran down her cheeks. "I've been so lost."

Papi held out his arms to her and she ran to him. Flinging herself against his massive chest, she buried her face in his white t-shirt. "I still miss Romero so much, but I can't hide from life anymore."

It had come knocking on her door in the form of Gabriel.

"I know. He loved you with everything he had in him."

"What am I going to do? How do I start over?" She sniffled and tried to dial back the water-works.

He hugged her tighter. "You do what he would have wanted you to do. You pick yourself up and fight. Don't give up. You're ready now. We'll finish your car and put his name on it to honor him. Every time it crosses the finish line, he'll be remembered."

Alena nodded. "He'd like that. We'll do it." She sniffled. "I love you, *Papi*."

"I love you too, *Pequeño Tigre.*"

"I don't like being so far away. I miss you and Carmen."

"Then you should come home."

CHAPTER SEVENTEEN

THE NEXT MORNING, Alena met *Papi* at Betmunn's garage. They had to get the wheels and new tires on her car, and take it off the blocks. It had been sitting a long time and deep-down inside she was afraid it was too old to race. Technology had left it behind but it could be a showpiece. If they dressed it up and put it out in front, the fans would identify with it. They'd see her car and know Betmunn Racing was on the track.

Papi must have read her mind. He'd been known to do that.

"Your car was ahead of its time. It can race with the right driver behind the wheel."

"It's not aerodynamic. It'll catch the wind." Alena ran her hand along the front fender.

"We can fix that." *Papi* popped the hood. "Have you forgotten it's the heart of the car that counts?"

She gazed at the engine compartment. "Romero put a lot into this when he was here. The two of you spent hours tinkering under the hood. That's what I remember."

"We race to win." He looked directly at her.

"We'll fix this car to take the championship. But I have to get us on the ticket first. I'll use a different car for that. Making my comeback is going to take time."

"The new season is coming." He waved at the men he'd selected to work on the car. "Come. Bring the wheels."

She looked up and caught the gleam in her *Papi's* eyes. "I'll talk to Dad about getting us set up with entry fees."

~

She settled in her room for the night and called Gabriel. Even with the time difference he should still be up.

"Hey, how are you? I was getting worried. It's kinda late."

"I'm staying at my dad's tonight. I spent the day with *Papi*." She giggled. "I'm trying to split my time between them so I don't wear either one of them out."

"Is everything okay? You sound tired."

"I don't know if there's such a thing as road-lag, but I think I have it. I'm still trying to adjust to the time change or something." He had no idea how emotionally exhausted she was and she was not about to tell him. That was on her.

"Have you figured out how long you're going to stay?"

"I don't know. I'm trying to work out some things with Dad and *Papi*. It might take a while." She wasn't ready to tell Gabriel about her plans to go back to racing. It might still fall through. She wanted to be sure before she said anything to him.

"What kind of things?"

"I'm thinking about going back to school." That was a safe subject. Nothing life changing or dangerous. She needed to get his mind off of her. "How's it going with Carlos? Do you have a court date yet?"

"Yeah, the first week of December."

"That'll be good. He could be home for Christmas." She didn't have a lot of faith in that but it was possible.

"What about you? Are you going to be home for Christmas?"

"I'll be here. *Papi's* birthday is Christmas Eve. I've missed the last few years and I'm not letting him down this time."

"Don't you think I should meet your family? Even if it's over the phone, it's only right. They need to know I'm serious."

"Are you sure you want to do that? *Papi* will probably ask you some tough questions."

"I'm ready."

"He doesn't like using phones. Um, he gets right to the point. I'm warning you, there's no beating-around-the-bush or mincing words with *Papi*."

"Fine. When can I talk to him?" Direct and determined, that was Gabriel.

"Okay. Well, how about Thanksgiving? That's only a few days away and he'll be in a good mood." He was boxing her into a corner. She needed to think fast.

"Great. That'll work."

"Carmen fixes dinner at Dad's and we all eat together. You can meet everyone at the same time." Dead silence at the other end of the line. "Gabriel?" Maybe he'd back off.

He cleared his throat. "Yeah, got it. Everyone at the same time."

"Perfect."

Hell, and be damned. She had to get her dad to keep their family name out of the conversation. She was not in any way ready to let Gabriel know she was a Betmunn. That would ruin everything. She wanted a man that loved her for herself, not her grandfather's money.

CHAPTER EIGHTEEN

THE FORT BEND Herald put the new trial of Carlos DeLeon on page three. Gabriel took time off from his job operating heavy equipment for the county to be in the courtroom with his grandmother. This time he'd get to see and hear it for himself from start to finish.

Word around town said the Juarez family, Michael's people, were outraged that there was going to be a new trial. For being so incensed it was curious that only the immediate family showed up at the courthouse. Some of them were on the witness list and had to be there. Alena was right, it didn't add up.

The District Attorney had assured him that the jury members had been grilled extensively. There wasn't going to be any screw ups this time. All the subpoenas were served to the witnesses that could still be found and everyone was on board.

The new defense attorney was ready for Sonja, and this time, she wasn't going to get off so easy. She was going to be treated as a hostile witness. She might not be guilty of a crime, but she wasn't exactly an innocent bystander either. If nothing else, Gabriel wanted the court to understand she'd played a part in what had happened.

He looked around the courtroom. His family was there, mother, father, and cousins all sat together.

Oddly enough no gang members came around. Michael had been a minor player on the fringe and not a seasoned member. Carlos was nobody to a small-town group of punks that could barely be called a gang on their best day. Back when it first happened, it was all a lot of hype and swagger for the newspapers but it wasn't gang related news anymore. No more badass publicity to make them semi-famous.

Gabriel sat between the door and his grandmother. She was an elderly lady, small in stature, and all he had left in the world from his old life. He didn't want her getting hurt if things got out of hand.

His mother sat in the row directly behind the defense table and never glanced in his direction. That was her way of telling the world that Carlos was her son, not Gabriel. Even if he was paying for this last-ditch effort to help his brother, she was not going to acknowledge him.

His grandmother patted his hand.

A minute later the court clerk called the room to order.

Gabriel listened to the proceedings. It followed the same story line that he'd gotten from Alena. He could tell there was a whole lot people weren't saying and the defense attorney couldn't force it out of them. The accounts of that night from the witnesses in the Laundromat hadn't changed. The witnesses from the laundromat still swore they didn't see or hear anything until the gun went off, and by the time they looked outside all they saw was Michael slumped over in his car.

Gabriel had never been so frustrated in his life. He finally under-stood why Alena had been upset with the whole experience. It was a miracle that she'd talked to him at all.

On day three, during a break he asked his grandmother, "What do you know about Sonja's mother? Why would she keep pushing Sonja to chase after Michael and Carlos?

"She was friends with your mother and Michael's in high-school. When your mother got pregnant with you, they had some arguments and never spoke to each other again. Nobody talks about those days."

Court reconvened before Gabriel could sort through what she'd said and ask any more questions.

Carlos stayed awake for the proceedings and he answered the questions exactly the way he had rehearsed with his lawyer. In the end, he walked away with six years' probation and time served for manslaughter.

It was a good day for the DeLeon family.

Michael's family, on the other hand, were not pleased.

Gabriel walked up to the defense table in time to hear Mr. Juarez snarl, "This isn't over. You killed my son," before being tugged away by his cousin.

Carlos grumbled, "Go to hell, old man."

Gabriel reached out for Carlos's arm. "Hey, keep it civil."

"Nobody disrespects me. Not anymore."

Gabriel stepped back and looked hard at his younger brother. "This isn't the brother I know. Didn't you hear the terms of your probation? You can't get in any trouble or you're going back inside."

Carlos wasn't soft anymore; there was hard muscle under the clothes. He'd worked out, trimmed down, and gotten an attitude. A bad attitude, a prison attitude.

Carlos shrugged. "Things change, man."

Gabriel shook his head once. "I gave up everything to get you out of that place. You mess this up, it's on you. I'm not saving your ass again."

"Thanks for paying the lawyer but I can take care of myself. I don't need you, and I don't need the Marines to teach me how to be a man."

With his jaw clenched tight, Gabriel kept his angry retort to himself. There was nothing to do but walk away. They'd both changed and there was no going back for either of them.

He didn't understand how they'd gone so wrong. They had both been well on their way to beating the odds in their neighborhood. Gabriel graduated from high school and went into the Marine Corps. Carlos planned to graduate high school and go to junior college. The DeLeon boys were gonna make something of themselves.

He walked their grandmother to his car. It had been repaired good enough to get him around and was parked in the same lot where Alena had damn near run him over. He grinned. That was the best day of his life. He hadn't known it at the time, but he wouldn't change it now for anything.

The ride home was quiet. His grandmother looked relieved but tired. He was sorry he'd put her through a second trial, but he was glad his brother was out of prison and had a chance to do something with his life.

He said, "I'm sorry you had to hear it all again. But he's going to be okay now."

"I hope so, *Mijo*. I hope so."

~

He needed someone to talk to. Thank God, Alena answered on the second ring.

First words out of her mouth were, "How'd it go?"

"Good. He got six years on probation." He should have felt relief or joy but he didn't. He couldn't explain the dread that lingered in his mind or the heaviness in his chest. Something still wasn't right.

Alena sounded cautious. "He'll be home for Christmas. Your grandmother will be happy."

He sighed. "Yeah, she's relieved he's out of prison. I think he's going to be staying with our mother." He didn't want to come right out and tell her what an ungrateful smart-ass his brother had turned into.

"He'll need time to adjust. So much has happened in such a short time, it's a lot to deal with."

"I get it. But he's changed. I don't know him anymore." And he didn't. "I got played. I was his ticket out of prison."

"Time fixes things. You did your best and that's all anyone can do. No regrets. He's got his second chance thanks to you."

He'd take her word for it. If anyone would know about that stuff, she would. "When are you coming home?" He needed her. He needed to hold her and although he'd rather sleep naked on a cactus than admit it, he needed her to hold him.

"Soon. I'll see you soon. I promise."

He caught the hesitation in her voice. "You're not telling me everything. What am I missing?"

"It's a secret. You'll see. It's nothing bad."

"I don't like secrets and I'm not a big fan of surprises. You can tell me."

"Not happening."

Gabriel chuckled. "All right but you just wait. I'll have a few surprises of my own waiting for you when you get here."

~

His version and her version of soon, were apparently two different things. He checked on her place, making sure it was ready for her return. Sometimes he'd sit and watch TV while pretending she was in the other room. There were evenings he'd lay on her bed and call her. They'd talk till she fell asleep.

He couldn't help retelling her all the things he'd heard during the trial. If he repeated it, maybe he'd discover something that would explain why he didn't feel better about the outcome. He was in the middle of describing the high points when Santiago Cordova's voice came on the line. He recognized it from their Thanksgiving conversation.

"Al is asleep on my couch."

Gabriel sucked in a deep breath and let it out. "Hey, yeah, this is Gabriel. I'm out here at her place keeping an eye on things for her."

What was he supposed to say to the man? *Hi! It's me, the horny guy who wants Al to come home so I can sleep with her.* Probably not a good idea if he wanted to keep breathing. If he had to bet, Mr. Cordova would not take that smart-ass kind of remark well at all. The talk they'd had at Thanksgiving had been politely civilized for propriety's sake and because Al was right there listening along with her dad, Montgomery. This was the, "what are your intentions," talk. He was ready.

"Al tells me, you are a Marine and you have an honorable discharge from the service. Are you an honorable man?"

He should have seen this coming. "Yes, sir."

"Good. She is working hard and needs rest. You can call her tomorrow."

Silence hung in the air. This was where a brave man would make his intentions clear. "I love Al. I'm going to ask her to marry me when she gets home." He sucked in a deep breath. "With your permission, sir."

"You may ask her. If you are half the man she says you are, I will not object."

That was good to know. "Thank you, sir. Goodnight." He disconnected the call and waited for his heartrate to return to normal. As soon as she got home, he'd find out what kind of man she'd made him out to be and what kind of expectations he'd have to live up to. No pressure there at all.

~

He called her the next evening, and try as he might to get it out of her, she wouldn't give him an exact date for her return. All she'd say was that she was working with *Papi* on a surprise. Screw the surprise, he was past wanting her to come home. He needed her back where he could see her, hold her and feel her arms wrapped around him. He'd be okay with her sleeping on his lap and drooling on his chest if she'd just come home.

He spent a quiet Christmas day with his grandmother. Carlos didn't come by to see her or even call. Whatever was going on with him was the best kept secret on the planet. And truthfully, Gabriel didn't care anymore. Carlos had made it clear that their family tie didn't matter to him.

Their mother had always favored Carlos. She'd given him her hugs and kisses. Gabriel got food and a place to sleep. It was his job to watch out for his younger brother when they were at school or on the playground. He'd never questioned it. It was what big brothers did for little brothers. Where had he gone wrong? The answer evaded him.

Christmas evening, he stretched out on the bed in his grandmother's spare bedroom talking on the phone with Alena. He imagined lying next to her and having Christmas sex, long, slow, under-the-covers sex. Long distance relationships sucked. It was definitely time to get on with his life. He needed to put the past behind him and reach for more. He would build the life he wanted with Alena, if she'd have him.

~

The next week leading up to New Year's crawled by. He was the new guy, so he got the privilege of working New Year's Eve. Quitting time arrived; he shut down the dozer and crawled his tired ass into the Monte Carlo. He'd have the holiday off to go check on Alena's house. Maybe sit and watch a football game and pretend she was going to bring him a cold beer at half-time. *Keep dreaming.* He'd pull her down and roll her under him and kiss her and tease her. He'd promise to do all kinds of sexy things to her once the game was over. Then he'd pray for the game to get over quickly.

By the time he pulled up in front of his grandmother's house his semi-erection had thankfully receded. His miserable condition was another indication that he needed Alena to come home. There were some things he was tired of doing for himself, especially when she was so much better at it. He walked through his grandma's front door frozen to the bone and inhaled the aroma of homemade pork tamales.

He called out, "*Abuelita*, I'm home."

"*Mijo*, get cleaned up and come eat supper."

"Okay."

He shuffled to the bathroom, stripped off his work clothes, and turned on the shower. The hot water could wash away the dirt and grime, but the empty aching space in his heart was killing him.

Their conversations had been short and she'd sounded distracted the last couple of days. Maybe she'd changed her mind. Maybe he was losing her.

He'd looked up Santiago Cordova and read every word he could find about the man. He was an old-school master mechanic. He had worked for Betmunn Racing back in the days when they were a force to be reckoned with on the race track. Picture captions said that his daughter accompanied him everywhere. After Benton Betmunn died, the company pulled its car from the track. Cordova and his daughter disappeared from the news until Romero stumbled onto her.

He stuck his head under the running water. What was the surprise they were working on, and why wouldn't she tell him? He stepped out of the shower and dried off.

After he put on a clean pair of grey sweat pants, warm tube socks, and a white t-shirt, he walked to the kitchen and took a seat at her ancient table. He was as ready as he'd ever be to share the tamales with his grandma and count down the hours to the New Year.

For his New Year's wish, he wanted Alena to come home, be his girl, ride with him, love him, and spend the rest of her days and nights with him.

He pictured her walking on a white sandy beach in the warm California sun. Texas and the Gulf of Mexico were probably the last things on her mind.

He wanted a beer, the colder the better.

After dinner he wandered to the living room and clicked on the TV. He watched the count-down celebrations from his corner of the old couch that had been there since he was a kid. When the ten o'clock news came on, he headed for the kitchen. The station switched to a live feed and he heard, "We're here at the River Oaks Country Club for the New Year's Eve gala fund raiser for the Children's Hospital. This year's guests include members from several entertainment venues, baseball, football, basketball, and we've heard there's some big news from the racing circuit."

He turned to see what was going on and glanced at the TV. A black limousine pulled up, and a doorman swung open the passenger door.

The reporter announced, "It looks like Alena Cordova is joining the gala."

What? Gabriel's eyes fastened on the screen. Sure enough, Alena stepped out and waved at the cameras. Reporters hit her with lights and microphones.

Gabriel shouted, "She's back! She's in Houston!"

CHAPTER NINETEEN

ALENA WAS BACK in more ways than one. She had a fine room in a four-star hotel on Post Oak Boulevard in the Galleria. It was convenient and showy. This was all about making an impression. A fancy hotel and a fundraiser at the River Oaks Country Club was her vehicle to letting people know she was alive and kicking. She was going to make an announcement regarding her plans to reenter stock-car racing. She had a New Year's party to attend and a New Year's resolution to keep.

She brushed her hands down the front of the designer royal-blue velvet evening gown making sure it was smoothed into place. She turned, peered over her shoulder checking the mirror one last time to be sure the elegant satin drape that flowed over her shoulder and down her back covered the scars. She sucked in a calming breath, swung the matching satin and crystal bead trimmed cape around her shoulders, and took the elevator down to the lobby.

As she walked resolutely to the front door, she saw heads turning and people's eyes following her. *Let them get a good look.* Head up and shoulders back, she looked straight ahead and kept moving. *Papi* didn't raise her to be a coward and she would do this for Romero. She was back and tonight she was coming out. Deal with it.

She stepped into the cold and nodded at the doorman. He waved to the waiting limousine.

She glanced at the hotels up and down the street. The Galleria was still in full holiday mode. Tiny clear bright lights twinkled in the trees. The doorman held the passenger door while she slid onto the leather seat and tucked her feet in. Cinderella was going to the ball.

The driver asked, "Are you ready, Miss Cordova?"

Alena looked into the rear-view mirror to see the driver's face and smiled. "Let's hope the River Oaks Country Club is ready for me."

The driver grinned and nodded. "Yes, ma'am."

A few minutes later, she saw the lights and the TV crews as they turned on to River Oaks Boulevard. Nothing like a New Year's Eve gala to bring out the cameras. Everybody loved a party with a purpose.

The club's liveried doorman opened her door. The cameras and lights all but blinded her.

"Ms. Cordova, are you returning to the track?"

"It's definitely a possibility."

"Do you have a car? Who are your sponsors? Who's on your crew?"

"We're in the planning stages. Nothing's been decided. Happy New Year to all our fans." Alena waved and walked toward the doors.

Once inside, she breathed a sigh of relief. She'd made it through the first step. Now, she had to keep the momentum building, get people talking and spread the word. Al Cordova was coming back to the track.

She was looking good from the glances she was getting from the other guests. She had her dad to thank for the dress. The high-end, brilliant crystal bling hanging around her neck and wrists set it off. They all needed to believe she had the backing to make her comeback happen. Tonight, she was all about sparkle and doing something good for the Children's Hospital while creating a favorable impression of her competitive position.

A waiter stopped to offer her a selection of wine on a silver-plated tray. She picked up something pink and nodded. "Thank you."

She sipped slowly, sauntered around the room smiling and quietly made her presence known.

The room buzzed with conversations and an underlying musical background. It was standard operating procedure for these affairs.

All she had to do was: stand, walk slowly and gracefully through several rooms, stand some more, pose for a few pictures, sit if she could find a chair, ignore the ache in her feet from the designer high heels, nod and smile, a lot.

She hadn't made it halfway across the room before she was waylaid by a rather notorious tire company representative.

"I couldn't believe my ears when I heard you were here. It really is you." He shoved his business card at her. "Give me a call next week. Let's do lunch."

Alena took his card while maintaining her practiced publicity smile. "I'm heading back to California as soon as the holidays are over, but I'll keep this handy."

She'd made it a few more feet before she was stopped again, this time by one of her competitors. Haloran was up in the ratings, racking up points, and keeping his name in the game.

"Hey, Al, good to see you. How's it going? Are you backing someone or planning to start driving again?"

"Tonight, I'm here to help raise money for the children's hospital." She tilted her head as if contemplating the thought and said, "Making a comeback would be a challenge but I'm definitely up for it. It would be great to compete again."

She struggled to hold back a satisfied smile at the sick look that spread across his face. Step two completed. The word would spread through the racing circles. Haloran couldn't keep quiet if his life depended on it.

He muttered, "Oh, sure, I'll look forward to having you back on the track," as he drifted away.

The evening went on like that, making rounds and small talk, lots of hints but nothing specific. She ate some high-dollar hors d'oeuvres, slowly drank a couple glasses of wine, shook hands, smiled for pictures, and planted the seeds for her comeback. The rumors would be spreading like wildfire by morning.

She found a semi-secluded spot near the French doors to the patio and took a break from the crowd. Romero's words echoed in the back of her mind. *"They can't beat you if you don't give up."*

She wasn't kidding herself. It was going to get tougher. She looked around the room and decided she'd done what she came to do. If she started now, she might make it to the front door in an hour. It was early enough that she'd still be able to get back to the hotel before the traffic became too congested. She migrated toward the exit and slid into her limousine with a sly remark to a waiting reporter. He looked young and hungry for a story. "I'll see you at the track. Look for me in the winner's circle."

Alena arrived at the hotel a few minutes before midnight. The people in the lobby bar were focused on the TV and counting down until midnight. She pushed the elevator call button. In a few more ticks of the clock she'd start a new year and a new chapter in her life.

She caught the elevator to her floor and slipped down the empty hall and into her room. From her window, she watched the fireworks going off around the city. She barely caught the sound of her cell phone signaling an incoming call.

She swiped the screen without looking at it and said, "Hello."

"You look beautiful tonight."

Gabriel. "Oh? How would you know how I look?" She smiled at her reflection in the window. A few thousand bucks could make any girl look pretty.

"I saw you on the news."

"Well, you can't believe everything you see on TV. But thanks." She focused on the Houston skyline.

"We've been talking every day. Did I miss something? Why didn't you tell me you were coming home?" Not quite grumpy but he didn't sound happy either.

Here's where it got tricky. She wasn't good at explaining herself. "I didn't want to argue with you. I needed to be seen in public, let people know I'm getting back into racing. It wouldn't be fair to drag you through that."

"Don't you think you should have told me? Maybe ask me if I'd be your escort? I clean up good."

"Okay, that's what I was avoiding. Reporters would ask questions.

They'd pry into your private life. You don't need that. Especially, not now." She frowned at her reflection.

"Have you forgotten I'm a Marine? We don't break easy and we can deal with anything that comes our way."

"Right, but things with me are a bit more complicated than average in case you've forgotten. You could get hurt in the process."

"I haven't forgotten anything. What aren't you telling me?"

"I needed to see how tonight went. People had to see me, not be distracted by you." Her reflection in the window didn't lie. The downward tilt of her mouth, the concern in her eyes. She could make a comeback but it could cost her Gabriel. They were going to have to talk about that.

"It sounds like you're ashamed of me."

Her forehead crinkled and her frown deepened. "What? No. What an awful thing to say. Where the hell did you get that idea?" She looked at the toes of her velvet shoes. Big difference from her non-slip, oil-resistant soled boots.

"It sounds like you don't want to be seen with me. You know damn good and well if I'd known you were in Houston I'd have been there."

"And you'd be on the news. Your face and name associated with mine and all the rumors and speculation that goes with it." She inhaled and muttered, "They'd take you apart like they did Romero."

"I'm not Romero. There's nothing they can do or say that I can't handle."

She stared out into the star-studded night sky. "That doesn't make it hurt any less."

"We're gonna have to get this stuff straight and we can't do it over the phone. Where are you staying? I can be there in an hour."

"You're not getting on the road tonight. I'm going to Galveston in the morning." She needed to feel the sand under her feet and remember who she was and how she'd come this far. She needed the extra courage she'd get from the comforting sounds of the waves.

"I'm off for the holiday. How about we get shipwrecked together?"

He remembered. It was a very tempting offer. In his most persuasive and hopeful voice, the man was doing his best to coax her into giving in to his wishes. She stifled a giggle. He didn't need to know he was getting to her.

"It's a long ride for you on the bike. Can you wait till I can get back to the house?" She didn't want him to freeze to death before she got the chance to scare him to death.

"I sold the bike. I'm in the Monte Carlo."

"That's better this time of year." She tried to sound supportive all the while knowing how much he loved riding that old Harley.

He'd been knocked down repeatedly. Some people would have given up but he was still holding on, and back on his feet. He was the right man for her.

He grumbled, "It's drier with a roof and windows I can close. I'll see you tomorrow. Where are you staying?"

"Same place we stayed last time."

"Should have known. Sounds good." Gabriel let out a breath. "Are you really going back into racing?"

Alena grinned at her reflection in the window. "I am. I can't change the past, but it's time to get back to being me."

"I'll leave early and we can talk about it when I get there."

He sounded tired and she knew the feeling all too well. The mess with Carlos had taken a toll on him, like it had on her the first time around. It was time to put it behind them and move on.

"Racing is a rough business. I'll understand if you're not up for it."

He huffed out a frustrated breath and grumbled, "This isn't working for me. I need to be where you are."

"No, not tonight. The roads are full of tired people that are half-asleep at the wheel. This is not the time to go and get yourself killed. I'm being selfish. I need you alive."

She couldn't have made it this far without him. Gabriel was strong enough to take the weight of being her man. Tomorrow she'd find out if he wanted to step up or walk away.

"You wear that pretty dress tomorrow night and I'll take you out to dinner. After that, we can get shipwrecked together."

"I sense an ulterior motive." She studied her reflection in the window.

"Yeah, I've got plenty of motive."

"So, let me see if I've got this right? We're stuck on a deserted island and I'm wearing an evening gown."

"Yeah, there was a big fancy party going on when pirates attacked. We had to jump overboard to get away. I'm the lucky guy who got to save you."

"Really? Are you sure I didn't save you?" She giggled. Teasing him was so easy and so fun. She'd missed that while she was away. Their phone calls had always been so serious.

Gabriel chuckled low in his throat and said, "I'm pretty sure I saved you. I'm a Marine, that's what I do."

"Huh, well, we'll see about that."

"Just meet me in Galveston."

The sky turned a darker shade of midnight and she could have sworn one of the stars winked at her. "I'll be there. I have a date with an archangel."

Hopefully, the stars were on her side. If her friend Banji wasn't dancing the night away in Paris and drinking pink champagne with her artsy friends, Alena would call and ask her to take a look in the cards. And then again maybe it was better not to know. This time it might be best to let fate surprise her.

CHAPTER TWENTY

IT WAS an easy drive to Galveston early in the morning. Everyone was sleeping off their hangovers. Everyone but Gabriel. He didn't have a hangover. The empty hollow ache in his chest hurt and there was only one way to fix it.

Other girls didn't get more than a passing glance from him; they never measured up to Alena. He'd made up his mind. Al was the one he wanted. She would have to cut him loose and even then, he wasn't sure he'd be able to give up on her.

He wasn't sure how he'd deal with it when she went back to racing. She'd be on the road, going from racetrack to racetrack, and only one crash away from getting injured or killed. He'd considered the possibility of quitting his job and going with her, but he wasn't a race car mechanic. His experience was in heavy equipment. That would be useless on her team. He didn't have an answer yet, but like all good Marines he could adapt and overcome.

His grandmother was never wrong. She'd told him to do the right thing, the honorable thing, and he was going to give it all he had. They'd figure out the details later. Al had stuck with Romero through the good and the bad. And that was saying something. If she was strong enough to stick with Romero, she was plenty strong enough to be with him if she wanted to. That was the question he was wrestling with. Would Alena want to tie herself to him?

He'd been a tough kid and a strong soldier. The Marines had made a solid man out of him, but he was still a man with some rough edges. Those edges didn't scare her. She might even be able to smooth him up a little bit. He was willing to try. He'd do it for her.

And then there was Santiago Cordova, her *Papi*. They didn't come any rougher than that and Alena adored him. The girl was fearless. That could prove to be his undoing.

CHAPTER TWENTY-ONE

AFTER ALENA DROPPED off her luggage, she went to the lounge. Even though it was still early, the clouds hiding the sun turned the sky a slightly lighter shade of grey than the waves. There wasn't a speck of blue anywhere except for the lights on the pier. Her faded blue-jeans and cozy cream-colored sweater kept her warm while the scarlet scarf added a touch of holiday color.

She was halfway through her Irish coffee when Gabriel slid into the chair next to hers. He still took her breath away with his broad shoulders and built-to-please body. The low-slung jeans hugging his hips and navy long sleeved Henley with the sleeves pushed up to his elbows suited him. God help her, she was so in love with him. The time for running away was over and she'd be so destroyed if he walked away. She wasn't up for another broken heart but she had to be ready for it.

"Hey, *chica*, it's good to see ya." He settled in.

"Well, *chico*, it's good to see you, too."

"And?" He focused on her face.

She studied Gabriel, trying to gauge how he was holding up. "I'm back in Texas to clean up the mess I've made. I'm through with hiding."

"Are you really going back to racing?" His eyes never wavered from hers.

"I am, if I can put together a team." She looked him over and asked, "Do you want something to drink?" He would never complain but the goosebumps on his forearms told her he was cold. "Maybe something warm?"

"I already ordered two more of whatever you're drinking. They'll bring it over. The heater in the Monte Carlo isn't working right now."

She nodded. "I'm drinking Irish Coffee. Do you even like Irish Coffee?"

"Never had it, but I'm gonna love it."

"And you know this because?" She let her words dangle.

"It's coffee and whiskey. What could be wrong with that?"

"Absolutely nothing." She chuckled softly. The ever-stoic Marine wasn't gifting her with any signs of how he was taking her news. "And it will warm you up."

"It's a start, but you could warm me up a whole hell of a lot better."

Ah, there it was, his Casanova grin wasn't wasted on her. She grinned back. "We'll get to that later. Right now, we need to talk about last night." She fingered her glass coffee mug. "I've set things in motion and it's not going to be an easy comeback. It wouldn't be fair to drag you through it. You've already been through so much with your brother."

He lost what little cheerful expression he had. "I think I messed up." His lips turned down and any happiness he'd had a minute ago drained from his face. Sadness and worry clouded his eyes. "I did what I thought was right, but it feels wrong. I can't shake the feeling I've made a terrible mistake."

"Messed up how? Carlos got probation. He has a second chance. You got that for him."

"He's thinking he's a tough guy since he's been in prison. He's already joined a rough gang. That's enough to get him tossed back inside if his probation officer finds out." He shook his head. "It's all over town how angry Michael's family is about the verdict. I'm thinking it's not really over."

"None of that is anything you can fix." She rearranged her fingers lower on her thick glass mug where it was warmer. "Carlos knows the consequences if he screws up."

"Maybe if I'd waited, let things settle down more, Michael's people would be taking this better. I don't know." Gabriel slowly shook his head and sighed. "He's not my little brother anymore, but he's still my brother. It was awful to see him locked up in that place."

"He's your family and you wanted to help the kid you remembered. The year he sat in jail awaiting trial didn't do him any good. He was already changing long before you got home."

The waiter brought their drinks and left.

Gabriel reached for his coffee mug. "I sold my Harley and cleaned out my savings to pay for his defense. I've got the car running good enough to get around and go to work. I'm still living with my grandmother and working for the county. It's like it was all for nothing." He stirred the whipped cream into the coffee and took a drink.

"It was for your brother. What he does with the opportunity he's been given isn't up to you."

"Sonja is back in town."

Alena's throat rippled as she swallowed hard. She quirked one side of her mouth and tamped down an unladylike snort. "Yeah, why am I not surprised?"

"She's back with Carlos." He took two long gulps of his coffee.

"No surprise there." She poked at the whipped cream with the stir stick. "That would be about right for her. She'll use him and she'll hurt him again. It's what she does."

"He's all in to taking her back. I've seen them together around town." His grim expression accompanied the deep tone of his voice.

"They're both adults. It's their life and their choices." Her gaze held his.

"It's hard to watch."

"I know." She swallowed another sip. "Give it time."

Gabriel downed more of his drink. "This is pretty good."

"Glad you like it." She'd add it to the list of things he liked. She could make Irish Coffee at home for him on cold winter nights. Provided of course that he came home to her. It was time to get down to business. "I had a lot of time on the road to think."

"I got that. So, what aren't you telling me?"

Was she that transparent, or was he that good at reading her? This was where a coward would look away, afraid to see her hopes smashed to pieces. She had to face it head on and do her best to live with the outcome. Her eyes met and held his.

She said, "The life I want means I have to make some changes. As much as I'd like to, I can't change the past. I've got my dad's support and *Papi* is good with my decision."

"I don't follow. What are you talking about?"

"I can't ignore what calls to my heart and soul anymore. Without my soul, I'm nothing. *Papi* told me that and he'd know."

So far, she'd danced all around the subject. She was going to have to cut to the chase. She tried again to gauge how he was taking the news. Dejection clouded his eyes. He couldn't hide it from her. She was making a mess of things.

"I'm back and I'm not quitting."

He took two long swallows of his liquid courage. "This isn't about racing, is it?"

"No, it's not. I can't keep hiding from the pain anymore. It's time I stand up, face it head-on and overcome it."

Gabriel swallowed hard. "I can help, if you let me."

Alena let the silence hang in the air. This was it. Her heart pounding double-time wasn't helping. She tightened her shaky grip and hoped the Irish Whiskey would hurry up and do something to control her trembling fingers. It was all she could do to take her next breath. Getting tongue-tied now was not an option. She looked away, gazing out the windows toward the rolling grey waves.

"There's a lot of distance between you and me. I'll be an outsider in your world." She was going out on a limb with him, giving him the power to slam her down hard if he wanted to.

"Well, right back at ya. Your people won't be any better."

"I know. I've been there." Her voice came out a little harsher than she'd intended.

"Right, and that was five years ago. Things are changing fast these days." His shoulders slumped. "I don't have anyone left to worry about except my grandmother."

Alena inhaled deeply and stared at the melted whipped cream floating on the surface of her drink. "I know it's risky, but anything worth having is worth fighting for. I think I have one more good fight left in me. *Papi* thinks so, too. He wants to meet you." She looked over at Gabriel.

He leaned forward focusing a steady gaze on her. "Does this mean you're not leaving me?"

"It means—I want to give this thing we've got every chance to work. I want you with me all the way."

Gabriel nodded. "So, I have to get approval from *Papi* Cordova and your dad?"

"I'm afraid so." She looked out at the horizon. "*Papi* said he picked up my phone one night after I fell asleep and you were still talking. I got the impression you two had an interesting conversation."

Gabriel smiled broadly and his eyes crinkled at the corners. "Yeah, we did."

"He likes you and he wants me to get back to doing what I love." She eyed her fallen archangel looking for some sign of how he was taking the news. "And that would be racing."

"And they're okay with you going back out on the track?"

"Yes, my dad is good with it and *Papi* is going to help."

He leaned back in his chair. "I don't know anything about fixing race cars. I won't be much use."

"That's not exactly true." She leaned toward him. "What I need you to do is catch me at the finish line. Can you do that? If you don't want to, say so, and I'll understand."

Gabriel grinned. "I can do that easy."

She sighed in relief and smiled back at him. "I was hoping you'd say that."

The sadness disappeared from his eyes and an encouraging smile spread across his face. "Right." He took her by the hand. "Would you like to get shipwrecked with me tonight?"

Her handsome archangel was back. "I'd love to. I think that would be a perfect date."

"I think we should have another drink. By the time we finish, our room should be ready. We can make sure the bed is comfortable, then change our clothes and go to dinner. I want to see you in that pretty blue dress."

148

Alena winked. "That sounds great, but I'm warning you, don't make plans for after dinner. You're going to be busy."

"You have no idea how glad I am to hear that."

Alena sipped her drink and scrutinized him over the rim of her mug. His eyes were a deeper brown in the island light and now they held a hint of mischief. It was a good look on him.

She commented, "Yes, we definitely need to take a nap. Something tells me it's going to be a long night."

CHAPTER TWENTY-TWO

ALENA'S GAZE focused on the mirror while she put the finishing touches on her makeup.

Gabriel called out, "Meet me in the lobby."

"Okay, just give me a couple minutes."

She shook her head and wondered what in the world had him in such a hurry to get to dinner. Left on his own, he forgot to eat half the time. She finished her makeup and checked the dress once more to be sure she was ready to be seen in public. The satin drape over her left shoulder hid the scars when it was perfectly in place. She picked up the matching velvet cape and evening bag.

When she stepped off the elevator, the lobby was unusually quiet, especially considering the high ceilings. The arched doorways and sparkling chandeliers offset the dark wood overhead. Alena walked toward the entrance, glancing from side to side until she saw Gabriel at the front desk.

He turned toward her and she had to remember to breathe. He was strikingly handsome in his black suit, pressed white shirt, bolo tie, and cowboy boots. When he got within arm's length, she stopped and held out her cape.

He draped it over her shoulders. "Come on, they're holding a table for us." He put his hand at the small of her back and guided her toward the front doors. As she walked through ahead of him, he looked back and nodded at the concierge.

The evening air was cool on their walk to the restaurant. Alena wrapped her arm through Gabriel's. She was holding her man, the one she wanted for all time. Even when he was having a complicated moment, like now. "Really, we're going to eat on the pier all dressed up?" She doubted she'd ever figure out the way his mind worked.

"I want to do it right this time. This is our special place."

"Okay, I'm good with that." It was starting to make sense. He was a romantic at heart.

He held the door open and she stepped inside. He gave the hostess his name and they were shown to a corner table with a view of the ocean. After their order had been taken and their drinks delivered, Gabriel reached across the table and held out a hand to Alena.

She looked at it, smiled slowly and then put her hand in his. That's when she felt the trembling in his fingers. What was he afraid of?

His thumb rubbed over her fingers.

She asked, "What?"

"I'm not good with this stuff, but I want to ask you something important."

"It's okay. Whatever it is, it'll be fine."

"We met rough, not all nice and polite like most people. I've got nothing much to offer you but I'm going to say this anyway." Gabriel never took his eyes off her. "I want to make you a promise." He swallowed hard. "I promise, I'm going to ask you to marry me someday soon, and I want you to think about what your answer will be."

She watched his smile fade in the seconds it took her to process what she'd heard. He loosened his hold on her hand and started to pull away. Snapping out of her trance, she grabbed his hand before he got completely free.

"Hold it." She smiled her best impish smile. "I haven't heard of a promise like that in a long time. It's very old-fashioned. I need to think about this."

"So, that's your answer? We can skip the promise if you want to." He reached for his water glass with his free hand and took a drink. "Alena, will you marry me?"

151

"Is this how you plan to fix things? I get the feeling your grandmother put you up to it."

"Yes, and yes. This is my best offer and she told me I could start with a promise ring to make my intentions known. I feel like we're living on a roller coaster. I don't want time to run out and we miss our chance to be together. I'm in love with you."

"Oh, well, since you put it that way, I'd be a fool not to take you up on it."

With a shaky hand, Gabriel pulled a small black velvet box out of his pocket. That wasn't like him. He was usually strong and steady. It was her fault. She'd done this to him.

Once before she'd accepted a ring with all the hopes and dreams that came with it. Delight danced a jig in her stomach. She stared at the box reveling in the elation that she had found a brave and honest man who was offering her his heart. Trepidation that she could break him and his heart scampered around the edges of her conscience.

She put her hand over his and whispered, "I didn't think I could fall in love again until I met you." Gabriel was one surprise after another. He left her breathless without even trying. She needed him in her life.

"Likewise. You blindsided me."

"No. I dragged you in off the porch." She snickered.

"Yeah, that too." He moved the box closer to her. "Will you wear my ring now? I want everyone to know you're spoken for."

Too choked up to speak right away, Alena nodded. She inhaled and willed her heart to slow down to something that didn't feel like a thousand butterflies were trying to escape from her chest. When she could get her lips to move, she murmured, "It's like the old days. I accept your promise."

The tiny sapphire band slipped on easily and fit perfectly.

"That's amazing. How did you know what size?"

Gabriel ducked his head. "I let myself in to your place and looked in your jewelry box."

"You broke in to my house?" She laughed out loud. "You're shameless."

"You told me I could check on the place. Remember? You said I could use the spare key in the shed behind the grill. So, I used it."

"I know I said it was okay if you checked on the place, but I didn't really expect you to do more than drive by." She laughed and squeezed his hand.

Gabriel swallowed a healthy amount of Tennessee whiskey. "A desperate man does desperate things."

∼

Their dinner date went off without a hitch, just like he'd imagined and prayed it would. If the concierge got the flowers and champagne up to the room like he'd asked, the night would be perfect.

They strolled slowly back toward the hotel with Gabriel's arm wrapped protectively around Alena's shoulders. He stopped when she slowed and watched the waves washing up onto the sand. She was stunningly beautiful, standing there with the sea breeze blowing through her hair and moonlight reflecting on the dark water. Magical was the word that came to him. "It feels like it's a shipwreck kinda night. If you listen, you can hear the surf."

She turned toward him and wrapped her arms around his waist. "I love you."

He pulled her close. His throat threatened to close. A growl rumbled from him before he forced the words out. "I don't want to live the rest of my life without you."

"It could be a lonely life. Holidays, there'll only be the two of us unless we go out to the coast. Are you ready for that?"

Gabriel grinned. "We'll have so many kids we won't have time to be lonely."

Her head shot up. "Hold it. Who said anything about kids?"

"I think I know you well enough to know you wouldn't wear my ring if you didn't love me a whole hell of a lot. And since you love me so much, we're gonna be a family with a yard full of kids."

Alena studied Gabriel's eyes searching for a clue and found a mischievous twinkle in their dark depths. What was he thinking? "How am I supposed to fit behind the wheel of a race car if I'm pregnant?" That ought to slow him down.

153

"You won't be racing forever." He grinned. "We'll figure it out as we go along."

"Seriously, you're a complicated man. We're barely engaged and you're already moving on to having kids. I think you skipped the part where we live together."

"I'll be glad to move in." He held her gaze. "War taught me time is the one thing you can't waste."

"I'll make room for you in the closet and dresser when we get home." She looked out over the waves and back up at Gabriel. "Tonight, we're here and we have the whole night ahead of us." She gazed into his eyes and saw the devotion shining there. "We're a couple of survivors washed up on the beach. What do you think we should do about it?"

"Just you and me?" Gabriel cocked his head to one side and gave her a lopsided grin.

"Yes, just us."

"We could get out of these clothes and get to knowing each other better, the best way, skin to skin close." Gabriel ran a hand up her back and back down, stopping over her hip, and pulling her up tight against the hard bulge in his pants. "That's what you do to me."

"Okay, then. It seems you have a condition I could help you with." She pressed a little closer, slipped her hand over from his hip and cupped his erection. "Yep, that's definitely a condition."

"Yeah, you've been giving me a condition since you bent over in those little black shorts last summer. You don't fool me, *chica*. You've been after my body from the start."

CHAPTER TWENTY-THREE

A MONTH LATER, Alena stood at the railing that circled above the pits. She spotted Tommy in the stands watching his kids working on their car and moved in his direction. His son, Trevor, was a good mechanic but Monica, his daughter, was the one to watch out for. She was a flaming ball of energy looking for a place to explode.

Trevor spotted Alena and waved. Tommy leaned forward in his chair and yelled, "What? I can't hear you."

Alena dropped her duffle bag next to his chair. "I think he's trying to let you know you have company."

Tommy looked up. A huge smile erupted on his face. "Oh, my God, where did you come from?"

"Here and there. I heard you were building a fast car and could use a driver. I thought I'd apply for the job." Her mouth quirked to one side emphasizing the question before she gave in to a smile she'd been holding back. Tommy knew her too well to hide her scheming ways from him.

"Yeah, the fastest car ever, and there she is."

"So, who's driving?" She eyed the maroon monster in the pit.

"Don't have a driver. Guess nobody thinks I can build a winning car."

"I believe you can do anything you set your mind to." Alena looked out over the track. "Any chance you'd let me drive your car? And I've got us a back-up driver."

"Damn, girl! I'd take you anytime. Who's the back-up?"

"He's a young guy, just out of the service. He's hell-on-wheels and pretty fair with a wrench, too. He has a little bit of a West Coast attitude but nothing we can't handle. I'm thinking we could put a team together."

Tommy rubbed his chin. "I'm flat broke, Al. I put everything I have and some that I don't, into that car down there. I can't pay a driver."

"I figured. But I've got a little cash. It's only an outlaw invitational, but it's a start. So, what do you say? How about you let me take a shot at it?"

"I've got no one else. You're taking a chance on a car that's never been driven in a race. My daughter has run it around the track and I know it's good to go, but you're still betting on a car that hasn't been really tested."

"And you're taking a chance on someone that hasn't raced in years, and on a new guy that hasn't raced on any official track."

"Hell, girl." Tommy patted Alena's arm, "Let's go tell the kids and see what your guy can do."

He turned to reach for his cane and stopped, "Hey, who's the big guy headed this way?"

"Shaved head?" Alena didn't turn around to look.

"Yeah, and a smaller version along with some long-haired, skinny kid that's got antique cameras hanging around his neck."

Alena gave him her best cagey smile and said, "Well, the big guy is Gabriel and we're together. As soon as they get here, I'll introduce you."

Less than a minute later, Gabriel put a hand on Alena's shoulder, and held out his other hand to Tommy. "Hey, how ya doing? I'm Gabriel."

"Tommy."

Alena motioned toward the other men. "This is Nate, the greatest mechanic's helper and my back-up driver."

Nate shook Tommy's hand. "Good to meet ya." He was a couple inches shorter than Gabriel and slimmer through the hips. He was well on his way to maturing into one hell of a fine-looking man. His big brown eyes and long lashes would have all the girls swooning.

She nodded to the skinny young man standing next to Nate. "And this is Sean. He's a sports reporter that's going to print only good things about our racing team and take amazing pictures."

The rookie reporter had the talent and the drive to make it. She'd found him a few weeks ago at a Houston baseball game scrambling for an interview with the winning team.

His well-worn clothes might be considered shabby, but his cameras were top dollar. Behind the dark glasses were blue eyes and a flare for capturing images on film. All he needed was a break. Her team was giving him one.

Sean held his cameras back with one hand and shook Tommy's hand with the other. "Good to meet you." He glanced at Alena. "This is great. Real behind the scenes stuff."

Tommy quirked a half-assed grin at the kid. "Okay. Well, welcome to the team."

Gabriel shifted toward Tommy. "Al says you have a fast car."

"Sure do. We're just headed down to take a look. Come on." Tommy grabbed his cane and led them to the pit.

Once they were all standing next to the car, Tommy introduced Trevor and Monica to Gabriel, Nate and Sean. Alena remembered them from the old days when Tommy loved showing her pictures of Trevor graduating high-school and heading off to college. Monica had been a senior going to the prom. The years had turned Trevor into a handsome young man and Monica was pretty enough to turn all the boy's heads.

Alena looked around and whispered to Gabriel, "This feels right."

Gabriel eyed the dark maroon Dodge Challenger and grimaced. "I'll take your word for it."

His hesitation wasn't lost on her. "My Nova looked worse. It's what's under the hood that counts."

"If you say so. Just remember, you're going home with me." He squeezed her hand. "I've got you at the finish line."

Alena smiled up at him. "I know."

Sean circled the car, frowning. "This is it? How am I supposed to make this look like a winner?"

157

Alena patted the hood. "Well, let me tell you how we're gonna fool them all. We stand in front of the car with only the corner of the grill showing. Be sure you get the Challenger logo real clear."

"Yeah, I guess that'll work." Sean shrugged. "Are you sure about this?"

"It's the Outlaw Invitational. We're good. After we win a few races we'll get her painted."

Nate muttered, "Are you sure it'll hold together?"

Tommy nodded at his son. "Pop the hood and show these folks what we've built."

Gabriel looked inside the engine compartment and whistled. "*Madre de Dios*, it's a monster."

Tommy rubbed his hands together. "It's 6.2-liters of 707 horsepower."

Nate whistled, "I've never seen one of these on the street."

Alena smiled at the greasy hunk of metal and said, "But we're not on the street." She patted the front fender. "I love it. I'm going to get my helmet and go for a ride. Come on Nate, you're going, too."

Gabriel and Tommy watched Alena trot up the stairs with Nate following close behind. When they were out of ear shot, Tommy turned toward Gabriel. "All I need to win is a great driver. Al's the best driver I know. If she says this kid is good, I'll take her word for it." Tommy fixed him with a calculating stare. "What I want to know is: are you gonna be able to handle her at the end of the race? It takes a strong man to keep a grip on her."

"I'll be there."

"You gotta do more than be there." Tommy gripped Gabriel's arm. "When she drives, the adrenaline rush, the vibration, and the force pushing on her body takes a toll on her. When she crawls out at the end of the race, she's shaking so bad, she hits the ground. If you're not going to hold her up, I'll get one of the crew to do it."

Gabriel blinked and cleared his throat. "I've seen the race reruns. I'll take care of her. She's my responsibility now." He stared down at

Tommy. "I take it, all that congratulating, crew chief walking her to the winner's circle show, is what's holding her up?"

"Yeah. By then she's worn herself out and there's nothing left. Time for Gatorade. There's always some in the cooler."

"How do you know all this?"

"Mechanics talk, pit crews talk. We talk about the drivers. We do all the work and they get all the glory. Romero didn't talk much. He just said it took everything he had to keep her on the track and thank God for Goodyear and Gatorade."

"How well did you know Romero?"

"Well enough. He always had the hottest broads on the circuit hanging around. Well, until he took up with Al. That was the end of that. His roaming days were over."

"Are you sure about that?"

Tommy nodded. "I'm sure. Romero lost that restless prowling thing he'd always done. Whatever he'd been looking for, he'd found it."

"He settled down?"

"When he and Al came back from their trip to California to meet her family, he was a different man."

"Different how?"

"Told me he'd met her *Papi*, and he had some big shoes to fill. It was time for him to be a better man."

Gabriel nodded, "I've talked to Mr. Cordova a couple times. He's got a seriously hard edge to him."

"After the shooting he came to take care of Al. I saw him carry her out of the hospital. Really pissed off the nurses." Tommy shook his head. "Scary looking man."

"Were you there the day she got shot?"

Tommy hesitated. "Yeah. One of the bullets hit me. I wasn't always like this."

"Hey, sorry. I didn't know."

"A lot of people got hurt that day. Snuffy just went nuts. Guess he'd lost once too often. Seeing Romero pull Al out of the winning car and them kissing and laughing must have been the last straw. Why are you asking all these questions?"

"She doesn't talk much and there's more to her than meets the eye. She's tough. She had to learn it somewhere." Gabriel eyed Tommy.

"Al was always strong. Probably got that from Cordova. The day she met Romero, she looked at him like they were old friends. It was strange to hear them talking like they'd known each other for years. When she gave him her phone number, I saw him smile. He never smiled. That's when I knew something had changed."

Gabriel grunted. "She has that effect."

They watched the Challenger fly past them on the track. So much for warming up. The engine roared, drowning out their conversation.

When the noise receded, Tommy added, "They were a winning combination. Some people were damn jealous. You might hear old rumors that Romero put some bruises on her, but don't believe it. Cordova would have killed him."

Gabriel's eyes narrowed. "Rumors or truths, which is it?"

"It's just sometimes she'd be bruised up." Tommy shrugged. "I took a look at the seat and harness in her car. They were okay. It wasn't the car."

"Did you ask her about it?"

Tommy shrugged. "I asked if she needed any help. She said she was fine."

Gabriel looked questioningly at Tommy.

"In all the time they were together, I never saw him get rough with her.

CHAPTER TWENTY-FOUR

GABRIEL SLID behind the Mustang's steering wheel. He watched Alena fasten her seatbelt and settle in for the ride home.

She gave a heavy sigh and giggled. "We did it. We've got a car to race and the beginnings of a crew."

Her excitement was contagious. Gabriel chuckled and started the Mustang. "You're amazing. You're really going to do this."

"We're in business. This is great. Tommy's a super mechanic. Did you see that Hemi? It's gonna tear up the track."

Gabriel smiled. "You and Nate are going to be hard to beat."

While he pulled onto the access road, Alena turned on the radio. Gabriel turned it off.

Her forehead wrinkled. "What? Don't you like the station?"

"No. The station's fine. I want to ask you something." It had been bothering him since Tommy had mentioned her sporting bruises back in her days with Romero.

She looked over at him, still wearing a grin. "Okay, do you want to stop for an early victory dinner in Houston? We're winning and I'm buying."

"That's not it."

"All right, so what's the question?" Her smile faded.

She was on to something good and he was about to burst her happy bubble. He hated doing it, but the knot in his gut wouldn't go away until he got answers.

He started with, "It's okay to tell me."

Alena's smile disappeared completely. "What are you getting at?" Her eyes flicked up and to the side.

He'd pushed her suspicion button. He spit out the question quick, before she had time to block him. "Did Romero ever disrespect you?" Gabriel glanced at her, then looked back at the road.

"What?"

There was no nice way to ask his next question. He hesitated for a hot second. He could back out altogether and change the subject, but it would eat at him until he had the truth. He struggled to keep his voice soft and low. "People saw your bruises. Did he hit you?"

"Where did you hear that?" Her brow wrinkled tighter and her eyes narrowed to questioning slits.

Gabriel frowned. He was in so much trouble if the look on her face was any clue. "It's just a question. He had a reputation."

"That's nobody's damn business." Alena crossed her arms over her chest and stared straight ahead.

"Hey, don't get mad. It's just something I should know."

She snapped, "That's it. Pull over. Get out. I'm not doing this. You're the one disrespecting me. What makes you think I'd let some man beat me? Not happening, ever! You can walk home and think about the awful things you've said."

Gabriel put a hard edge on his answer to make his point. "No. I'm not pulling over and we are going to talk about it."

"Double damn, this is so messed up. That never happened, ever."

"So, tell me what really did happen and it won't be messed up anymore."

"Screw you."

She moved as far away from him as she could get. *Please, Jesus, don't let her crawl out the window.* He'd really hit a sore spot that wasn't going to go away easy this time. He had to see this through or he'd never have peace of mind.

"Alena." Gabriel's gruff voice issued a warning. "I'm not going to let this go. If he hurt you, I need to know."

She hit the door with the edge of her fist. "Fine. Yes, Romero hit me but he didn't mean to. He had terrible nightmares. He'd wake up screaming, punching, and kicking. I didn't always wake up fast enough to get out of the way. It really tore him up when that happened. He wanted to call it quits but I wouldn't let him."

"He had nightmares?"

"Anybody can have nightmares. You told me you have them some-times. Maybe I should worry about you hitting me."

Gabriel flexed the muscles in his jaw and rearranged his grip on the steering wheel. This was not the time to get into a shouting match with her. He purposefully lowered his voice. "And you stuck around? Even with all that?"

"It wasn't his fault. It didn't change the way we felt about each other. We talked about getting a king size bed and putting those divider pillows in the middle, but I wouldn't do it. I didn't want anything to come between us. I couldn't put him at a distance. That was on me." She scrunched tighter against the door.

"Is that why you bought a place so far out of town? That way people wouldn't hear him, wouldn't see you all banged up? You had to be crazy risking your life to protect that bastard."

Alena's head snapped in his direction. He'd stepped over the line. Volcano Al was about to blow. Suddenly, it was too hot in the car. He turned up the air-conditioning.

Alena let her breath out in a huff. "I warned you not to call him that. It was my life and my decision to stay."

Guilty as charged and no defense in sight. He kept his eyes on the road and prayed she didn't smack him. Not that he'd blame her.

Luckily, she only stared across the car at him with a look that could have incinerated a lesser man. "We were on our way back to Houston and we drove through the country for a change of scenery. It was so peaceful. We saw the sale sign and thought it would be a good place to just be ourselves."

"Weren't you afraid?"

"Of what? He was doing better. It was getting longer between episodes. Especially after he spent that week working with *Papi*, things really calmed down. He was feeling better inside. He said he'd found peace. They had a lot in common." She looked down at the floor and then back at Gabriel. "I think he could tell *Papi* things he couldn't tell anyone else."

"Okay. So, you both lived there?"

She repositioned herself properly in her seat. "No. We were in the process of buying the land when he was killed." Alena turned her head away from him and toward the crowded buildings edging the express-way. "After I got out of the hospital, I ordered the house. It takes about three months for the factory to build one. Once it was set up, I moved out there. I needed the quiet. There wasn't time to build a house on site."

"Okay, I get it." He let out the breath he'd been holding.

She glared at him. "You can relax. You're not sleeping in Romero's bed. Now, pull this damn car over and get out!"

"No." Gabriel hit the automatic locks to be extra sure they were locked.

Alena glared daggers at him. "We were having a great day. Why'd you have to go and start this?"

"I'm trying to find out what I'm dealing with so I don't get blind-sided by some reporter." He couldn't tell her that the idea of anyone hurting her had brought him to the edge. He'd been ready to drag Romero out of his grave and pound him to dust.

"Really? Well, that's interesting because most men don't give a shit what happened with the last guy. The less they know the better. Were you part of an Intel unit? Is snooping how you get your kicks?"

"I told you a long time ago you'd have to tell me about yourself."

Alena crossed her arms over her chest. "Fine. You'd better find a drive-thru. I'm not fixing dinner. You can starve for all I care."

"No problem. Sugar Land is full of fast food places."

"Good."

"What do you want?" He looked her way.

"I want to slap you," she muttered.

"To eat. What do you want for dinner?"

"It doesn't matter. Get whatever works for you. I'm not hungry anymore."

"Alena?"

164

"What?"

"Did Romero ever tell you he beat a man to death with his bare hands when he was sixteen?"

"Yes. And he had every right to do it, too. He was never prosecuted."

"But didn't that scare you?"

"No. He had his reasons."

"Really?" He looked her way for a split second and then back at the road.

"Yes, really," she snapped.

"Anyone with any sense was afraid of him. What if he lost control? He could have killed you. He'd done it before."

Alena was quiet for the better part of a minute. The hum of the Mustang's engine was the only sound between them. He barely caught her quiet words.

"Yes, okay there was one time I was afraid when we first got together. I was scared he was going to figure out I had no idea what I was doing. He always had experienced women that knew every-thing about doing what he'd like. I hadn't been with anyone else and I was pretty sure I'd be a terrible disappointment to a man like him." Alena glared hard at Gabriel. "That's the right term, right, a man like him?"

Gabriel grumbled, "Quit it. We've already been there and settled that." Damn, Romero had been her first lover. And from the looks of her place and the way she'd talked, there hadn't been anyone in between.

"So, nobody between him and me?"

"No. I told you I was boring."

He was the second man in her life. That was a heavy burden and a lot to live up to.

"It makes more sense now why you were afraid of us getting to know each other." He gave her a quick glance out of the corner of his eye.

"*Papi* told me not to waste myself on unworthy men. I was heart-broken and not looking to try again. You came along and started pushing me towards something I was terrified of."

165

"That wasn't my intention but, if it helps, I felt it too. I wanted to know the brave girl hiding inside, even if she scared me."

"You, scared? Not." Alena scoffed. "Marines aren't scared of anything living or dead."

"Hell, yeah, we get scared but we figure it out and we deal with it. I wanted to hold someone accountable. You were there and being angry at you wasn't working worth a damn."

"Could have fooled me."

"No, I don't think I've ever fooled you." He kept his eyes on the road ahead.

They were passing the tollway interchange when Alena sniffed and quietly said, "I'll understand if you want your ring back."

"Not a chance. It needs to stay put till I trade it up to an engagement ring. I'm just trying to know more about you before we go see the justice of the peace. You'd kill 'em at the poker table. You don't even blink."

"It comes from years of having my life shredded and dissected in public." She stared straight ahead. "It's called self-defense."

"That kind of helps clear up why you were so attached to your sunglasses during the trial. If the news got out that Romero's fiancée was on the jury there'd have been all kinds of reporters with questions."

"I was only a small fish in a very small pond. I never made it to the really big money."

He grinned. "You would have. When I deployed, your team was on the edge."

"That was a long time ago," she muttered.

He shrugged the shoulder nearest her. "Have it your way. Why don't you go back to working at a hospital?"

"No."

"Why?" he challenged. "It would sure be easier." He was poking at a tiger. If he miscalculated he'd be a cat snack in minutes. She'd chew him up and spit him out.

"I don't want to."

He moved his hands higher on the steering wheel. "So, how do you plan to make a living? This racing thing will take a long time before it pays off."

Alena smirked. "I'm going to marry you for your money."

"Well, that's just great, because we're gonna starve. The county doesn't pay much. We're barely scraping by living together."

"No problem, my dad is going to help me so I can finish my business degree."

"Yeah? I'm good with school. But not with your dad having to help."

"I can finish on-line pretty quick."

"Why a business degree?" She'd ignored his concern and moved on. He quirked an eyebrow. What was she up to?

"I was headed for business management before I went crazy and ran off to the races."

"I don't get it. It doesn't sound like you."

"Someone will have to manage things for the team. I guess it's time for me to shape up and accept responsibility for my choices."

"Is that everything? It sounds like there's something else you haven't told me."

"I owe people. Tommy and the crew. They got hurt in that mess with Snuffy. It's time I did something to help them out."

"When were you planning on telling me all this?"

"When it happened." She looked over at him. "I wasn't sure Tommy would be interested in letting me drive his car. I'm partly to blame for his injuries. He tried to stop Snuffy. I was taking a chance he wouldn't be angry with me for what happened."

"What about my job?"

"What about it? We don't race during regular business hours. You won't miss work."

"I don't make enough to support us both."

"You don't have to. I have some money saved up to cover my end of things. You just worry about fixing the air-conditioning in your car." She snickered. "Summer's coming and you're gonna need it."

CHAPTER TWENTY-FIVE

ALENA WOKE up the next morning and peered over the top of the pillows lined up down the middle of her queen-size bed. If Gabriel thought he'd gotten away with his inquisition into her past, he'd found out soon enough that he was sorely mistaken.

He'd refused to sleep out on the back porch with the mosquitos, which, in her opinion, was where he deserved to be. After he declined to stay in the guest room, she'd taken pity on him and built a pillow-fort. God help her, he was stubborn like an Army mule. Marine mule? Did the Marines even have mules? Never mind. She had bigger problems to solve.

He didn't open his eyes when he mumbled, "Are you done being mad yet?"

"No." She flopped down on her side of the fluffy boundary line.

She felt the mattress move and then his brawny arm came over the top.

"Tough. Cuz I'm through with this." His hand grabbed the pillow it was resting on and gave it a fling.

Alena let out a surprised squawk and scrambled out of bed.

Oops, she'd apparently pushed his last button. The man launched out of bed behind her, putting NASA's rockets to shame. Shit! How fast could she run?

She rounded the couch and glanced back over her shoulder. He was standing in the bedroom doorway smirking. Really?

She stopped behind the back of the couch and stared at him. "What's so funny, *chico*?"

"You are. Your butt cheeks are hanging out of your shorts." He snickered. "It's cheating to distract a man like that."

She twisted around to look. "My butt's not hanging out."

His arms wrapped around her before she could react. His triumphant rumble in her ear was all male smugness.

"Gotcha, *chica*."

She tried to wiggle free but was unsuccessful. Of course, she hadn't tried very hard. She was such a fool for him it was pitiful. But even a fool had to keep up appearances.

"That's what you think."

"It's what I know. I'm in it for the long haul. Your *Papi* made it real clear and easy. I could get it together or get on down the road. I had to decide what I wanted and make the commitment. You're it. This is it. There's no turning back for me. We're going to the races."

"And I guess now, you expect me to make breakfast?"

He scooped her up. "Maybe later. Right now, there's something I need more than food." He headed for their bedroom.

"You're shameless. You know that, right?" She gazed up at him. His features were somehow softer this morning. All the hard angles were relaxed and the corners of his mouth were slightly curled up, hinting at a grin.

"When it comes to you, I have to do whatever it takes." His knees hit the mattress and he lowered them down into the mess of pillows and twisted blankets. He braced his arms on either side of her and looked straight down into her eyes. "I'm in love with you and we're gonna make this work if I have to keep you in this bed all day."

"Wow, that's one hell of a promise. Do you think you're up to it?" She snickered and grinned.

"Oh, that's it. Game on, *chica*."

CHAPTER TWENTY-SIX

ON RACE DAY, Alena's team was all over the news. Potential sponsors and people in the racing business stopped by her pit to wish her luck. She fielded questions and noted possibilities. She needed to win this race to get back in the game.

Alena walked toward her pit and stopped dead in her tracks. Sonja stood at the lower edge of the stands bordering the pits waving at Gabriel. *Oh, hell no. Not gonna happen.*

Sonja was nothing but trouble. Trouble nobody needed, especially not Gabriel. Zeroing in on her, Alena dragged in a deep breath and put one foot in front of the other. Nothing got in her way until she stopped directly in front of Gabriel. She watched Sonja simper and roll her shoulders back effectively thrusting her boobs enticingly at anyone that might be watching.

Alena didn't smile and her voice rolled out low and ferocious. She snarled, "You're not welcome here. You, your fake eyelashes and push up bra need to get back up in the stands or I'll have the boys show you where we put the garbage."

"You can't tell me what to do. I have every right to talk to anybody I want to."

"That might be true but not hanging over the rail to my pit. This is off limits to you."

Sonja flung her long black hair over her shoulder. "Anybody can be here. I have a ticket like everyone else."

Alena squared her shoulders. "You have no business with Gabriel. You're done here. You should move on while you can."

Sonja turned her attention to Gabriel. "Tell her how I make you happy. Tell her you want to be with me like before and you're leaving her."

Gabriel's response came out cold and hard. "What are you doing here? You rode to Houston with me and left with someone else. That's the same trick you pulled on Carlos. Was I supposed to fight Julio and end up in prison like my brother?"

"No, of course not. It wasn't like that with us." She leaned forward exposing her cleavage for all to see.

Alena's fingers itched to throw a tarp over her.

"There's no, us. Never was, never will be." Gabriel rubbed his hand over his mouth. "Stay away from me and my family. You've caused enough trouble."

Alena scowled. "You were never going to marry Carlos, ever. You wanted Michael, but he wasn't falling for you, even if he did booty-call you when he couldn't talk anyone else into it."

Sonja's cheeks turned scarlet and she said in a haughty voice, "You're just saying all this because you're jealous of me."

"No. I know where you've been. I know Julio, his habits and how he likes it. I've seen his girls come and go. He uses them up and throws them away." Alena glanced over her shoulder at her crew. "Guys, show this worn out trash bag to the dumpster."

Two of the crew stepped forward. Before they'd made it three steps, Sonja spun away and slowly climbed the stairs back up to the bleachers. Her hips swayed seductively in the skin-tight jeans that left very little to the imagination. When she got to the walkway between the sections, she looked over her shoulder and sneered at them before disappearing into the crowd.

Gabriel said, "I don't need you to protect me from her, but it's nice to know you care."

"Nobody jacks with what's mine. Ever. I'm funny that way." She kept her eyes on Sonja's retreating figure. "If you want her, you'd

171

better say so now."

"Not in a million years. I'm right where I want to be." He reached around and hugged her back to his front. "You're my *chica*."

When Sonja was at a safe distance, Tommy turned to Alena and lightly gripped her upper arm. "You and Sean go take some pictures with the car and Nate. Open the hood, point at something inside like you're telling him something important. The fans like stuff like that. Makes them think you know something no one else does."

Alena turned to him and said, "You're right. We want them to think we've got this."

～

After she'd gone, Tommy touched Gabriel's arm getting his attention. "Man, tell me you did not have a go at that tramp."

Gabriel turned, squaring off with Tommy. He wasn't smiling. "What the hell?"

"I'm telling you, we could lose everything if you did. Al won't stand for it. I gotta know. How much trouble are we in? Everything I've got is riding on this."

Gabriel scoffed. "We're not in trouble. I've never been desperate enough to get with Sonja. She's anybody's lay and everybody knows it."

"If you do Al wrong, break her heart, we'll all pay for it. *Papi* Cordova isn't an ordinary man. I met him once and that was enough. He's something straight out of the South American jungle. I'm pretty sure he can rip a man to pieces with his bare hands." Tommy dipped his head. "He'll come to her rescue. He was the only thing holding her together when she lost Romero." He nodded toward the stands. "So, what's that bitch talking about?"

"She's just trying to make trouble. I wanted to get the truth about my brother out of her and we rode my bike up to the Finish Line. She went to flirting with the other men there and left with Julio. I think she was trying to make me jealous. Maybe get me to fight him, beat him up, and end up in jail."

Tommy shook his head. "She's got that look. She's not done with you. Watch your back. And for all our sakes, stay out of her panties."

"That's not a problem." He patted Tommy on the shoulder.

It was damage control time. With a determined stride he headed toward the Challenger and Alena. When he reached her, she slipped her arm around his middle and hugged him instead of hitting him with the socket wrench she had in her other hand. That was a good sign.

She looked from Sean to Gabriel and smiled while saying, "Look down at the engine, smile and nod. Come on Nate, make happy faces like we're sitting on a winning secret."

Gabriel did as instructed. Then he looked at Alena, wrapped both arms around her and kissed her. Let the crowd check that out. She was his woman now. He whispered so only she could hear, "You're my *chica*, I've got you."

He watched her win that race and several more. As promised, he was always there to catch her at the finish line. Sean snapped hundreds of photos of the team's fight back into the top slots driving Tommy's Challenger.

On a hot summer Saturday afternoon Gabriel had his arm around Alena's waist, anchoring her close against his hip as they walked back to their pit. He whispered quietly for her ears only, "You're worn out. You've gotta get more rest."

"I'm okay."

He said, "Things will get better now that I've been promoted to foreman. We'll get by, hang in there with me."

What would he do if he lost her? Even with his promotion he wasn't making near the money it would take to support them for very long with her not working. Her savings wouldn't last forever. No way could he expect her to live on his salary.

He put her down on a bench while he dug a bottle of Gatorade out of the cooler. He handed it to her.

"Here ya go. This'll make you feel better. It's extra hot today; we're all sweating like pigs."

"Yeah, thanks."

Her hands shook so much she could hardly keep a hold of the bottle. Try as he might, he couldn't hide the concerned look on his face.

She softly said, "I'm okay. It's fine, really. And we won."

"It scares me. I can't help it."

"I know and I'm sorry. A few more races and we'll be set for next season. Then it'll be easier to manage things. It'll be good for all of us."

Gabriel tamped down the skepticism threatening to escape his tight control. "How do you figure?"

"It's getting time to hand it off to Nate. He's up for it."

"And your degree, how's that coming?" One more thing for her to do and him to worry about. Once things settled down, he needed to try getting his on-line college education but now wasn't the time.

"Not much more to go. Almost done."

"Then what? Will you go to work in some office while managing the team?"

Alena shrugged. "Um, I'm not sure yet. I have something else I want to get started on."

Gabriel straightened. "What?"

What could it be? He couldn't imagine what project she'd come up with. Was there no end in sight?

She grumbled, "Oh, hell. This isn't exactly how I wanted to do this."

"Do what?"

"Tell you I've been thinking about what you said about starting a family, having some kids. I'm thinking we need to do that before we get too old."

Gabriel couldn't speak. He was at a loss for words. Hitting him with a stun gun would have been just as effective. He wasn't moving. He wasn't even sure he was breathing.

"Gabriel?"

"What? I mean, you want to have kids now?" He sucked in much needed oxygen.

"Well, no, not this minute, but we shouldn't put it off too long. We gotta get married first, settle down and fix up a room in the house. I thought you wanted kids?"

Gabriel sat next to Alena and put his hands on his knees. "I can't support you and a bunch of kids right now. I don't make that kind of money."

"Hold it. Back up. Do you want kids or not?"

"Someday." He turned toward her. "I want us to have a family. You know, we'll have all the kid things to do. Sunday dinner at my grandma's, summer vacations at the lake, little league, Christmas and Santa pictures. And you'll be home taking care of them."

She shook her head slowly. "I'm not planning on staying home. Working moms are the norm these days." She drank several gulps of Gatorade before stopping to breathe. "We can take them to Carmel for Christmas to see their grandfather and *Papi*."

"How do you figure?" His forehead crinkled and his fingers dug into his thighs. He had to hold it together.

"You're working, I'm working. We've got money saved. The team is going to be running in the black soon and won't need me every minute of every day. It's a great campaign. The house is paid for. We're good." Alena smiled at him encouragingly.

He thought he might throw up. "We don't make that much after expenses. It's gonna be tough to make ends meet." He wasn't sure about all this.

"It's okay. We don't have to do this right away. It was just an idea for after we're married." Alena gulped down more electrolyte and fluid replacement.

Gabriel sucked in a deep breath. "If it'll get you off the track, I'll do my best to get you knocked up."

Alena spit out a mouthful of blue fluid and shrieked, "Knocked up? Knocked up? I don't think so." She shook her head and hurled the plastic bottle across the dugout portion of the pit. "I won't be getting knocked up."

"What? You just said you wanted to have kids." Gabriel threw his hands in the air.

"Knocked up is a mistake that happens to girls who aren't careful. My children will not be mistakes." She got to her feet and tottered off in a huff, head thrown back and muttering, "Knocked up. I don't think so. Not gonna happen, *chico*."

Gabriel stifled a laugh watching Alena do some kind of rubber-legged stomp and shuffle maneuver leaving him behind sitting on the bench. She was mad and she'd sure told him. Yeah, he was gonna have fun knocking up his wife when the time came. And no, his kids weren't gonna be mistakes. He'd be real careful to do it right. He had absolutely no idea how, but they'd get by. He was a Marine, he'd handle it. Everything was going to be all right. He sat there grinning, giving Alena time to cool off.

A minute went by before Tommy ambled in. "Hey, I just saw Al. She looks mad. What's going on?"

Gabriel chuckled. "Wrong flavor of Gatorade."

CHAPTER TWENTY-SEVEN

GABRIEL DROVE them home while Alena looked either straight ahead or out the passenger window. She didn't fall asleep either. Nope, she was still stressing. Gabriel smiled into the darkness. He'd fix it when he got her to the house and tucked into bed. Yep, this was gonna be good.

They pulled into the driveway and he shut off the Mustang. She got out like she was being chased by the devil himself. Well, he was a good likeness to the devil on occasion and this might be one of those times.

She had the front door open by the time he got there. He watched her walk in, drop her duffle bag on the floor, and head for the master bedroom. He called after her, "You're gonna have to talk to me sometime."

No response. Great.

He locked up the house and followed her into their bedroom. The door to their bathroom was closed and he could hear the shower running. She was right on schedule. She'd take a shower, dry her hair, and come to bed. And he'd be waiting.

At the sound of the bathroom door opening, Gabriel looked over, Alena had gone in but, from the looks of it, Al was coming out. He was ready for her.

He was bare chested, propped up on a pile of pillows with the covers tucked around his waist waiting for her and grinning. He wasn't going to sleep till they got this settled.

She picked up the covers and slipped into bed. "Good night." She rolled on her side, turning away from him.

This was all wrong. He hadn't handled it right. But she'd caught him off guard. Gabriel's movement caused the mattress to shift. His hand slid gently along her shoulder as he moved in close. His lips rested close to her ear and he softly said, "We gotta fix this."

"There's nothing to fix. You don't want kids. I get it."

He pulled her over onto her back. "Look at me. You've got it wrong. I'm your man, good or bad." He leaned down and kissed her long and slow. "I love you, *chica*. But I've seen things, been places, and I know what's out there. I don't want my kids growing up with all kinds of bad stuff to deal with. I want them to have good things."

"It's never going to be a perfect world. But we can raise them to be good people. We can give them a good home."

He was hard and getting harder. "We're gonna be making us some babies."

Alena's hand slid up his arm and rested on his shoulder. "What am I gonna do with you?"

"Fuck me real good." He smiled and kissed her again, harder this time.

She kicked off the covers and urged him onto his back.

"I'm ready." The gravel tone and rumble of his voice gave him away. He was more than ready to let her take him down.

"I can see that. But you like it when I make you wait." She straddled his hips.

"I've been waiting all day. I'm done waiting." His hands fastened on her waist; he sat up and rolled them until he was on top with her legs wrapped around him.

She stopped giggling and looked him in the eyes. "You've never been any good at being patient. But it's okay. I'll take you any way I can get you."

"Earlier today you announced to everyone within earshot that I was yours." He quirked an eyebrow. "Remember that?"

"Um, sort of." She snickered. "I may have overstated things a little."

"I don't think so. I'm all yours but you're mine. That's how it is and has been since I put that promise ring on your finger."

She cupped his cheek with her hand and softly said, "I love you. You have no idea how much."

"This would be a good time to show me." He nudged her slick opening with the crown of his cock. "Tell me again."

"I love you, Gabriel." Her heels rubbed the backs of his thighs. "I want you now and for always."

CHAPTER TWENTY-EIGHT

A MONTH LATER, the racing season was half over and the victory party was in full swing at Gabriel's grandmother's house. He had a yard full of guests and meat sizzling on the grill. The aroma from the smoked sausage, chicken, and brisket filled the air. Music wafted from his old boombox on the porch. The thing was ancient but his grandmother had kept it for him, a dusty souvenir from his past.

Alena's crew entertained the neighbors recounting the events of the latest race while sitting in the shade on the front lawn. Her team had won again, they were racking up points, and more sponsors were coming around. It was a great day. Looking at all the happy faces, Gabriel realized he had a lot to be grateful for.

Earlier, Roberto Sanchez, a neighbor kid, had pulled up in his old yellow Mustang, mumbled something about it wasn't running right and asked Tommy to take a look at it. Seeing them bent over the fenders with their heads under the hood and Alena supervising made him grin. She had brought laughter back into his world, something that had been missing since he boarded the bus to boot camp.

Grandma worked on a giant pot of borracho beans simmering on the stove in an effort to teach Tommy's daughter how to cook.

Gabriel walked in and hugged his grandmother. "*Gracias, abuelita.* You're the best."

"*Mijo*, you make me so proud. But how am I going to get this girl a husband if she can't cook?" She nodded at Tommy's daughter, Monica.

"You'll think of something." Gabriel's smile didn't waver.

"Of course. I'll think of something," she grumbled.

His help wasn't needed in the kitchen so he headed for the front yard. Stepping onto the front porch, he caught movement down at the corner of the block. He stared at his brother's brown Camaro as it rolled up and stopped behind the yellow Mustang.

It wasn't so much that Carlos had come to the party that had his hackles up. It was the sight of Sonja sitting in the passenger seat that jolted him right down to the soles of his boots. There was a lull in the conversations as heads turned to see what was going on.

Carlos shut off the Camaro and got out. He hustled around the front of the car and opened the door for Sonja. She wiggled her way out. She wore an oversized blouse. If he wasn't mistaken, she appeared to be in the early stages of pregnancy and wearing a big diamond ring on her left hand.

The party was over for Gabriel. He looked around the yard for Alena. He caught sight of her over by Tommy and prayed she'd stay put. No cat fights in Grandma's yard today, please.

Carlos put his right arm across Sonja's back and walked her to the bottom of the steps.

He gave Gabriel a lopsided half-grin smirk. "Hey, bro, we came by to let Grandma know we got married. She's gonna be a great-grandma.

"Well, congratulations. It looks like things are working out for you." Gabriel didn't smile.

"Yeah, funny how things turned out. I'm gonna be a dad and you've got Romero's crazy left-over piece who put me in prison." Carlos sneered and shouldered his way past Gabriel. "I want to tell Grandma the good news."

Gabriel tamped down his anger. He was not taking the bait. Marines keep it under control. He gave a curt nod, "She's in the kitchen cooking. Be careful, she's got her big spoon."

Carlos winced.

Sonja looked pointedly at Gabriel wearing a smirk on her ruby red lips. "I guess we're family now."

Gabriel ignored Sonja and muttered to Carlos, "In grandma's mind, we're not too big or too old to be smacked with that thing. Don't upset her."

"You've always been afraid of her," Carlos grumbled, and disappeared inside the house with Sonja sauntering ahead of him.

Gabriel strolled to the curb and stopped next to Alena. He eyed at the grime-covered V-8 engine and said, "This thing is filthy. How can you tell what you're doing?"

Tommy turned his head and grinned. "It's all in the hands. You've got to feel your way." He wiggled his grease covered fingers at Gabriel. "Anytime you want to get your hands dirty, let me know."

Gabriel stepped back and looked at the house. People had gone back to talking and grilling. The muffled noise coming from inside the house was a clue that Grandma Marta had heard the good news.

The screen door flew open and Sonja hurried down the stairs, not looking to the right or left as she marched toward the Camaro. Carlos wasn't far behind her.

He yelled over his shoulder, "Okay, Grandma, stop hitting me. We're leaving."

Marta stopped in the doorway, shook a huge, wooden cooking spoon and shouted, "Don't be coming around here until you learn to have some respect for your family. You hear me?"

Gabriel chuckled. "I think the whole block heard her."

Tommy snickered under the hood. "Yeah, I'd say you're probably right."

Gabriel slipped his arm around Alena's waist and squeezed. "Grandma's still got it."

She smiled at him. "I'll go see if I can help bring out the food. I think it's time to eat before anything else happens."

∼

In the kitchen, Monica patted Marta on the shoulder. "It'll be okay, Miss Marta. Don't worry, he'll figure things out."

Alena stopped in the kitchen doorway. "Hey, the meat's ready, let's get these beans on the table. They're going to be perfect."

Monica replied, "Miss Marta let me help. She says I need to be able to cook before I get married. They might not be all that perfect, but they're good."

"Well, let's let the hungry crowd decide."

Monica swallowed and blurted out, "I'm going to marry Roberto."

Marta wailed, "*Dios mio*, Roberto Sanchez! Aye, I need to sit down." She stepped back from the stove and sank onto a kitchen chair.

Alena jogged to the sink and filled a glass with water. She handed it to Marta. "Take a drink. It'll help." She looked at Monica and asked, "When did this happen?"

"He asked me last Friday after the race. He's going to talk to dad today."

"Well, that's the honorable thing to do. I guess this means you love him, right?"

Monica giggled. "Yes, I'm in love with Roberto."

"Well then, we're good. A wedding it is."

Marta mumbled, "His mother was kind of one of those fast girls back in the day."

Alena's forehead momentarily crinkled and she grinned. "Well, her son turned out pretty good."

Monica laughed. "And Alena, I want to be like you. I want to drive."

Marta flung her hands up. "*Aye, mas agua*, more water. I'm going to faint."

Monica patted Grandma Marta's shoulder and giggled. "It's okay. It's going to be okay."

"I will call the dressmaker." Marta smiled up at Monica and asked, "You're sure he's the one?"

"I'm sure."

Alena shrugged. "Your dad is going to kill me."

They got pot holders and Monica carried the steaming pot through the house with Alena opening doors for her.

People grabbed paper plates and plastic forks to devour the feast. Tommy frowned at Monica when she sat under an old oak tree shoulder to shoulder with Roberto.

Alena followed his gaze and swallowed. "So, Tommy, how's it going with Roberto's Mustang?"

"Awe, it's nothing serious. I think that kid goes home and breaks it just so he can come around and get me to fix it."

"Maybe he wants to get better at fixing cars?"

"Nope. He wants to spend time with Monica."

"Really? How can you tell?"

"Just look at them. That's how I can tell. I'm a dad, you know. A dad knows these things." Tommy forked another helping of beans and chewed.

"Gabriel says Roberto's a good kid. Lives with his folks, works, and is almost finished with junior college. He's here with all of us watching every move he makes. Give the kid a break."

"I'll break his arm if he touches my daughter, that's what I'll break."

"Not a good plan. Besides, I think he's got more in mind than just touching her."

Tommy quit chewing and swallowed. "I'm gonna kill him."

Alena patted his arm that was resting on the weathered wooden picnic table near her. "No, you're not. You can't kill your soon-to-be son-in-law. It'll put a terrible pall on the wedding."

Tommy glared at Alena. "Monica's too young to get married. And not to that kid. How's he going to take care of her?"

"They'll take care of each other. You can't get in the way of young love unless you want to push your daughter away."

Gabriel put his plate down next to Alena and sat. "What's going on? You two look like you're planning a tactical assault."

Alena grinned. "Tommy is planning on killing Roberto to stop him from marrying Monica."

"Well, that's not good. Grandma's on the phone talking to the dressmaker."

Tommy looked down at his plate and muttered, "I'm out-numbered, beaten by an old lady. This is the worst day of my life."

"It's going to be fine. You're the father of the bride. Picture it. A church full of flowers, a flowing white gown, a handsome groom in a fine tux." Alena sighed, "She's going to be the most beautiful bride ever, in all of Texas."

Tommy smiled for a second, then frowned. "I'm gonna kill him."

Alena giggled as Tommy kept glaring at Roberto, and trying to smile at Monica at the same time which made him look like he was suffering from the worst case of heartburn ever in the history of barbecue.

A few minutes later, Roberto held Monica's hand when they walked up to Tommy. He cleared his throat and looked Tommy in the eyes.

"Excuse me, sir. I'd like to ask you for your daughter's hand in marriage. We want to get married."

Alena squeezed Gabriel's leg under the table.

Gabriel whispered in Alena's ear, "You're going to fall off this bench if you don't stop bouncing."

She did her best to sit still and keep an eye on the flexing muscles in Tommy's jaw. His face was unreadable, it could go either way.

She poked Tommy on the arm. "Say, 'yes.'"

"OW! Fine, okay, yes. There, are you happy now?" He glared at Alena.

She patted Tommy on the shoulder. "You're the father of the bride. How exciting!"

A few of Roberto's friends showed up to drink some beer and congratulate him. The party lasted late into the evening. After the crew left, the neighbors slipped away slowly.

Gabriel picked up the yard and made sure his grandmother was safely inside for the night. Once on the road out of town, he glanced over at Alena. "It was a great party."

"Monica and Roberto are perfect together."

"I haven't been to a wedding in years."

"We'll get you a tuxedo. You'll be the handsomest man there." She giggled and teased. "It'll be hard to keep my hands off of you."

CHAPTER TWENTY-NINE

THE TIME LEADING up to the wedding went by in a blur. Alena caught sight of Tommy looking like he might be in danger of suffocating in his tuxedo. Roberto stood tall and handsome as only an excited young groom could.

The candles were lit and the church filled up as the organist played Moonlight Sonata. It was a good evening for a wedding, not too hot, not too humid, a pleasant breeze, and a glowing full moon had slipped into the night sky. Alena's cocktail dress with sequins and crystal trim at the princess neckline sparkled in the candlelight.

It's a magical moonbeam kinda night. Banji would love it. According to her it was all in the cards. They'd had a couple long-distance conversations and one card reading. The way had been cleared for transformation. Fairness and emotional balance seemed to be working. The King of Cups was on her side.

Alena hugged Gabriel's arm a little tighter. He was so striking in his black tuxedo. She gazed deeply into his sinfully sexy eyes and whispered, "I'll love you forever."

"Alena?"

"I want you to know that."

He leaned in close so only she could hear. "*Mi corazón.* I love you with all my heart. I don't need some church wedding to prove it."

"I know. But as long as we're already here, I wanted to tell you."

"Does this mean you'll dance with me later?"

She couldn't resist his devasting grin. "I'll save all my dances for you."

"Good. That's my *chica*."

"There are more guests coming. You'd better go help them get seated. It's about time to start. Go on. I'll be right here waiting for you."

She watched Gabriel walk to the front doors of the church. He had that military posture. Tall, proud, a Marine. And he was hers. It wouldn't make any difference if they had a church wedding or not—his, folks wouldn't come. He'd told his mother he was engaged and she'd slammed the door in his face. Alena hadn't been surprised, but she'd been sad for Gabriel. He kept trying to please a woman that clearly didn't care about him.

Her mother wouldn't dream of coming. Her dad and *Papi* would, but it would be a long flight for a short ceremony. Hers was going to be the smallest wedding in history, if it happened in Texas.

If they got married in Carmel it would be a little better. There, the backyard overlooked the Pacific Ocean. It would make for the most beautiful wedding ever. *Papi* and Carmen would be there and Sean could take pictures. With enough notice, she had a few friends who might be able to fly in from wherever they were working. They'd all scattered to the four winds after graduation taking jobs around the world.

She could invite the people she'd met from Kington House. If all went well, Betmunn Racing was going to need a truck to haul race cars and parts. And the good news was, she liked Esmiralda Kington. She was different but interesting, very interesting.

Marta settled onto the pew beside Alena, bringing her out of her musings. She slipped a fragile hand over Alena's.

Alena glanced questioningly at her and quietly asked, "What? Is everything okay?"

Gabriel's grandmother whispered, "You look beautiful."

"Thank you." Alena glanced at her lap and smoothed the amethyst satin skirt over her knees.

"You make my grandson happy." Marta's worried expression was at odds with her kind words.

"I love Gabriel."

"I know. Don't stop. He was always a good boy."

Alena's brow wrinkled. "I don't understand. Why would I stop?" She focused her gaze on Gabriel's grandmother.

"We're in church. There's something you should know before you get married." Marta stared straight ahead. "My son, Enrique DeLeon isn't Gabriel's father. I've never told anyone that before, but you're going to be his wife. And it'll be important when you have children."

Alena blinked. "Okay, now I know, but it doesn't change the way I feel. He's still Gabriel, and I still love him."

"He's grown into a good man." Marta patted Alena's hand.

Alena sat in stunned silence through the ceremony. Monica was radiant. The modified A-Line satin gown with crystal beaded lace appliques at the Princess V-neck twinkled in the soft candlelight lending an ethereal quality to the scene. It was lovely: the music, the singing, the candles glowing, the promises made. The bridesmaids were picturesque in their soft mint green dresses, the groomsmen handsome in their black tuxedos. It was all so romantic.

Gabriel was still the same man she'd fallen in love with months ago when he took his seat next to her. His hand holding hers was as strong and warm as it had always been. She didn't give a rat's ass who his father was.

When the church service was over, they rode to the reception in her Mustang. Gabriel drove while she sat back and took in the fine man who was all hers. For the first time in years, she was content. It hadn't come easy but he was so worth it.

He momentarily glanced her way. "Are you okay?"

"I'm fine. Better than fine. I'm in love with you."

His lips morphed into a sexy grin. "This is gonna be a great night. I can feel it coming on. We gotta go to more weddings."

"Um, I think it's the tux. You're so dashing and handsome in it. Irresistible actually. But then, you're irresistible out of it." She leered at him. He was so easy to tease.

He had that self-satisfied male smirk men get when they've just been laid and she was definitely going to lay him down when they got home.

"You'd better quit while you're ahead. Keep talking like that and we won't make it to the reception."

"We'll get you a really nice tuxedo for our wedding. Something really sexy."

Gabriel shot her one of his *I'm coming for you* looks. "If you don't stop talking like that, I'm gonna pull over right here."

"You're so hot when you go all masterful on me. It gives me chills." She shivered dramatically for good measure.

"That's it. You're asking for trouble and I'm the man who can deliver." He chuckled.

CHAPTER THIRTY

ALENA LOVED SUNDAYS. She curled up on the couch with Gabriel. He watched football, she watched him. She wiggled closer. They were a perfect fit.

His phone binged and he glanced at the screen. "I gotta get this. It's Grandma."

Alena got up and walked to the kitchen, giving him some space. She could only hear Gabriel's side of the conversation but it didn't take a genius to figure out something was seriously wrong. Things had been quiet in the three weeks after the wedding. Too quiet in her opinion, but she kept that to herself.

"It's too soon." He sat up. "Okay, do you need a ride to the hospital?"

Alena looked at him. He had that knit brow, worried look. That wasn't a good sign.

"I know you don't like Sonja but it's your first great grandchild. Don't you want to be there?" Gabriel pulled his boots on. "Okay, I'll come get you."

Gabriel disconnected the call and looked over at Alena. "I gotta drive Grandma to the hospital. Sonja's in labor."

"Yeah, I got that."

"You wanna come?"

"Um, no. I'll fix dinner and keep some warm for you. Drive careful. And take the Mustang. Don't make your grandmother ride in the Monte Carlo. It doesn't have air conditioning."

He scooped up her car keys, kissed her, and walked out. Squeezing himself behind the steering wheel of the Mustang, he adjusted the seat to fit his taller frame. Yeah, he was making himself real comfortable like always. An amused grin materialized on her lips. And like always the computer would reset the seat to fit her when he shut off the engine. Yeah, she loved technology.

~

She drifted off to sleep in front of the TV after eating a hearty bowl of vegetable beef soup and woke to the clomping of Gabriel's boots across the front porch. The door opened and the look on his face was a dead giveaway that things had not gone well at all.

She asked, "What happened?"

Gabriel grabbed a can of beer out of the refrigerator and downed half of it before stopping to take a breath.

Alena twisted around on the couch to watch him. She'd never seen him act like this, not ever. Something was really wrong.

He put the can down and pressed his open hands down on the counter. "It was a little girl. She didn't make it."

"She was very premature but there's a lot they can do these days."

"The doctor said she'd been dead for days. Something about Sonja using too much cocaine."

"She should know not to take drugs while she's pregnant. Unless that was her plan." Alena winced at the grim look Gabriel shot her way. "Carlos wouldn't give it to her, would he?"

"Not Carlos, Julio."

Alena shook her head. "That can't be right. Julio likes to party but he knows better than to give a pregnant woman coca. He wouldn't do that. He's got sisters with kids. I'm sure he wouldn't do anything to hurt a baby."

"Maybe he would if the baby was his and he didn't want it."

"No. I don't think so. He's cold but not that cold. Not Julio."

191

"They have Sonja on morphine and she kept saying Julio forced the cocaine into her. When Carlos asked her why she'd gone to see Julio, she said to tell him it was his baby."

"What? Come again? They've been broken up too long for it to be his. Think about this a minute. She's not making sense."

"It makes perfect sense if you consider she might have been sneaking off to meet him for a quick lay."

"I don't think so. When Julio is done with a girl, she's gone. He doesn't recycle them. His sperm count is very low from an old injury. He never talks about what happened but his chances of having kids is close to zero."

"You're talking like those girls were nothing."

"Well, to him they're disposable. I told you way back that he's a ruthless player. Maybe I wasn't clear enough, but girls don't last long with him. They never have. They come, he uses them, they go, that's it."

"And you know this how?" His eyes narrowed and the muscles along his jaw bulged.

"People talk." Alena looked away. She'd stepped in it this time.

"Hey, look at me, don't shut me out. It's important. So, tell me how you know all this?" He stepped out of the kitchen advancing in her direction.

She sank onto the cushion keeping the back of the couch between her and Gabriel.

She said, "Julio was on a crew. They all hung out at the Finish Line. Romero liked to stop in sometimes. He had a share in the place, and sometimes I'd go with him. I've got two eyes and I could see for myself the goings on. And the guys would make comments. It doesn't take much to put two and two together and get a real clear picture."

Alena turned her gaze away, again. She wasn't lying exactly. But there were some things he didn't need to know.

"Alena." The warning in his tone was plain.

"What?" She needed to think fast. She was going to have to answer him but there were things she didn't want him to know. Not yet anyway.

"How do you know about the thing with him not having kids?"

192

Alena focused on Gabriel's face. He was as serious as she'd ever seen him. She chewed on her bottom lip and sucked in a deep breath.

"Romero was at the bar getting us a couple drinks and I sat down at our usual table. Julio was already there and pretty drunk. Drunker than I'd ever seen him. I asked him if he was okay. He shook his head. I asked if I could help and he said, no. Then he told me there was nothing any of us could do. He'd been in love with this woman when he was young and stupid. That's how he put it, and he'd just found out that she'd died from a drug overdose." Alena stopped talking long enough to collect her thoughts. This was delicate territory. She didn't want to discuss Julio's personal issues with Gabriel or anyone else.

She chewed on her bottom lip before saying, "Back when he was going with her, she'd come to him telling him she was pregnant and it was his. He said he could have forgiven her for cheating on him, but not for lying. He would have married her and raised the baby as his own. It was the only way he'd ever have a child. But because she was a liar, he'd never be able to trust her."

She stopped to catch her breath. "I told him she probably lied because she was afraid. Then he asked me if I'd ever lied to Romero. Well, he had me there. I never lied to Romero. I knew he could forgive me for just about anything else but he'd never forgive that." She shrugged her right shoulder. "I loved him too much to hurt him that way."

"You dodge answering a lot of my questions. Let's get this out in the open. I want to know. Have you ever lied to me?"

Alena leaned forward. In a deliberate, controlled voice she said, "Believe me there have been times I thought about it but then I'd lose your trust along with my self-respect. We'd be over." She pinned him with her stare. "No, I have not lied to you."

Gabriel winced but didn't look away. "I'm sorry. I don't know where that came from."

"I know exactly where it came from. It's Sonja. She's never going to stop. As long as Carlos is breathing, she's going to keep tormenting him. And when she's done with him, she'll be coming after you, again."

"It won't do her any good. I've got you to protect me. So, what do I do now?" Gabriel gave her a weak half-smile.

"Not much. Carlos has to get over Sonja and let her go and I don't see that happening. She's got a hold on him. There's something that goes way back to the old days. Carlos and Michael have been fighting over Sonja since they were in grade school."

"I asked my grandma but she didn't know. My mom isn't going to tell me anything and my dad is still avoiding me. We haven't had much to say to each other since Carlos was born." Gabriel finished the beer in his hand, then fished another out of the refrigerator.

"Gabriel?"

"Yeah."

"When you were in the Marines, how many whorehouses did you visit?"

"What? That's low, but I guess I have it coming. Do you really want to know?"

"No. Not really. Just wanted to see if you'd tell me the truth." She sighed.

"Alena?"

"What?"

"Are you ever gonna forgive me?" He rubbed his hands over his head and down to his neck.

"Yes. I love you too much not to."

Gabriel sat at his end of the couch and looked at her curled up at the opposite end. "Um, do you think you might come a little closer? I could use the company."

Alena scooted over. When she settled in next to him, he put his arm over her shoulders and snuggled her up against his side.

She quietly asked, "How's your grandmother taking this?"

"Not good." He kissed the top of her head.

"She's had a rough day."

"Yeah, she worries about Carlos."

"When it rains, it pours." She turned toward him and wrapped an arm across his midriff. He was nice and warm and he needed to be held even if he couldn't come right out and say it. She was getting good at interpreting his hints.

"I know." He clicked to his favorite late-night show.

She hadn't lied to him, but there were things she should tell him. She'd put it off because figuring out how to do it was not easy. *Oh, by the way, I'm Alena Betmunn y Cordova and I'm going to be sitting on the Board of Directors of Betmunn Racing and we're going to be living in California. How soon can you pack?*

There was still time for things to change. If the team didn't win, if the car wasn't good enough and if her father didn't want a loser on the company's board of directors, it wouldn't be an issue. She wouldn't be going anywhere. She'd find a job in Houston and they'd get by. She wasn't exactly lying. She was protecting him from disappointment.

Gabriel still carried the weight of his brother's mistakes. It would take time for him to let it go. She couldn't control Carlos, or Sonja but she could keep her end of things simple, at least for now. Moving to California would be a couple years away at best. He didn't need to worry about that, yet. That was on her. She'd handle it.

Alena fell asleep cuddled up to Gabriel picturing her wedding ceremony on the cliffs overlooking the Pacific Ocean. Banji would stand next to her. They would wear gorgeous A. Crystal Foxz designer dresses and *Papi* would give her to Gabriel. Beautiful.

CHAPTER THIRTY-ONE

THE NEXT MORNING, Alena woke up on the couch stiff with every ache and pain known to mankind. "What the hell?"

It all started coming back to her. She reached for her neck. "Oh, ouch. What happened?"

Gabriel laughed, "You fell asleep on me."

"Well, you make a lousy pillow. My neck is killing me."

"I love you, too." He winked at her.

"Right." She looked around and sniffed. "Coffee?"

"Ah, no. It's not good for you if you want to get pregnant."

"Excuse me?" That wink and Gabriel's sexy I'm-hungry-for-you smirk was not working on her. "I need coffee."

"No caffeine, no alcohol, no going to smoky places."

"I don't like you very much right now. I'm suffering over here."

"I don't get any either, so you're not suffering alone."

"That does not make me feel better." Grimacing, she massaged her neck. "You'll get yours at work. You're not giving up anything."

"Yeah, actually, I am. It's not fair for you to be the only one having to adjust."

"Oh lord, you're going to be grumpy." She arched her back, bent side to side then rolled her shoulders.

"Not any worse than you."

"Well, we're not married. So, no kids yet. I need coffee and one of those gooey cinnamon rolls. They're my favorite."

"We'll be married soon enough. I figure it's time to start getting in shape." He took a small plate down from the cabinet.

Alena locked eyes with Gabriel. "I should have run you over when I had the chance. That was my first mistake. I'm sure of it."

"I would have made a terrible dent in your car. Torn up the ground treatment and wrecked the suspension." He snorted softly and grinned.

"Probably." Her brow wrinkled while she contemplated a comeback. "Why did I ever answer the door? I should have known better."

"I'm glad you let me in. It's the best thing that ever happened to me." He nabbed a cinnamon roll out of the bakery box and put it on her plate.

"You looked so beat down and pitiful, I couldn't leave you on the porch. Then you turned your big brown, puppy-dog eyes on me. It was all a plot wasn't it?"

"Not at first." His phone rang and he grabbed it. "Yeah, what's going on?"

Alena could hear Carlos's voice from where she sat but couldn't make out the words.

Gabriel winced. "Hey, take it easy and calm down. I'm not getting you a gun. Not now, not ever. You need to think about this before you go getting all worked up."

Carlos yelled some more and Gabriel held the phone away from his ear. He raised his voice, "Don't go doing something you'll regret. Wait till Sonja is off the pain pump. Drugs mess with a person's mind. She might have things confused. It won't hurt to wait and be sure. Let them do a DNA test on the baby. It could be yours."

Carlos was still talking but he'd stopped yelling.

Gabriel said, "Okay, call me later and we'll talk."

He disconnected the call and looked at Alena. "He's upset, talking crazy. He's going back to the hospital to see Sonja. Maybe she can straighten this out." He carried the plate over to Alena.

After settling into a more comfortable seated position, she accepted the plate. "She won't do it. You know that. Right?" A dozen ugly possibilities swirled through Alena's mind. Sonja would do and say anything to hurt the DeLeon's. "She's gonna twist the knife as hard as she can. She's gonna gut him like a fish."

Gabriel shook his head once slowly. "And I can't stop her."

"Is there anybody he'll listen to? Someone that might get him to slow down and think?" Alena pulled a chunk of roll loose and popped it in her mouth.

Gabriel shrugged. "Our mother, maybe."

"Can you call her?"

Gabriel got his mother's voice mail. "Hey, Mom, Carlos just called. He's pretty upset. Can you talk to him, try to calm him down some? I'm worried about him." He disconnected the call.

He looked at Alena and shrugged. "I don't know what else I can do. If I go to the hospital, I can try to talk to him, get him to listen."

"Getting between him and Sonja isn't a good idea." Alena desperately wanted to talk Gabriel out of going near Sonja. Her inborn instinct to protect him came storming to the surface. *Get a grip. Don't blow this.* "Slow down and think. Marines always have a plan."

"If it wasn't Julio, who was it? Where'd she get the drugs? If she knows we don't believe her story, maybe she'll say what really happened." Gabriel paced the living room.

"And maybe she'll just tell more lies. She's good at it. And she's angry at Julio for dumping her. She's getting even with him and using Carlos to do it. It's the perfect plan." Alena watched him pace. "If she drags you into it, even better. She's killing two DeLeon's with one lie."

"So, I should look the other way while my brother screws up his life, again?" He ran his hand over his head and huffed out a breath.

Alena settled deeper into the cushions, finished her pastry and put the plate aside. She followed Gabriel with her eyes. He could pace a rut in the carpet for all she cared. She could replace it. She couldn't replace him. "Not look the other way but get him someone he'll listen to. Why don't you go talk to your grandmother? She's been watching all this for a long time. She might have some ideas."

"Okay, I'll call in late to work and go talk to her."

"That sounds like a good place to start." She watched him pick up his car keys and trudge out the front door.

Alena's stomach curled up in a tight knot turning her cinnamon roll hard as a rock that no amount of coffee or tea was going to fix.

There wasn't anything she could do to help Gabriel this time. Not at this end anyway. She picked up her phone and called Emilio. He'd know how to get in touch with Julio and warn him to make himself scarce for a few days. That might buy enough time for Gabriel to talk some sense into Carlos.

CHAPTER THIRTY-TWO

ALENA ROLLED over and got out of bed when Gabriel's car rolled up in the driveway. She hustled to the living room as he trudged in, his face pale. He closed the front door with a shove, walked past her without saying a word and went straight to the bathroom. The sound of water spraying in the shower was hardly a greeting.

It wasn't like him to say nothing. It had to be bad, really bad for him to be so quiet, so distant.

She tossed his dinner in the microwave. It was warm when Gabriel emerged from their bedroom in grey sweatpants and a raggedy, black t-shirt.

"I got your dinner ready." She watched for clues and met his gaze.

Tired eyes and slumped shoulders were not his usual posture. Something was very wrong. He sat next to her, slumped forward with his arms resting on his knees and stared at the ottoman.

It took several seconds before he spoke, "Enrique DeLeon isn't my father. He's Carlos's but not mine."

"Um, do you know who is?" Alena didn't move.

"Rogelio Juarez. Michael's father. Michael was my half-brother."

"Oh, lord, that's rough." She put one hand on his shoulder and the other on his arm. "I'm so sorry."

Gabriel looked at Alena, his voice barely audible. "I'm not who I thought I was. I'm not a DeLeon."

Alena slipped off the couch and knelt in front of Gabriel. She gently took his face between her hands. "Look at me, really look at me."

Gabriel blinked and slowly brought his eyes to meet hers.

Her fingers moved gently over his cheeks as she continued cupping his face. "Listen carefully. I love you, only you, just the way you are. I love Gabriel."

"I know, but you shouldn't." He sucked in a shaky breath and let it out.

"Well, I don't always do what I should. I do what's right for me." She searched his eyes looking for a hint of what was going on inside his head. "You're what's right for me."

"Mom said Rogelio dumped her when she got pregnant with me and moved on to dating her girlfriends. That was the reason they all stopped speaking to each other."

"He married Michael's mother instead." Alena sat back on her heels. "What a mess."

"It's all been lies." His body shook and he closed his eyes.

"Not everything." She took him by the shoulders. "Listen to me." He opened his eyes and focused on her. "Your grandmother loves you and I love you. You were smart enough to get out of this town and join the Marines. You did your duty and came back alive. You work and take care of your family. That's the truth of your life. You did your best to help your brother."

"Carlos killed Michael. How do I make that right?" He rubbed his eyes with the heels of his hands sucked in a shuddering breath and let it out slowly.

"That's not up to you. You only wanted justice. You only wanted a fair trial." She put a hand on his knee. "This is all too coincidental. I'd bet there's still more to the story. Stuff we'll never know and don't want to know. This tragedy has been festering for years. You didn't have anything to do with it."

Gabriel never took his eyes off hers. "You didn't sign up for any of this. If you want me to leave, I'll understand."

"No. I'm not letting you go. You belong to me now. They can all go to hell." She came up on her knees, wrapped her arms around him and pressed her head against his chest over his heart. "I love you and none of this changes the way I feel about you."

"Are you sure?"

"I'm sure. I'm planning on spending my life with you. You're my Gabriel." Alena tilted her head so she could look him in the eyes. "You made me a promise."

"You think you can still love me?" He inhaled deeply through his nose.

Grown men don't cry, so no sniffling. Especially, not Marines. Alena recognized the condition. Her man had a tender heart. Good to know. "Yeah. What have I been down here on my knees telling you?"

"Only *una chica loca* would stay with me."

"There you have it. You're stuck with me, craziness and all. How's that gonna work for you?"

"I'm good with it." A faint smiled teased the edges of Gabriel's lips before he wrapped his arms around Alena, pulled her up against his chest and hugged her tight. He whispered against her neck, "I was so afraid you wouldn't want me."

She whispered back, "No. Not gonna happen, *chico*. It's you and me for as long as you'll have me."

⌇

When they slid into bed, Alena fell asleep with her hand resting on Gabriel's arm. He'd never been so grateful for simple human touch as he was that night lying there in the dark. She wasn't letting him go.

Gabriel stared at the ceiling. He'd spent a lot of nights staring at that ugly, plain, brown ceiling fan and something told him he'd spend more in the future. One of these days he was going to replace it with something half-way attractive that didn't hurt his eyes to look at.

He'd been so sure he was doing the right thing by getting Carlos a new trial. He didn't understand how it had turned out so wrong. He wasn't a DeLeon and he wasn't a Juarez. He was nobody. When he married Alena, he could be a Cordova if she'd let him. He'd have to get permission from her *Papi*. He had two reasons to go see the man. Asking something like that over the phone was disrespectful. He'd never imagined he could love anyone as much as he loved Alena. Thank God she loved him back. His eyes drifted shut.

A couple hours later, he bolted upright in bed, yelling at the top of his lungs. "No! Don't go."

Alena's eyes flew open instantly and she grumbled, "What? What's happening?"

She sat up and looked around the room. "Everything's okay. We're okay."

Gabriel's chest rose and fell, sucking in air and letting it out like he'd been running a race. He swiped at his cheeks brushing away the tears that had escaped from his eyes.

He was still shaking and he didn't want Alena to see him like this. "Go back to sleep." She was still there next to him. He could breathe; it had all been a terrible nightmare.

"Gabriel, it's okay. You're home. Gabriel? Can you hear me?"

He shook his head. "Yeah, I hear ya. I said go back to sleep."

"Are you all right?"

"Go back to sleep. It was just a nightmare. I have them sometimes."

"You told me that when we were in Galveston." She touched his shoulder. "Can I get you anything?"

He shrugged her hand away. "No, I'll be okay. This one wasn't so bad. Go back to sleep." It had only felt like his heart was being ripped from his chest. The replay in his mind of her leaving him wasn't going to stop any time soon.

She settled down, lying on her side and watching him intently.

He hated making her worry. "It's okay. I won't hurt you."

Alena answered softly, "Of course you won't. I'm afraid the trouble with your family has brought this on. I hate seeing you like this."

Gabriel rolled to his side and brushed her hair back from her face. "As long as I've got you, I'll be okay. Really." He kissed her soft and slow. "Don't worry."

He let go of her, sat up and propped his pillows against the head-board. He needed to sit up and let the adrenaline rush back off. He glanced at Alena who was tangled in the covers and breathing easy. Thank God he hadn't hit her. She didn't need to go through that shit again and he didn't need it on his conscience.

Didn't she realize the gossip that would spread through town once it got out who his father was? And it would get around. He was Rogelio Juarez's bastard son. People would be pointing and giving her looks for being his woman. He was no better than Romero. The tables had turned on him and judgement day had come home to teach him a lesson.

More staring at the hideous ceiling fan.

Marines don't run. A man admits his mistakes and faces the consequences. Right. The only mistake he'd made was trying to get a better life for himself and Carlos. He looked over at Alena sleeping next to him, trusting him to be the man she needed. He had to get it right.

CHAPTER THIRTY-THREE

FOR THE NEXT WEEK, Alena kept a close eye on Gabriel. He went to work every morning and came home to her tired and dirty every evening. Her worst fear was the possibility that someday he might not come home. His pride had taken a devastating hit and a lesser man might walk away. She was counting on his male stubbornness to keep him next to her.

Saturday morning, he changed the ceiling fan in their bedroom. Alena wasn't about to complain. The beautiful creation of cut-glass and polished brass had no doubt cost him a pretty penny. He had excellent taste. Talk about elegant and romantic, even a little sexy with the dimmer feature.

When she'd first seen him taking the box out of the car, she'd half expected the Humvee version of something dreadfully bold and male with gargantuan fan blades. Not in her bedroom. She'd braced herself for war and been cheerfully disappointed. Damn, maybe a good fight would rattle him out of his funk. But no, he wasn't going to unwittingly accommodate her.

While Gabriel assembled the ceiling fan, she went outside and called her dad. When she asked if they could get married at the house in Carmel, he'd been thrilled. Her second call was to *Papi* to let him know he had to give the bride away. Her wedding plans were going to work out. She'd get a pretty dress and buy Gabriel an amazing tuxedo. Her heart tended to pitter-patter thinking about how super sexy he looked all dressed up. Yes, their wedding would be beautiful. She smiled to herself, enjoying the feeling of being in-love again.

Gabriel had mentioned renting a tuxedo but she'd put an end to that idea quickly. If things went according to her plans, they'd be going out to very nice events and he'd get plenty of use out of one tailor-made for him. She had to start mentioning those plans to him pretty soon before he got suspicious. More suspicious. The clock was ticking and the wins were adding up. She was running out of time.

Afternoon slowly turned into evening, Alena shooed Gabriel outside to start grilling the meat while she daydreamed, fixed her part of their dinner and half-way listened to the news on TV.

Her hands stopped moving when she heard a reporter say, "We're here at the Finish Line Tavern where stock car driver Julio Garza was shot and killed earlier this afternoon. The assailant got away before police arrived. Witnesses said the man drove away in a dark-colored sedan."

She forgot to breathe and a cold dread instantly sent a chill to the pit of her stomach. She dropped the wooden salad bowl on the counter, ran outside on the back porch and shouted, "Julio's been shot and killed at the Finish Line."

Gabriel's head jerked up from staring at the flames. "Did they catch who did it?" He put down the long-handled fork and walked toward her.

"No, just that he drove away in a dark-colored sedan."

"That could be anybody." He stopped at the bottom of the steps.

He didn't have to say it but she could see he was thinking it from the wrinkle in his brow to the flicker of doubt in his eyes.

Alena nodded. "I know. But the timing is just so bad. It could be Carlos. He was so mad when he called you. I could hear him yelling through the phone."

"I'll call him." Gabriel pulled his phone out of his back pocket. He kept his eyes on Alena while it rang. When he got the voice mail, he said, "Carlos, call me when you get this. I'm worried about you. There's stuff on TV about Julio. Okay, just call."

Her lips parted and she inhaled deeply. She'd held her breath and prayed silently for everything to be all right.

He shook his head. "It's not him. After what he went through with Michael, he wouldn't do something like that. He doesn't want to go back to prison."

Alena nodded. "I know. It's probably somebody Julio pissed off. It's Houston, stuff happens all the time."

"It's not good no matter how you look at it. He told me about Julio and Sonja, so he probably told his friends. I'll go over to his apartment. Sonja might know what's going on."

"Okay, shut off the grill and we'll go."

"You don't have to. I can take care of this." Gabriel walked back to the grill.

"I know you can, but Sonja is a piece of work and you shouldn't be alone with her. There's no telling what she'll cook up to make more trouble. I'm going with you."

Gabriel grabbed the Monte Carlo keys on his way to the front door. Before his hand grabbed the doorknob, Alena dangled her keys in front of him. "Let's take the Mustang. It's got air conditioning."

Gabriel shot her a knowing look. "You've got a thing for air conditioning, don't ya?"

"Yeah, I like staying cool. And it keeps me from hurling. I tend to get car sick if I'm in a hot car and not driving. So, unless you want your car to be worse than it already is, we should take the Mustang."

"I like how you're always worrying about me."

"Absolutely. You're my man and it's my duty to take care of you." Alena flashed him a smug grin. "And I love you."

"I know. That's what worries me. Now, let's go."

She followed him down the steps. "What's that supposed to mean?"

"I'll explain it in the car."

They were about two blocks away from the apartment building when Alena saw emergency responder lights blinking in the dark and uttered, "Oh, no. That's not good."

Gabriel said, "That doesn't mean it's them. It could be someone else."

"I hope so but what are the odds? It would be the worst timing ever." She pointed at the curb flanked by a tall overgrown hedge. "Pull over here and we can walk. It's not that far and we can get closer on foot."

Gabriel parked the Mustang in the dark, far away from the nearest street light. "You stay here. You don't need to be out there. Understand?"

"No, I do not understand. I don't want you going alone."

"You'll only make things worse. You'll stick out in the crowd. I'm going to see what's going on and come back. I need to know you're safe while I'm out there. Got it?"

Frowning, Alena grumbled, "Yeah. I'll be here. You be careful." He'd made it very clear on the drive to town that he'd be the one protecting her and not the other way around. Fine, if that's what it would take to make him happy for the time being, she'd do it.

"I will." Gabriel kissed her and got out.

Alena locked the doors and waited quietly in the dark while Gabriel disappeared into the crowd. Some of the onlookers held their positions watching the action while others shuffled around the edges. There was no way Alena could see what was happening: She'd have to wait for Gabriel to come back and tell her the news.

Gabriel returned fourteen minutes later according to the Mustang's clock. Even in the dim light, there was no missing the grim set of his mouth.

"Well, what is it?"

"Sonja's been shot. The EMT's are working on her."

"Did she say anything?"

"No. The neighbor's kids heard the shot and went to look. She's been unconscious the whole time." He gripped the steering wheel and stared at her. "Who would want to kill Sonja and Julio besides my brother?"

"Probably nobody. Is there someplace Carlos would go? Someplace he likes to hang out?"

Gabriel shook his head slowly. "He was still a kid when I left, not old enough to get into the bars. Since he's been out of prison, I don't have any idea who he runs with."

"What about your mom, would she know?"

"I doubt it but I can try to ask her."

They left the apartment complex and drove through his old neighborhood stopping in front of a plain white, clapboard house.

Gabriel said, "Stay here. I'll go see if she'll answer the door."

Gabriel climbed the stairs and knocked on the door. Nothing. He knocked again. The door cracked open and then closed quickly. Gabriel slid into the driver's seat and pulled away from the curb without saying a word. They rode in silence until they turned onto Highway 36.

Gabriel kept his eyes on the road. "Do you want to get something to eat on the way home? We can stop at a drive-thru."

"Not unless you want to. I can finish cooking supper when we get there." Alena ran a finger along the groove where the window slid into the door. "I'd feel better if we were home."

"Okay." He kept his eyes straight ahead.

He'd been in enough battles to keep it together under fire. She wanted him to focus on the immediate problem of getting them back to the house. Eventually, he'd have to deal with Carlos, but the uninterrupted drive would give Gabriel the time he needed to think, to pull his thoughts together. It was a sure bet that Carlos was in big trouble and Gabriel was still his brother. If Carlos, by some miracle, had not shot Julio and Sonja, he was going to be high on the suspect list. This was going to get rough.

Gabriel interrupted her thoughts. "My mom already knew about Sonja. The neighbors called her."

"Did they say if they saw who did it?"

"No, and they won't. It'll be up to Sonja to say what happened when she wakes up."

Alena mulled it over for several seconds. "That'll be a while. She's going to be sedated, under the influence of narcotics. She'll probably need surgery. It could be a day or two before the police can get anything reliable out of her."

"If Carlos calls, I can talk to him and find out what happened before the cops arrest him."

"Yeah, that would be good."

They rode the rest of the way to the house in silence.

Gabriel called Carlos, got voice mail, and then called his grandmother while Alena finished putting their dinner together. By the time he was through talking to her, dinner was ready and he wasn't hungry.

Alena made him a plate and put it on the counter. She said, "I hate eating alone. Can you try to choke down a couple bites?"

"I'll try." He sat down next to her, stared at his food and picked up his fork. "How do you manage to put up with me?"

"That's a no brainer. You're mine and I love you."

"Same as your *Papi*?" Her statement from way back when they'd first started going together flashed across his brain. *Papi* was hers. At first, he'd thought it was a figure of speech but now it was having a familiar ring. And she was fierce when it came to protecting what was hers.

"Exactly. Have you got a problem with that?" She took a bite of her dinner and chewed.

Gabriel turned his head toward her and grinned. "No, no problem. I kinda like the sound of it."

CHAPTER THIRTY-FOUR

ALENA JUMPED when the doorbell rang. Who the hell was on her porch early on Sunday morning? Not that she really wanted to know. She was still in her yoga pants and tank top, not exactly dressed for company.

She answered the door to find two scowling men frowning at her through the screen.

It didn't look good considering the cheap suits and cowboy boots on their feet. She said, "Good morning," even if the odds were against it.

"I'm Detective Reynolds and this is Detective Williams." They both extended their badge holders for her to see. "We're looking for Gabriel DeLeon. We were given this address."

"Okay." She shrugged.

"Is he here?"

"Yes, he's in the shower. We just finished breakfast. Give me a minute and I'll go tell him you want to talk to him."

She left them on the porch. It wasn't polite but neither was arriving unannounced, even if it was their job.

Alena knocked on the bathroom door. "Gabriel there's two detectives here to talk to you."

"Did they say what they want?"

"No, but I'm pretty sure it's either about Sonja or Carlos?"

"Okay, let me get some clothes on and I'll be right out."

She walked back to the front door. "You can come in. He's getting dressed."

The two men entered the living room, taking positions facing the master bedroom door.

Gabriel walked into the room barefoot, wearing faded jeans and a Marine Corps logo t-shirt. "I'm Gabriel DeLeon."

Detective Reynolds said, "Mr. DeLeon, we need to ask you a few questions."

"All right."

"Is Carlos DeLeon your brother?"

"Half-brother. We have the same mother." He gave a short, curt nod.

Detective Williams asked, "Do you know Sonja DeLeon, Carlos's wife?"

Gabriel looked from Reynolds to Williams. "Yes."

"Are you involved with her?" Detective Williams raised an eyebrow.

"No. I went out with her a couple times when Carlos was in prison. Why?"

"Do you know anyone that might want to hurt her?" Detective Reynolds wrote on his note pad.

"I can't say for sure. I don't know her that well."

Williams asked, "Are you aware she was shot last night?"

"Yes. Alena and I went to their apartment so I could talk to Carlos. When we got there, we saw the emergency vehicles and the neighbors told me she'd been shot."

Reynolds was next up to ask questions. "Did you talk to your brother?"

"No, he wasn't there."

"Do you have any idea where he might be?"

"No. We haven't been close for years. Not since I left to join the Marines. I enlisted when I got out of high school."

"If you hear from him, this is my number. Call me." Detective Reynolds handed Gabriel his business card.

"Okay." He accepted the card without looking at it.

They nodded in Alena's direction and left. Alena closed the front door and leaned against it. Neither she nor Gabriel said a word until they heard the car pull out of the driveway.

She stared at him. "Are you okay?"

"No, not really. They're just getting started."

"I'm afraid so. I'm so sorry." She stepped away from the door.

"I was hoping when Carlos got married, things would settle down and turn out all right."

"I suppose it was a possibility but with Sonja's mother and Michael's dad being so close, it probably wasn't a good bet."

"You weren't at the second trial. Nobody said anything about those two coming out of the bedroom."

"Read the transcript from the first one if you don't believe me."

"I don't need to read the transcript. If you say it was testified to, I believe you. I just don't see what difference it makes."

"Revenge, that's what difference it makes. All three of these women were involved with Rogelio Juarez. Your mother had you, Sonja's mother is still sleeping with him and he's married to Michael's mother. Every time Michael beat up Carlos, Michael's mom was getting even with yours. If you went to jail for fighting with Julio, you'd have a criminal record for the rest of your life. Sonja is collateral damage. They'll all be crying big salty tears for the cameras, the jury, and anybody dumb enough to listen. Same as last time."

Gabriel rubbed his neck and rocked his head from side to side. "What's it gonna take to make this stop?"

"Old grudges die hard. We could move away from here."

～

The rest of Sunday went along quietly with Gabriel nervously waiting to hear something. He took out his frustration on the yard. He called it landscaping, she'd called it destruction and stomped back into the house.

Alena hid from him in her office mumbling about working on the team's books. Okay, so he was in a bad mood that got worse the more sweat dripped into his eyes and ran down his back. Around one o'clock she came out long enough to fix their lunch and scampered back to the safety of her office.

At dinner time there was still no word from Carlos. She settled Gabriel on the couch with a cold beer and rubbed his shoulders. He was going to be sore in the morning but the yard looked great.

"You did a great job on the yard. You've got our place looking good." She concentrated her fingers on an especially hard knot in his right trapezius muscle. His body had gotten a tough workout.

"I needed to keep busy." He leaned his head back and sighed. "That feels so good."

She smiled. "Glad to hear I haven't lost my touch."

She came around and sat down next to him so they could watch the ten o'clock news together. She was not leaving him to get through this alone. They were both hoping to hear something about Julio or Carlos but there was nothing. She yawned and said, "Let's get some sleep. You have to go to work in the morning. You can't be late."

"I know but I don't think I can sleep. Carlos is out there somewhere doing God only knows what."

She smiled. "I'll rub your back and anything else that needs attention."

A little after midnight, his eyes flew open. The side gate opened and closed. It had a squeak he should have fixed weeks ago but hadn't gotten around to it yet. He'd been too busy hacking limbs off trees.

He whispered, "Alena, wake up."

"Hmm. What?"

"Shhh. Someone's on the back porch."

Alena rolled over faster than an alligator caught in a net. "How do you know?"

"I just heard the back gate open and close."

There was a soft thump and a scratching sound.

Gabriel mouthed, "Stay here."

He was up and pulling on his sweatpants. No time for jeans and shoes. They had a space invader. Uninvited, unwanted, unannounced trouble in the middle of the night. Never a good thing.

Gabriel walked slowly toward the back-porch door. He didn't hear anything. He crouched and looked out the window.

Someone sat at the patio table not moving. He had a sneaking suspicion who their uninvited guest was. But, to be on the safe side, he called out, "Who's there?"

A familiar voice answered, "It's me, *hermano,* your brother, Carlos. What? You don't recognize me anymore."

Gabriel stood and opened the door. "No, not when you're hiding in the shadows. That kind of thing can get you killed."

Carlos tapped the gun lying in front of him on the table. "Not anymore bro. I'm the man with the gun."

Gabriel stepped out onto the porch. "So, what do you plan to do with that?"

"Keep it handy till I'm over the border."

"You're gonna run?"

"Yeah. I ain't going back to prison." Carlos looked steadily at Gabriel. "I killed them."

Alena poked her head out the door. "Do you boys want some iced tea?"

Carlos snarled, "Fuck you!"

Gabriel kept his eyes glued to Carlos and the gun. "Sure, babe, that'd be great."

Alena closed the door.

Gabriel growled hard and low. "That's my woman and you'll respect that, or you can get the hell off our place."

Carlos smirked, "She helped put me away."

"She kept you from getting a life sentence and she helped get you out." Gabriel sat down across from Carlos.

"Whatever."

The back door opened, Alena put two tall glasses of iced tea down in front of Gabriel and Carlos, followed by packets of sweetener. "I'm going back to bed. You know where to get a refill if you want more."

"Thanks. I'll be in soon."

"Take your time. You guys need to have a good long talk." She disappeared inside the house.

The only illumination was a dull glow from the light in the range hood over the stove. It was enough so they could make their way to the kitchen but not enough to light up the back porch. Gabriel's lips curved up into a small smile. She should be calling the police but instead she was giving him a chance to help his brother, half-brother. It would take time for him to get used to that change.

Carlos grumbled half-heartedly. "I should go. She's probably in there calling the cops. She'll get us both arrested."

"She's going to bed. A couple detectives were here this morning right after breakfast. They didn't say anything about a warrant for your arrest. They wanted to know where you were."

Carlos picked up the nearest glass and took a couple long gulps. He put the glass down. "I killed Sonja last night."

"No, you didn't. They took her to the hospital. They don't know it was you, unless she woke up and told them."

"She'll tell 'em it was me and I'll be in a shit-load of trouble." Carlos looked away. "After I killed Julio, I went home and told Sonja she didn't have to be afraid of him anymore."

Gabriel leaned toward his brother letting the silence draw him out.

Carlos grimaced and tilted his head to the side. "She laughed. She said I was a fool. Julio hadn't done anything. She'd taken the cocaine on purpose to get rid of my kid. She was glad it was dead." He leaned back staring at the roof over the patio. "She hoped I'd rot in prison. She was going to Los Angeles and have some fun before she got too old. I don't know what happened. The gun just went off."

"She set you up." Gabriel leaned back in his chair.

"Yeah. I guess. But I need some money to get out of here."

"You should turn yourself in. That's the right thing to do."

"I already told you, I'm not going back to prison. They'll have to kill me first." Carlos finished drinking his iced tea.

"Don't talk like that. It was one of those crimes of passion. A good attorney can use that."

"The man is dead. I should be sorry but I'm not. He was another

216

fucker that thought he could get away with laughing at me when I told him I was Sonja's husband."

"You shot him for laughing?"

"Damn right. Nobody laughs at me."

"Did Michael laugh at you?"

"Yeah, for about a second. Soon as he turned his head away, pop, no more laughing."

"Oh my God!" Gabriel ran his hand over his mouth. "What were you thinking?"

"Look, just give me some traveling money and I'm out of here." He nodded toward the house. "And you can go back to bed."

Gabriel's jaw clenched and his hands fisted. He made a conscious effort to force himself to relax. Anger would not help Carlos. "Okay, but you have to go tonight. Once there's a warrant out for your arrest, you won't be able to get across into Mexico."

"Yeah, I know. I can't come back."

Gabriel inhaled deeply and exhaled. "There's one more thing. How long have you known we don't have the same father?"

"I heard mom and dad fighting the day he left." Carlos tipped his head to the side. "I figured you didn't do anything about Michael beating up on me cuz he was your brother too."

"That's not true. Michael was your age. I couldn't go around beating up a little kid. I didn't find out about dad until this week."

"Yeah, mom told me when I stopped by her place to say goodbye."

Gabriel shook his head slowly. "I'll go get the cash. Where's your car?"

"Out by the road in the trees." Carlos tucked the gun into his jacket.

"I'll bring you the money and I'll see what food I can find for you. Sitting in a café gives people too much time to recognize you." Gabriel stood up, turned and went in the house.

He grabbed his wallet off the dresser top and counted out all the cash except for a couple of dollars. He dug in Alena's purse and did the same with it.

She quietly asked. "What ya doing, *chico*?"

"Helping my brother." Gabriel didn't raise his head or move his hand. He said, "You never agreed to any of this."

"Exactly, I didn't give you anything."

"I know." When he turned around, Alena was facing away from him so she couldn't have seen him take it.

Gabriel raided the pantry and then the lap drawer of Alena's desk where she kept an emergency stash of cash. He walked to Carlos's Camaro and handed him the money through the window along with a bag of snacks. "Take care of yourself."

"Thanks for the plates off the Monte Carlo." He clicked on the headlights and pulled away.

Gabriel stood in the road and watched his brother disappear into the dark. He'd have to borrow the money for new plates from Alena.

He went in the house and locked the back door. By the time he'd rinsed their glasses and put them in the dishwasher, Carlos was down the road. By morning, there'd be no sign that he'd ever been there. He slid into bed with a heaviness in his heart that he couldn't easily explain.

Alena's eyes drifted open. "Are you okay?"

Gabriel sucked in a breath. "Yeah, it was a set up. You were right. Julio wasn't the baby's father."

"And an innocent man is dead." She closed her eyes.

Gabriel spent the next hour staring at the new ceiling fan. It didn't help. He got up and went to the living room so he wouldn't wake Alena with his fidgeting. He wasn't sure he'd ever be able to sleep again. He'd helped a murderer escape. He'd helped his half-brother stay out of prison. It was a hell of a spot to be in.

He picked the detective's card off the kitchen bar and called the number on it. He left a voice message, "Carlos came by tonight and told me he's leaving town, headed for Mexico."

He stepped over to the refrigerator and opened the door. He needed a drink, a beer, anything with alcohol. He didn't reach for it. He shut the door and jumped when Alena said, "It's okay. I figure you really need that beer right about now."

"What the hell?" Gabriel shot her a look over his shoulder. "Have you got mouse ears? Do you hear everything?"

"Um, yeah, pretty much." Alena smiled as she walked to the couch. "Put the coffee on and come sit down. We can probably find some old movie to watch while you drink it. You can't be late to work again, and you can't smell like beer if you want to keep your job."

Gabriel put together the coffee and sank down on the cushion next to her. "I'm sorry about Julio. He didn't deserve this."

"No, he didn't but fate had a different plan for him." The Devil card had turned up in the last reading Banji did for her. She'd been so afraid it was going to be Gabriel. She wiggled around and snuggled in close to him. She whispered, "I'll have to go to his funeral."

Gabriel hugged her and said, "I know."

"He wasn't a bad man, just a sad and disillusioned one. I always hoped he'd find someone to help him get over his heartache."

"I keep thinking I should have done something more but I don't know what." He exhaled and leaned his head back. "I never imagined my brother could be capable of killing someone on purpose."

"You aren't responsible for this. I heard you warn Carlos to calm down and think before doing something he'd regret."

"I could have called the police sooner."

"And I could have called them while you two were talking on the back porch but it wouldn't have changed anything. It wouldn't bring Julio back and you needed to clear things up between the two of you."

"If I'd left it alone—left Carlos in prison—this wouldn't have happened."

"And you'd have blamed yourself for the rest of your life because you weren't here to protect him." She put her arms around him. "You did the best you could. That's all anyone can do."

"Where would I be without you?"

"Living with your grandmother." She hugged him harder. "Come on, let's get some coffee in you."

CHAPTER THIRTY-FIVE

THE FUNERAL WAS JUST THAT, a funeral. That part was behind her now but the sadness still weighed on Alena as she trudged into the house. Julio's life was lost and Carlos's life was destroyed. Sonja was recovering in the local hospital and naming Carlos as the man who shot her. There was a warrant out for his arrest.

It was a huge mess. She flopped down onto the couch, toed off her shoes, and took a deep breath. Only a few days remained till the season's final race. She wasn't driving because the car was in a good starting position and Nate was ready to take over. She'd also promised Gabriel she'd stop driving so he could quit worrying so much. He didn't need to know she'd be spending her time on the test track with *Papi*, if all went according to plan.

She leaned her head back and closed her eyes. Where had it all gone off the tracks? Gabriel's voice startled her and her eyes flew open. She hadn't heard him walk up.

"What the hell is this?" He waved a handful of papers in front of her face.

"What?" Her forehead crinkled and she sat up trying to get a better look at the papers in his hand.

"I was putting back the money I borrowed from you and I found these." He dropped the papers in her lap and stood over her glaring.

She looked down at the scattered papers and then back up at him. "These deposit slips are mine. They're to my rainy-day fund."

"I'd say more like hurricane wreckage day! We're struggling to get by and you're sitting on this stash. Is this your traveling money when you leave me? You're gonna take the money and run?"

"Screw you." Alena lurched to her feet, tripped over her shoes and bounced off the ottoman. She crashed to the floor flailing and yowling.

In a flash, Gabriel reached to catch her but missed. "Are you okay?"

"Get away from me. I don't need you. I'm so done with this mess." She pushed herself up slowly.

"I'm sorry."

"Not sorry enough. That's my money. It's for when the world goes bat-shit crazy and there's no place to hide from the insanity. It's for shipwrecks. And it's my share of the bar money. I own the Finish Line since Romero died. You know, the tavern where your brother shot an innocent man." She jammed her hands on her hips and shouted, "How the hell do you think I pay for all this?"

"I wondered how you did it, but I was so damn happy to be with you that I really didn't care. I figured you probably had some money from the old days and your dad." He pointed at the bank statements. "I don't know, but that's a lot of money."

Alena walked away instead of answering.

"Don't turn your back on me. We're not done talking about this." Gabriel followed her until the bedroom door slammed in his face.

When he tried the door knob, it didn't give. "Alena, open this door. We have to talk about this."

He heard her muffled response, "No, we don't."

He yelled, "You have to come out of there sometime and I'm going to be right here waiting for you. Do you hear me? Right here, I'm not budging."

"Good, you stay right there."

∼

After a couple minutes, he heard the bedroom window slide open.

"Oh, shit." he turned and ran down the front steps two at a time. He sprinted across the yard and stopped in front of their window.

Alena glared down at him.

He glared up at her. "Where do you think you're going?"

"Away from you."

"Not happening."

"Really?"

"Yes. Really. Shut the window and meet me in the living room. We're gonna work this out."

"Fine." She shoved the window down and turned the lock.

It took her a hot second to get to the front door and lock it before he got there. Gabriel grabbed the door knob but it didn't turn. His keys were sitting on top of the dresser.

"Fuck." He yelled, "Open the damn door."

"Not till you apologize."

"For what?"

"Being a jerk and thinking bad things about me."

He hung his head. "You're right. I'm sorry I said those things."

"That's better." She unlocked the door. "But I'm still mad at you."

He stood face to face with Al. "There's enough there for you to leave and start over. I'd like an explanation."

"There's more than enough and I don't owe you an explanation. If you'd bothered to look, you'd see those are automatic deposits from my dad or the bar. None of that is your money. Where would I even get your money? We don't share an account."

"I don't know but it's what girls do."

"Well, that's an interesting theory. I'm not hiding my money, unless keeping the statements in my desk constitutes hiding. It's right there on that statement."

"A buddy of mine got home and his wife had taken everything and run off with another man. House, car, bank account, everything gone." He shoved his hands in his pockets.

"What's that got to do with me?"

"Everyone else has left me. Why not you?"

If you don't know the answer to that, we have a problem." She picked up her car key-fob. "I've got a race tomorrow. I'm going to the shop and make sure we get loaded up. Don't wait up for me."

~

She pointed the Mustang toward Houston and didn't stop until she pulled in at the shop. The lights were on and the guys were hustling to get the equipment organized. The shop's fluorescent lights lent and eerie glow to the Challenger. It reminded her of a hungry animal waiting to pounce. And pounce it would. Tomorrow was the day the team would put the competition in the rearview mirror.

Tommy walked up to her. "I didn't expect to see you here tonight."

"I needed to go for a ride and thought I'd stop in and make sure we have everything we need. I can call the local distributor if we've forgotten anything. He'll bring it to the track tomorrow morning."

"I've double checked and we're good." He quirked an eyebrow. "Anything else I should know?"

"Not right now." She looked down at the toes of her shoes. "When we win tomorrow, things are going to change. I want you and the crew to know we're staying together. We didn't come this far to give up."

"I'll remind the guys." He dipped his head a fraction while keeping focused on her. "Anything else?"

"The tribute car is on the way. Kington's driver is on schedule."

"Is Santiago coming with it?" Tommy shifted his weight and repositioned his cane.

"No, Carmen isn't feeling well. He has to take care of her."

"Anything I can do to help?"

Her gaze met Tommy's. "Can you be sure we get good video? *Papi* likes to watch the race in motion. Sean is great with the cameras but he might need help getting a good vantage point to shoot from."

"I'll take care of it. What else?"

"Nothing. I think that's it." She patted Tommy's arm. "We've got this."

They watched the Challenger roll up onto the trailer, followed by the guys securing the spare tires and tools.

She gave the crew a thumbs up. "Looks good. I'll see you all tomorrow."

One of the guys would stay overnight in the shop to make sure nothing happened to the car in the middle of the night. The rest of them would come back early and move it all to the track.

She started the Mustang and poked her console icon for Banji.

The ever-cheerful voice of her long-distance friend came over the dashboard speaker. "Hey, girlfriend, I knew you'd be calling." She giggled. "It's the night before the big race and you want to know who's going to win."

"And you're going to tell me the cards don't work that way. I know." She pulled out onto the access road. "Actually, this time I'm hoping for general good news. Gabriel's gone dark on me. Thinks I'm planning on leaving him."

"Hang on. Let me get my deck."

After a quiet ride home with Banji for company, Alena crawled into bed. She was somewhere past tired and approaching exhausted. After tomorrow she'd take a few days and rest. A week would be good.

She scooted over and pressed her front to Gabriel's back and slipped her arm around him. He was sound asleep. If she'd been an enemy sneaking up on him, he'd be dead. Okay, he was faking it. The man could hear a pin drop in the next county. No way had he slept through the Mustang growling in the driveway, the front door opening and closing, and her getting ready for bed in the bathroom. Nope, he was awake and playing possum.

She whispered against his back. "I promised I'd love you forever. You might want to get used to it."

His breath hitched and the movement of his six-pack abs changed under her hand. He'd definitely gotten her message.

CHAPTER THIRTY-SIX

THE MORNING of the season's final championship race, Tommy was in the pit along with the rest of the crew when Alena arrived.

She asked, "Where's Nate?"

Tommy grimaced. "He's stuck on the freeway coming in from Baytown. There's a wreck that's got things shut down and backed up. You're gonna have to drive."

Alena pulled the Mustang key-fob out of her pocket. "Jake, can you go out to my car and get my race bag out of the trunk?"

He nodded and she pitched him the key.

She turned back to look at Tommy and said, "We need to talk."

They stepped over to the edge of the pit by a stack of tires and stopped. Tommy adjusted his weight to be comfortable.

She leaned in and quietly said, "Kington's truck is here with the tribute car. We have to win this race so we can roll it out and go public with our new team. Gabriel doesn't know about it. When he shows up don't tell him I'm driving. Don't lie, just don't mention it. If you need to flag me, have Jake do it. Anyone else and I won't pull in. Got it?"

"Yeah. I got it."

"When Jake gets back with my gear, I'll go change. Have the Challenger ready. I need to be in it and on the track. With my helmet on, Gabriel won't know the difference between me and Nate."

Tommy's forehead wrinkled. "Al, what's going on?"

"He's having a hard time of things since Carlos shot Julio." She inhaled a deep breath and let it out. "He found the money from the Finish Line and my dad. He thinks I'm hiding money from him so I can leave him."

"Anyone that knows you would know that's nuts!"

"What do you think he'll do when he finds out about the rest of it?"

"Oh, hell!"

"Yeah, I'm not going there. I don't lie, I don't cheat, and I don't steal." She shoved her hands into her back pockets.

"Of course not. I know that."

"Well, he doesn't."

Tommy ran a hand over his mouth. "I'm sorry."

"Me too. Keep this to yourself. The crew doesn't need to know my personal business." She squeezed his arm. "Let's win this race, then we'll fix what we can and move on. Okay?"

"Okay." He gave a short nod.

"Jake's got my bag. I'll go change."

Alena grabbed her bag and key from Jake and strode off toward the ladies restroom. It was a short walk and only took a few minutes to get into her gear. She stashed her bag in the crew area behind the tool chests. Then she headed toward the Challenger. She climbed in and started fastening her harness.

Tommy waited and checked the clasps. He leaned down. "Al, you get us to the finish line and I'll handle the rest. I won't let you down. That's a promise."

Alena didn't move except to adjust her hands on the steering wheel. "I know. We race to win. My grandfather didn't believe in losing and I'm just like him. I can do this. *Papi* said so and I believe him."

"From what I've heard, Benton Betmunn was one hell of a man."

"That's what they say." She stared straight ahead.

"Okay, then. Get out there and warm her up."

"When we win today, we become Betmunn Racing." She pushed back in her seat. "Are you good with that?"

"Hell yeah. You bring home the trophy and I'll do the rest."

Tommy stepped back and Alena pulled out onto the track, letting the Challenger warm up and letting the crowd get a look at a winner. They'd come for a show and they were going to get one. She pulled around and got in line for the start of the race.

The staring lights blinked: Red, yellow, green. It was go time. Alena's foot pressed down on the accelerator.

∿

Tommy glanced quickly to his right when Gabriel stepped up next to him.

Gabriel planted his hands on the railing and leaned forward. "How's it going?"

"Good. We're good. How about you?"

"Holding on."

"Oh?"

"I heard Nate's driving this race but Alena left early to be here for the start. I saw the Mustang in the crew parking area."

"Well, if it's here, she's here."

"Yeah, I know that's right." Gabriel recognized the word game. He could play too. "So, have you seen her?"

"She was around earlier."

"Tommy."

"What?"

"She's still my fiancée."

"Yeah, and you'd better fix whatever in the hell you did, if you want it to stay that way."

"What did she tell you?"

Tommy looked up and over at Gabriel. "She said, she doesn't lie, cheat, or steal. So, best as I can tell, whatever you did falls in there somewhere."

"I found statements for a fat bank account. I said some stupid shit. I didn't know she owns the Finish Line and she forgot to mention her dad sends her more than tuition money. She has secrets."

"Yeah, she dipped into her savings when we were first starting up. She told me about it then because I couldn't make the books match what we were spending. She loaned the team enough to get us on the map. When we win today, the team will be able to pay her back."

"I screwed up."

Tommy nodded. "I'd say so. You know, back in the day, there were rumors about Romero's cars. Some people said she was paying for them."

"Damn, that fits. She told me about a time when he was trying to talk her into changing cars. But if they were his, he wouldn't have had to ask. She bought the cars, he fixed them, and she drove them." Gabriel looked out at the track. "She's been hiding stuff from me all along."

"What do you think would have happened if people found out she was the money behind Romero?" Tommy fixed his gaze on Gabriel.

"He'd never have been able to live it down."

"Yeah, and a man has his pride. Right? Same as you. She won't do anything to take that away from you." Tommy held out an empty parts box. "What's that say on the back?"

Gabriel took the box and turned it over and read the fine print, "Betmunn Racing Equipment. So?"

"Yeah, her grandfather, Benton Betmunn's company. They make the best and most expensive racing equipment and we have it. As much as we need, thanks to Al."

"But her name is Cordova."

"That's Santiago's name. She took it years ago. She loves that man."

"I can't deal with all these secrets. I never know what's coming next." He crossed his arms over his chest, "Who is she?"

"She's Alena Betmunn y Cordova. Santiago Cordova is Betmunn's chief mechanic, garage boss, shop foreman. He taught her to fix the engines on her grandpa's race cars."

Gabriel jammed his hands on his hips. "And I bet there's more I don't know."

"The way I see it, if you don't trust Al, there's a serious issue somewhere you need to deal with. And here's some news for you, everybody has secrets. Even you."

"Nothing like this."

"She never tells anyone about Betmunn. She wants to make it on her own." Tommy stopped talking as the Challenger flew by them. "Do whatever it takes to fix this mess. Do you understand me?"

"Yeah." Before he had time to say another word,

Nate ran into the pit. Breathing hard from exertion he huffed, "Sorry we're late. Roberto is parking the car. Who's winning?"

Gabriel's eyes hunted for the Challenger on the track. "Al's driving, isn't she?"

Tommy mumbled, "We didn't have any choice. If we don't place, we won't be in a good starting position next year. If we win, we're at the top. The car had to make this race."

"She promised me she'd stop driving." Gabriel glared at Tommy.

"As long as she's breathing, she's not going to let us down. Any of us. Hang on to her and it'll work out."

Gabriel grumbled, "I'm not so sure about that." He turned to Nate and asked, "What do you know about Santiago and Al? I know you work for him, so don't try to hide it."

Nate stepped back. "He's Betmunn's shop foreman."

"And what else?"

Nate shrugged. "Back when her grandfather was still alive, she'd spend the summers learning to work on cars and racing. The old timers gave her a cap to cover her hair so other crews wouldn't laugh at them having a little girl on the team."

"And Santiago, what do the old timers say about him?"

"He came to America from Buenos Aires with gang brands and tats all over his body." Nate shrugged. "He's scarred up bad. Old man Betmunn gave him a job picking up the garage and washing cars until he figured out Santiago had a talent for engines."

"And?"

"And Al latched on to him. There was only one problem."

"Which was?"

"She'd go home with Santiago. She learned his language and ate lunch and dinner at his house. The nanny would go nuts looking for her. One day, she came into the shop hunting for Al and Santiago sent her running back to the main house."

"Did he get his ass chewed?"

Nate shook his head. "No. The nanny spent the rest of the summer sitting in the shade by the pool, drinking lemonade and reading."

"Al was good at getting her way even back then." Gabriel grinned.

Nate nodded. "One time, Al caught some new guy making fun of Santiago and she fired him right there in the shop."

Tommy grumbled, "Figures she would. No fear in that girl."

"The old guys told me to be careful if she came around. That guy laughed and said she was cute. But he wasn't laughing when Benton walked in and handed him his severance check. From that day on, everyone knew who the real boss was. And the big man protects her."

"She's been holding out on me all along. I don't really know her at all."

Tommy's eyes stayed glued to the track. "She did not lie to you. She just didn't tell you everything. You know her well enough." He leaned forward and shouted, "She's closing in on Hal. Shit! That old car won't take much more. It'll come apart."

He grabbed at his mic, "Goddammit! Slow down, slow down, you're going too fast into the curve!"

Nate growled, "Don't insult my car."

"Go Al, go!" Monica pumped her fist in the air and shrieked, "Yeah, kick his ass!"

Nate threw both fists in the air and shouted, "Al's got it."

Gabriel shook his head.

Monica squealed, "Did you see that? She's blowing past 'em like they're in slow motion. She's driving to win, yeah!"

Nate grabbed the headset off Tommy, yelling, "Push it, Al, hold on tight and push harder."

The rest of the crew lined up at the edge and started chanting along with Monica, "Drive faster, race to win."

Gabriel looked at Tommy and shrugged. The crowd came to its feet. The cheer went up as the Challenger screamed over the finish line.

Tommy grumbled, "At least it's not smoking. We can fix it." He pulled out his cell phone and tapped on it. "She's done it. Roll out the car and set up. We're announcing the new team."

Gabriel's head snapped up. "What new team?"

Alena eased up on the accelerator, letting the car slow a little at a time as she made the victory lap. The faces were a blur, the noise was deafening. Her rapidly pounding heart made it hard to breathe and her numb fingers refused to let go of the steering wheel. It would be embarrassing if she couldn't stay on her feet when she finally crawled out of the car. She made a second lap and forced herself to focus. Mind over matter: She had to make it look good.

She pulled in to her pit and stopped. Her numb fingers made it impossible to unfasten the harness and get out of her helmet. She needed help.

When she looked out her driver's window crawl-space, she came nose to the zipper on Gabriel's jeans. "Oops."

Gabriel's hands reached for her. "Come on, I've got ya."

"Um. Maybe I'll just sit here a minute."

"The fans are waiting for you. You can't let them down and you can't make your team look like pussies because you can't get out of your car. Come on. Trust me on this. It's okay."

She looked past Gabriel. Her crew, her responsibility, they were waiting. This wasn't the time to go all cowardly. *Papi* and Romero would be ashamed of her. "You need to unfasten my harness."

She grabbed onto Gabriel's arm and let him pull her out. When her feet hit the ground, she realized her legs were shaking too badly to walk. She leaned against Gabriel.

He muttered under his breath. "I'm here for you. It's my job, so let me do it." His hands gripped her waist and he lifted her. "Now, wrap your legs around me. You can do it."

Her legs were more than wobbly, but with his help, she hitched them over his hips while clinging to his shoulders.

"For heaven's sake, wave at the crowd. You just won. The least you can do is smile and wave."

Gabriel walked to the edge of the pit and turned full circle. When that was done, he headed for the back wall where she could sit and recover.

By the time he got there, Alena was limp with her head resting on his shoulder.

He quietly said, "You're gonna have to turn loose so I can put you down and get you something to drink."

"No."

"No? What the hell? I can't reach the cooler with you hanging on me like a monkey."

"I don't care. I'm fine like this."

Gabriel sat down on the back bench with Alena still plastered to him. "You're dehydrated. What do you want?"

"Nothing."

Gabriel rubbed her back with one hand while holding her steady with the other. "Come on, pull it together. Let's get your helmet off and walk out to the winner's circle. People are waiting for you to accept the trophy and say all the right stuff. Come on."

"Not yet."

"Fine, but let's at least get this brain bucket off your head. You need to breathe." He unbuckled her helmet, lifted it off and set it aside. "You gotta talk to me. I hate secrets. That shit never turns out good."

"You didn't ask." She shook her head from side to side freeing her hair.

"Got it. I'll ask more questions in the future." He rubbed her back.

"Okay. That feels good. You have great hands."

"Only you would say that." He tightened his grip on her. "I want to be your main man. Can you add me to the list with your *Papi*?"

"Sure, if that's what you really want. Maybe you should think about it."

"Okay, I'll think about it and you can add me to the list."

Alena untangled herself from Gabriel one limb at a time. "I'm okay. I'm good." She flexed her fingers and worked her gloves off.

Gabriel stepped over to the cooler and twisted the cap off a bottle of water. "Here, try to drink at least some of this. It will help."

She took a few swallows and made a scrunchy face. "It tastes weird."

"It hasn't changed."

"When did you become an expert on water?"

"Fine. We'll get you a different brand. First it was the Gatorade and now it's the water. Can we do this later? Right now, you need to get out there and smile for the fans and cameras."

They walked out together with his arm around her waist keeping her steady. Alena put on her victory smile and waved enthusiastically. Surrounded by her crew, they made their way to the winner's circle. She accepted the trophy on behalf of her team and held it up for everyone to get a good look. The cameras clicked and flashed with Sean in the forefront.

She looked at his camera dead-on and smiled. "I want to thank all the fans for coming out today. And I want to announce the new Betmunn Racing Team will be here next year to continue what we've started."

The questions came fast after that. She kept smiling and repeating, "Betmunn Racing is back on the track. Stop and take a look at the Romero Vasquez Tribute car on the way out".

Her team was on the map: they were back in a big way. When the photo taking was over and the crew had gone back to the pit to pack it all up, Alena left to change her clothes.

Gabriel stopped her along the way. "Why didn't you tell me about Betmunn Racing?"

"Because if I lost today, it probably wouldn't happen. It was a gamble and you didn't need to worry about it."

"We are going to have a serious talk. You can't keep doing this to me."

She ran her fingers through her damp tangled hair. "Can I change clothes first? And I really need to pee."

Gabriel choked out a short chuckle. "You always say the damnedest things." He shook his head. "Go get changed."

Trudging down the hall, it was evident that she was tired and worn out. Thank God the season was over so she could get some peace and quiet. Galveston would be the perfect place to rest and do some serious thinking.

～

Back in their pit, Tommy grabbed Monica by the arm and whispered to her, "Go check on Al. She's been in the ladies room a long time."

"Sure, Dad."

Two minutes later, she whispered to her dad, "She's not in there."

"Damn," escaped from Tommy's mouth.

Gabriel frowned. "She's gone, isn't she?"

Tommy nodded. "Now, what are you going to do?"

"I'll call her phone. Maybe she'll answer."

"And if she doesn't, then what?"

"It's too late tonight to go hunting for her in the dark. If she's in Galveston, they won't give me her room number so I'll have to wait till tomorrow. If she's not at home, I'll take a ride over and see if she's there. It's her favorite place."

"Okay, sounds good. You find her and make this right."

Nate disconnected his call, looked at Gabriel and Tommy. "Santiago says it's time for her to come home."

Tommy's eyes went wide. "Uh-oh. You are so screwed."

Gabriel turned to him. "Why? What's it mean?"

"You're going to California."

"Why?" He rubbed his hand over his head. "I have a job. I can't up and leave."

Nate answered, "They're rolling out the car she built with her granddad and Santiago."

Tommy cleared his throat. "It's already here."

Gabriel muttered, "What? Where?"

"Weren't you listening to her talking to the reporters? The new Betmunn Racing Team is us. We have a car. The Romero Vasquez Tribute is our new car."

Gabriel hung his head and muttered, "He's back and she's driving."

Nate looked from Gabriel to Tommy. "I'm driving. Unless you know something I don't."

Gabriel glared at Nate. "So, how's this supposed to work?"

Nate shrugged. "I'm driving, Tommy's crew chief, and Betmunn is bankrolling us. Al is the division head, Santiago is Master Mechanic, and you're in charge of transportation. She got us a dedicated driver with Kington Trucking. The team is staying together."

Tommy eyed Gabriel. "You're sticking with the team, right?"

Time stopped for Gabriel. Everyone turned and stared at him. They had that look. Like they were depending on him to make or break their futures. Was he going to screw up their team? It was the highway or the raceway. He had to choose.

He put one foot in front of the other. "All right. Let's go take a look at our new car." He clapped Tommy on the back. "This is gonna be fun."

CHAPTER THIRTY-SEVEN

GABRIEL ROLLED SLOWLY along the seawall in his classic Monte Carlo. He'd gotten Santiago to agree to help him rebuild it into the fine car it once was. Of course, he had to get Alena to take him home to Carmel first. Funny thing was, he actually wanted to go.

That early the street was pretty much deserted. He was almost to the Pleasure Pier when he spotted a familiar figure sitting on the edge of the concrete wall looking out to sea.

Sitting on cold concrete wearing jeans, and a Galveston Island jacket, she had to be freezing.

He parked the car and walked over to Alena. "Is it okay if I sit down?"

She didn't look up. "Yeah, it's still a free country and this is a public beach. You can sit anyplace you want."

Gabriel sat and swung his legs over the side. "It's cold out here this morning."

"There's a change in season coming. I can feel it in the air." She swung her feet and glanced his way.

"You really kicked ass on the track yesterday. It's all over the news. You're back."

"Betmunn Racing is back. I told you I needed to fix the mess I'd made. Things are going to be okay now."

"Tommy says his phone's been ringing non-stop." He looked at the white capped waves. "Reporters are asking if you'll be driving the tribute car?"

"No, Nate's the new team driver. We'll have to find him a back-up driver." She kept looking out at the endless waves.

"Don't you think it's about time you tell me what your plan is?"

"Grow up. Take my seat on the company board. Make sure my team has everything it needs. Take care of *Papi* and Carmen."

"What about me?"

"Your grandma will take you back. You could stay with her till you get your own place."

"I'd rather stay with you."

"I can't imagine why. You don't seem to like me much these days. It can't be any fun living with someone you think is stealing from you."

"You're not stealing from me. But you weren't exactly honest with me either. You're Betmunn Racing Equipment. Your grandfather left it to you."

"Who the hell told you that?"

"Your dad, he called last night to congratulate you on the win and on taking your seat on the Board of Directors. Then there's the parts box Tommy handed me yesterday."

"Bunch of blabber mouths. I changed my name so this shit wouldn't happen."

"*Papi* told Nate to tell you that it's time to come home."

"I know, he called me last night. Carmen is sick."

"I called you last night."

"You just wanted to yell at me some more."

"I wasn't yelling. You'll know when I'm yelling. All these secrets are killing me. I think I finally know you, then something else blind-sides me and I realize I don't."

"You know I love you. What more do you want?"

"I want you to trust me. You can tell me anything. I've got your back no matter what." He inhaled a deep breath and let it out. "It's all or nothing, Al. We can't go on this way."

"Fine. Ask your questions." She speared him with a glance. "I hope you're ready for the answers."

"Why did you take Santiago's name?"

"Because he's my *Papi*."

Gabriel shook his head. "That's so twisted."

"Maybe to you but not to us."

"Can you explain it to me?"

"His dad moved the family to Buenos Aires. They were poor and the gangs pulled him and his brothers in. They tortured *Papi* and made him do terrible things." She looked over at Gabriel.

He nodded. "Go on."

"He escaped and made it to America. Granddad's personal car was giving him fits. Papi worked on it one night after everyone else had given up. He fixed it. After that he worked on all our engines."

"Okay. So, where do you come in?"

"I followed Granddad down to the garage to see what the mechanics were doing. When I saw *Papi*, I knew he was the smartest. Granddad said I could have him."

"Having him show you mechanics was stretching things. You were too young."

"*Papi* held me over the engines so I could reach the tiny places his big fingers wouldn't fit. Guess he didn't get your memo."

"He's a dangerous man. They had no business leaving a little girl with a man like that."

"Oh, hell! Here we go again. I'm not doing this." She shifted away from him.

He inched closer. She wasn't getting away. "Yes, we are. His name, why did you pick his name?"

"He's my *Papi*. How many times do I have to tell you? He kept me with him and took me home so Carmen could feed me. I was always hungry. We took care of each other and we're still taking care of each other. He's mine. We're family."

"You said, I was yours." He pinned her with a stare reserved for desperate measures.

"I didn't hear you agree. You're still free to go."

Gabriel brushed his hand over his mouth. "There's this thing called 'family friends'. That's more normal."

Alena speared him with a look that could have killed. "Normal is for somebody else. Not me. Carmen and *Papi* couldn't have children. I'm all they have."

Gabriel shook his head. "You could have told me about the Finish Line Tavern and your allowance. Even if you didn't want me to know it was from Betmunn. Lots of parents send their kids money to help with the bills."

"I wanted you to love me for me. Not for what I could buy you."

"And I fell for you without a clue that you were the heiress to Betmunn Racing Equipment."

"It's not a good life never knowing if people like you for you, or the money. I left all that behind me and moved to Texas where nobody'd ever heard of me."

"And how did you explain it to Romero?"

"That was a bad day." Alena looked at Gabriel. "Are you sure you want to hear it?"

"Yeah, we can't keep on having all these secrets from each other."

Alena took a deep breath. "The Nova was broken down again and we had zero money for more parts. We were going to lose the season. I phoned the regional manager and picked up what we needed the next morning. When I gave them to Romero, he wanted to know how I'd gotten them."

Alena looked at the sand beneath her feet. "I had to tell him the truth." She glanced over at Gabriel. "I was a rich spoiled brat playing games to hear him tell it. Well, more like he yelled as if we were all deaf. But he wanted to win more than he wanted to be mad. He had a hard time believing I could love him the way he was. Stubborn, like you and *Papi*."

She shifted her weight from one hip to the other and looked over at Gabriel. "I knew Romero was another *Papi*, he needed to be the one protecting, doing, providing. I couldn't take that away from him. I needed him to fix the cars and he needed me to drive them. We were always a team."

"But Santiago had taught you how to fix cars. You could fix your own car."

"No, mostly he showed me how to fix engines. My mother took me away before we got to the other parts."

"So, when you met Romero, how did that work?"

"I kept quiet and sometimes helped him figure things out when he got stuck."

"But you weren't hooked up with him yet?"

"No. Racing was his business. He'd made a name for himself. If people got the idea that I was his meal ticket, they'd lose respect for him. I couldn't let that happen." She pinned Gabriel with a questioning look. "So, now what? Are you leaving me? Spit it out, say it and get it over with."

If she'd stabbed a frozen ice pick deep into his heart, it wouldn't have hurt worse. This was not the time to let his pride get in the way. The corners of his mouth curved upward. "I'm yours. I'm not going anywhere without you. Guess you'll have to get used to it".

She snickered. "I knew it. You were awake."

"I was." He turned his head and grinned at her. "You never quit, do you?"

"Ah, no. I tried once but this hard-headed Marine wouldn't let me."

Gabriel lost his smile. "He had no right to do that, not when his life was so messed up."

"He didn't know that then." She hitched her hip back from the edge and turned toward him. "Some things are fate and meant to happen. I wouldn't change it, even if I could."

"I wouldn't either, but if you stop to think about it, everything I believed about my life has been a lie. The man I grew up thinking was my dad, isn't. My real father won't acknowledge me. My younger brother is a half-brother. He killed my other half-brother, then he killed Julio, and shot his wife. Carlos is a man on the run forever. I don't even have a respectable name to give you."

Gabriel cleared his throat. "The only good thing I had was you and I believed you were with me through all that because you loved me, the real deal. Why else would you stick by me?" He shook his head. "Then

240

I find you have a fat stash of money in the bank while we're barely making ends meet. It scared me."

He pointed at the Monte Carlo sitting at the curb. "Do you see that? I'm still driving the Monte Carlo and coming home to you every night."

Alena glanced down at the sand below. "I warned you the day would come when you'd resent me. I guess it's finally arrived."

"I did not drive all the way over here to leave you. I want you to come home with me. We've got some stuff to work out but nothing so bad we can't fix it." Gabriel grinned. "And your dad is expecting us to get married in his backyard. He's having a gazebo built for the occasion. I'm supposed to tell you that he and Santiago will be giving the bride away and he's inviting everybody."

Alena bit her bottom lip and kept looking at the Gulf of Mexico.

Gabriel stared at her profile. "I'll get on my knees and ask you to forgive me."

Alena's eyes met his. "No, I love you too much for that. Sometimes I think that you don't know me at all."

"I know you but I can't believe it's real. I say stupid stuff and I'm sorry as soon as the words come out of my mouth."

"I will always love you, Gabriel. It's in the cards. Banji told me and she's never wrong. What I want to know is, can you love me back unconditionally?"

"I wouldn't be here if I didn't." He looked down at the toes of his boots dangling over the sand. "I'm shameless when it comes to you." He turned his gaze on her. "I'm in love with you, plain and simple with no way out."

"I think I love you more." She laughed softly.

Gabriel looked out over the waves. "That would be hard to do."

"I'll take your word for it." Alena bumped his shoulder with hers.

"Can we go home now?" Gabriel put a hopeful hint in his voice. "I miss you crowding me in the middle of the night."

"In a few minutes. I'm not done listening to the surf."

"Aww, here we go again. Shipwrecked." Gabriel scooted over till they were hip to hip. He put his arm around her shoulders. When she rested her head against him that was the signal he'd been praying for.

241

They were going to be okay. Reaching for love had forced them to cross over every dividing line there was. He'd come out a stronger man. This was what survival felt like. He was going to live his life with *una chica loca.*

"Alena."

"Um?"

"I like being shipwrecked with you."

"You saved me." She snuggled closer.

"When we get home, we've got some making up to do."

"How do you mean?"

"I mean, I'll be reminding you just how good we are together."

She sighed, "That would be nice. I was afraid you'd forgotten."

Gabriel snorted. "Not in this lifetime."

"I'll meet you there, *chico.*"

"Don't keep me waiting."

"So bossy." She wrinkled her nose and grinned. "I think you're the one that needs a head start."

CHAPTER THIRTY-EIGHT

WHEN ALENA PULLED up in the driveway, Gabriel was waiting for her with his legs spread and his hands planted on his hips. The only thing missing from the gunfighter stance was a gun belt and six-shooter. She got out, shut the Mustang's door and asked, "What?"

He dropped his hands to his sides and stalked toward her wearing a grimace he used to frighten everyone in his unit into instant obedience. He pointed to the new, gleaming, Midnight Blue Harley Deluxe sitting in front of the Monte Carlo and demanded, "What is that?"

Alena frowned and shot back, "Your wedding present. I ordered it from the factory months ago."

Gabriel balled his fists at his side and growled, "My wedding present? What are you talking about? Are you paying me to marry you?"

"No. It's tradition. The bride and groom give each other wedding gifts. I got you a new Harley. It takes months to build one to order. How was I supposed to know it would take us forever to get married?"

"Just how long have you been planning on marrying me?"

"That would be since you gave me a promise ring in Galveston."

He winced and hung his head. "And exactly how am I supposed to pay for this bike?

"Well, it wouldn't be much of a gift if you had to pay for it. It's yours free and clear."

Gabriel opened and closed his mouth without making a sound.

Alena bit her lower lip. "You love to ride. Let me do this for you."

Gabriel inhaled in a deep breath and turned away. He mumbled, "I don't know anything about all this stuff. I didn't get you anything."

Alena walked up behind him, slipped her arms around his middle and softly said, "It's okay. I've got you. That's all I want."

Gabriel lowered his voice and asked, "What am I gonna do with you?"

Alena smiled against his back. "Well, we could go inside and you could take off all your clothes for starters."

Gabriel patted her hands that were still holding him prisoner. "You still want me?"

"Always."

"I think this is where I get down on one knee and ask you to marry me."

"Yeah, this would be the right time."

The End

NEWSLETTER SIGNUP
Stay up to date
If you would like to stay up to date on news and releases, please sign up for my email newsletter.
Sign up at NellieKrauss.com
Amazon: amazon.com/Nellie-Krauss/e/B08LF2K8K6

Keep reading for a look at: Sea Storms

Banji ambled along the tideline, looking for anything of interest that might have washed up on California's beaches during the storm. Something like the ruins of her career, or a clue to her future. Something, anything was better than another fruitless day of searching for a way to fix her professional reputation and coming up empty.

She glanced up and saw the big man from up the coast. He liked to walk at sunset. For days she'd watched him and wondered who he was. A middle-aged, handsome man like him walking alone day after day was unusual. Well, in California anyway. If he'd been jogging alone, that would put him in a different category. Lots of married people jogged alone. Curiosity was her downfall. It killed the cat, and her career. If she hadn't been so damn curious she wouldn't be living like a hermit in her Gram's oceanside, summer cottage with freaking winter closing in.

Usually, they passed with only a quiet, "Hello." But today she was going to say something. He drew closer and she inhaled a steadying breath. She plastered a friendly smile on her face and said, "Hi! The storm was sure a wild one last night."

"Yes." A slight nod while he kept walking.

Great. The strong, silent type. The width of his shoulders and the denim hugging his thighs hinted at the muscles underneath. His flannel

shirt told her the cold didn't worry him. He was definitely still attractive for a middle-aged man. His long, coal black hair matched his
neatly trimmed moustache. And there was something about him that
told her his dark brown eyes had seen more of the world than she
wanted to know about. There was nothing innocent or naïve about him.

She glanced at the grey, churning waves and shoved her hands
deeper into the pockets of her old, burgundy parka. The deep wine
color was still vibrant on a cold winter's day even if the material was
fraying at the cuffs.

She looked down the beach at his receding figure. Ah-ha. She
caught him. He glanced back over his shoulder at her. Yes! She stifled
a giggle. She would work on him a little at a time until she got a
complete sentence out of him. She'd found her new purpose in life.
Well, at least until she found a job.

She continued her walk a little longer and then turned around. The
deserted beach and a few seagulls made for peaceful company and a
routine ending to a quiet day.

Santiago glanced over his shoulder at the young woman who had
spoken to him. She was pretty but the dark circles under her weary
eyes told him she had history. He knew this stretch of beach between
Kington House and the Betmunn estate by heart. He lived and worked
on the Betmunn estate. Twenty-six years of building race cars and
restoring antique vehicles made him a good living. But he'd been
lonely and walking the isolated stretch of sand seemed to help.

He could say something to her next time they crossed paths. His
English was near perfect when he chose to speak. Today, she'd taken
him by surprise. He'd do better. He stopped beside the dunes and
watched her climb the hill to the widow's little house. For years,
Missus Lori made the best apricot pies and shared them with the neighbors. Then one day she didn't wake up. After that, the family rented
out the house every summer. A tenant in the winter was something
new.

He could ask his daughter, Alena, if she'd heard anything about the new tenant but that might bring up questions he didn't want to answer. Alena Betmunn had adopted him to be her *Papi* when she was a child and she'd made it legal when she was twenty-one and racing with her own team. In case anything happened, she'd wanted him to have rights to her estate.

She considered herself his daughter with all the accompanying rights to snoop in his life. He chuckled softly. Without Alena, he'd have no one. And she could snoop all she wanted. There was nothing happening in his world outside of work. But that might be about to change. The pretty girl on the beach had actually spoken to him first. It wouldn't hurt to talk to her. Maybe she was lonely too.

Banji locked the kitchen door and shucked out of her coat. A cup of hot chocolate sounded good. She'd have to settle for the store-bought, instant version but it would be fine. She was not known for any cooking ability. More like inability. Odds favored her burning whatever it was to tiny meteorites regardless of how many cookbooks her friends gave her for Christmas.

While the water heated she looked through Gram's vinyl albums. Another antique feature she enjoyed. Watching the turntable spin always fascinated her. The old songs resonated with her current life, a little raw and scratchy but still good.

She placed a black disk on the spindle and pressed start. The walk to the kitchen accompanied by the pulsing drumbeat lifted her flagging spirit. She was still standing, barely, and she could get past the wreckage. It would take time but she'd figure it out.

Her phone signaled an incoming call from her least favorite person in the world. She could answer it now or later but she would talk to her father. Lloyd Preston could be extremely and annoyingly persistent when he wanted to be. And since she'd dragged the Preston family name into the gutter he'd been determined to make her life a misery.

"Hello."

"Finally. I've been trying to get ahold of you all day."

"I've been busy." Auction houses were few and far between and none of them were looking for disgraced appraisers. Art, and estate jewelry were her specialties. At least they had been.

"What's that god-awful racket?"

"Gram's stereo."

He grumbled, "More worthless junk."

"What do you want?"

"I'm losing business. People don't want anything to do with Preston Auction House in case you're working for the family. You have no idea the influence the Floods have."

"I can't help that. I wasn't working for Preston Auction when I did their insurance appraisal so it really has nothing to do with you."

"The Floods are threatening to file a law suit for the damages you've caused them."

"They won't. The test results back up my reports and they wouldn't want to have that confirmed in open court. The tests don't lie. It's more tabloid fodder." She leaned against the tile counter.

"And where are those documents?"

Ah, now the real reason for the call. "In my safe deposit box."

"Which bank?"

"None of your business. I don't work for you. I'm not part of Preston Auction."

"You don't work for anyone and you're not going to at this rate."

"If there's nothing else, I need to go." She didn't bother masking the heavy sigh. She'd had enough of this conversation.

"There is one more thing. We'd appreciate it if you didn't come to Caroline's wedding. We'd like it to be a pleasant occasion."

"No problem. Give my half-sister my regrets, or not. I really don't care."

"That's the problem with you. You don't care about your family. You never have. Not since you were a little girl."

Banji rested her fist on the tile countertop. "You're right. I don't care about the cheating bastard that drove my mother to suicide."

"She was depressed. It wasn't my fault. Someday you'll wish you had a family."

"I have a family and you're not in it. Don't ever call me again. You can crawl in a hole and pull the dirt in on top of yourself." She disconnected the call.

Well, that had gone better than expected. At least he hadn't yelled obscenities at her. That was a nice change. She walked back to the living room, turned up the volume on the stereo and gazed out the window toward the open sea.

Freedom was out there. The tall, dark and handsome man standing in the dunes glanced up and caught her gazing out the window. Okay, now that could make any girl smile. He was a fine-looking devil. Well, for a man his age. Lucky for him she liked antiques.

AFTERWORD

Tarot Cards:

Wheel of Fortune: Good Fortune, Destiny, Future

5 of Pentacles: Feel isolated and alone

Ace of Wands: Success in all aspects

10 of Wands: Challenges, intense pressure

Death: Clearing the way for transformation

Justice: Fairness, balance, integrity

King of Cups: Emotionally balanced, compassionate

Devil: Violence, Fatality

ALSO BY NELLIE KRAUSS

If you liked this book check out these others

Galveston Island Series

#1 The Moon Over Sea Wolf Bay

#2 Desperado Lucky

#3 Valentino's Fire (forthcoming in Fall 2021)

Other titles

East of Baghdad

Queen of the Black Roses Ball (Short Story)

Sea Storms (Summer 2021)

Amazon: amazon.com/Nellie-Krauss/e/B08LF2K8K6

ABOUT NELLIE KRAUSS

Nellie Krauss is a Pro member of Romance Writers of America and San Antonio Romance Authors. She writes contemporary Romances with sassy heroines. Her cross-cultural stories are inspired by her time spent living with Native Americans on the Pine Ridge Reservation in South Dakota. The Renaissance Fair is her favorite place to be when she's not in the Black Hills or at the beach. Her biggest thrill is hearing the roar and rumble of her Harley's engine on the open road. She has travelled the Caribbean, the Bahamas and Western Europe in search of adventure. Her next destinations are the romantic Greek Islands. Opa!